Enigmatic Promise

Eva Sage

Published by Eva Sage, 2024.

This is a work of fiction. Similarities to real people, places, or events are entirely coincidental.

ENIGMATIC PROMISE

First edition. October 30, 2024.

Copyright © 2024 Eva Sage.

ISBN: 979-8224409655

Written by Eva Sage.

Chapter 1: The Fractured Connection

I stood on the bustling streets of Ashwood, the crisp autumn air swirling with the scent of fallen leaves and the distant aroma of roasted chestnuts. My heart raced as I spotted him across the way—Liam Callahan, the man who had unknowingly shattered my peaceful life just months before. We were supposed to be competitors in the local art festival, but his arrogance and smug confidence had turned every encounter into a battleground. I took a deep breath, reminding myself of my resolve to avoid him at all costs. But as fate would have it, the universe had other plans.

His tousled chestnut hair glinted under the golden sun, a halo of mischief that perfectly matched the devilish smirk plastered across his face. I cursed the way he carried that same nonchalant air, as if the chaos he created around him was merely a side effect of his brilliance. He was a canvas of contradictions—both a tantalizing mystery and an irritating puzzle I couldn't quite solve. My heart thudded loudly in my chest, not just from the anxiety of confrontation, but from an inexplicable pull toward him that I had spent months denying.

"Is that a scowl I see, or are you simply pleased to see me?" Liam called out, his voice smooth like honey but laced with a teasing edge. He took a few confident strides toward me, hands casually tucked into the pockets of his navy jacket. The moment felt suspended in time, like the golden leaves fluttering from the branches around us, each twist and turn echoing the tension that simmered just beneath the surface.

"Just admiring how you manage to look so insufferable, even in autumn," I shot back, unable to resist the temptation of sparring with him. The words slipped out before I could stop myself, sharp as the brisk wind. I stood my ground, challenging him with a glare that was half exasperation, half undeniable fascination. The corners of his mouth twitched, a mix of surprise and delight, as if I had just delivered a rare piece of art rather than a mere retort.

"Touché," he replied, chuckling softly. The sound was rich, like the scent of mulled wine drifting from a nearby café, and for a split second, I felt my resolve wobble. His laughter had a way of drawing me in, making the air around us thick with unspoken tension and lingering possibilities.

I forced myself to look away, focusing instead on the street vendors setting up their booths, each stall bursting with colorful creations—ceramic mugs glazed in shades of sapphire, delicate scarves woven with threads of gold, and paintings that captured the very essence of autumn. The festival was the heart of Ashwood, a celebration of creativity that brought together artists from every corner of town. My small pottery studio was among the many participants, and this year I had poured my soul into my pieces.

"Are you ready for the festival?" he asked, his tone shifting from playful to sincere, cutting through the haze of tension like a knife through soft clay. I could feel his gaze probing me, searching for something I wasn't quite prepared to reveal. "I hope you've got something special lined up. Wouldn't want to disappoint the masses, right?"

"Right," I replied curtly, feeling the weight of his scrutiny. The truth was, I was terrified. My latest project—a set of bowls inspired by the seasons—was meant to encapsulate everything I felt about change, loss, and resilience. It was raw and unfiltered, a reflection of the turmoil that had come to define my existence since our last clash. But the last thing I wanted was for him to see the cracks in my carefully curated façade.

"Still so guarded," he mused, his brow furrowing slightly as if he was genuinely trying to understand the enigma before him. "It's like you're encased in your own little bubble. Don't you ever want to burst it?"

The audacity of his observation made me bristle. "And what would you know about breaking bubbles, Mr. Callahan? You thrive on your own inflated sense of self-importance." I crossed my arms defensively, wishing I could summon enough strength to withstand his charm.

"Oh, I've popped a few bubbles in my day," he said, his voice low and inviting, the weight of his words hanging between us. "Though I'll admit, I'm more of a sculptor than a bubble-popper. What about you? Are you ready to let your art speak, or are you content with keeping it trapped inside?"

I faltered, taken aback by his insight. It was as if he could see through the layers I had built around myself, exposing the fear that lay at the core of my creativity. But I wasn't here to bare my soul to Liam Callahan—not when every fiber of my being was screaming to retreat into the safety of my studio, where I could hide behind my pottery and paint.

Before I could respond, a gust of wind swept through the street, sending a flurry of leaves dancing around us, momentarily distracting me from the intensity of his gaze. I glanced around, pretending to admire the vibrant colors of the foliage, but the truth was, my heart was racing—not just from the encounter but from the thrill of the challenge he presented.

Liam took a step closer, his expression shifting from playful banter to something more earnest. "You know, beneath all that tough exterior, I see a real artist—one who isn't afraid to explore the depths of her own emotions. You just have to be willing to let go."

In that moment, surrounded by the laughter of festival-goers and the crackling energy of autumn, I felt a flicker of something—hope, perhaps? Or maybe it was simply the realization that the barriers I had so meticulously constructed were beginning to crack. But before I could respond, a shout from across the street drew our attention, and just like that, the spell was broken.

"Liam! Come help us set up!" called a fellow artist, waving her arms in exaggerated desperation. He turned back to me, and I could see the lighthearted mischief return to his eyes.

"Duty calls," he said, a lopsided grin spreading across his face. "Don't think this conversation is over, though. I'll be watching your booth, and who knows? Maybe I'll let you win this time."

With that, he sauntered off, leaving me standing there, a whirlwind of emotions swirling inside me—confusion, intrigue, and the tiniest hint of excitement. I couldn't shake the feeling that this festival would become something more than just a competition; it would be a reckoning. A chance to confront not just him but also the buried fears that had been holding me back, and perhaps even rediscover the passion that had initially drawn me to art in the first place.

The bustle of the art festival wrapped around me like a well-worn scarf, its vibrancy both comforting and chaotic. I strolled through the sea of booths, my fingers brushing against the cool ceramics and warm fabrics displayed under twinkling fairy lights. Each piece told a story, a fragment of someone's soul laid bare for the world to admire—or criticize. I inhaled deeply, the mingling scents of spiced cider and freshly baked pastries filling my lungs, a welcome distraction from the tension lingering in the back of my mind like an unwelcome guest.

But even in this lively atmosphere, I couldn't shake the memory of Liam's smirk, nor the intensity of our brief exchange. It clung to me, electrifying the air between us, making it hard to focus on my own work. My booth was a colorful array of pottery, each piece crafted with care, designed to resonate with the beauty of the season. Autumn bowls adorned with intricate leaf patterns and mugs that captured the spirit of cozy nights by the fire, all waiting for eager hands to take them home. Yet, as I arranged my creations, my thoughts wandered back to him—his laughter, his confidence, the way his presence commanded attention.

As I adjusted a particularly vibrant bowl, a voice interrupted my reverie. "These are stunning!" A petite woman with a cascade of curly hair stood in front of my booth, her wide eyes sparkling with enthusiasm. "I've never seen pottery that looks so alive!"

"Thank you!" I replied, my heart warming at her praise. "I like to think of each piece as a little story. This one, for example," I gestured to a bowl swirling with oranges and reds, "is meant to capture the essence of autumn leaves tumbling in the wind."

"Gorgeous! I can practically hear them rustling." She picked up the bowl, cradling it as if it were a fragile treasure. "How do you come up with these ideas?"

I felt a flutter of pride and vulnerability as I explained my inspiration, sharing how I poured my emotions into every piece, crafting not just ceramics but reflections of my inner world. The conversation flowed easily, a welcome change from the chaos of my thoughts about Liam.

Just as I was starting to enjoy the moment, a voice called out, smooth and confident, slicing through the air like a knife through warm butter. "Now, if you want to hear about real artistry, you should come see my work. It's what I like to call 'intricate genius.'"

My heart sank as I turned to find Liam, striding toward my booth like he owned the place, hands casually resting on his hips. He stopped a few feet away, a smirk playing at the corners of his mouth.

"Liam, how charming," I said dryly, my voice betraying none of the tumultuous emotions roiling beneath the surface. "I didn't know this was a competition for the most grandiose self-introduction."

"Why not? It's clearly a talent of mine," he quipped, his eyes sparkling with mischief. He leaned in slightly, examining the bowl the woman still held. "But I see you've gone for a more subtle approach. How quaint."

"Subtlety has its merits," I countered, a smile teasing my lips despite the irritation that bubbled beneath. "Unlike the over-the-top dramatics you seem to favor. I'd hate to distract the audience from your genius with mere decorations."

"Ah, but isn't art supposed to provoke thought? To spark conversation?" he asked, his voice low and playful. "And what better way to do that than with a little flair?" He gestured flamboyantly, as if he were unveiling the next great masterpiece rather than standing in front of my pottery.

The woman, clearly entertained by our banter, giggled. "You two are hilarious! Are you always this entertaining?"

"Only when there's a worthy opponent," Liam replied, his gaze locking onto mine, a challenge lingering in the air between us.

"Oh, I wouldn't say you're a worthy opponent," I shot back, a rush of adrenaline fueling my words. "More like a comedic sidekick."

"Comedic? You wound me." He placed a hand over his heart, feigning deep injury. "I thought I brought a certain charm to the festival."

"Charm? More like chaos in a well-fitted jacket," I retorted, unable to hide my grin.

"I prefer to think of it as... unpredictability," he replied smoothly, leaning closer, his eyes twinkling with mischief. "The festival could use a bit more excitement, don't you think? And who better to provide it than me?"

I rolled my eyes but couldn't help the warmth creeping into my cheeks. "If your version of excitement involves stealing the spotlight, I think the festival might survive without it."

As our repartee continued, I felt the barriers I had built begin to crack. Liam had a way of drawing me in, of making the tension between us feel charged with a different kind of energy—one that was thrilling and terrifying all at once. Just as I was starting to lose myself in the banter, a loud crash broke the moment.

Turning to see what had happened, I saw a nearby artist's easel had toppled over, sending canvases tumbling to the ground. The vibrant colors splayed across the pavement like a shattered rainbow. My heart sank for the artist, who rushed forward, panic evident in her eyes.

"Sorry! I thought I secured it better!" she exclaimed, scrambling to gather her fallen pieces.

Liam and I exchanged a quick look, the competitive energy morphing into something else entirely. "Let's help," I said, my irritation with him momentarily forgotten as a sense of camaraderie took hold.

"Agreed," he replied, moving to assist her. We both knelt on the ground, carefully picking up the canvases, our hands brushing against each other inadvertently, sending a jolt of unexpected warmth through me.

"Thank you, thank you so much!" the artist gushed, her hands trembling as she accepted her work back from us. "I'm so embarrassed. It was a last-minute addition, and I thought I could manage it."

"It happens to the best of us," Liam said, his tone soothing as he helped her straighten the easel. "Just take it as a lesson in securing your artistic brilliance."

I smiled at his genuine kindness, surprised by his unexpected compassion. Perhaps beneath that smug exterior lay a heart capable of empathy. As the three of us worked together, the atmosphere shifted. The laughter of festival-goers faded into the background, and for a brief moment, it was just the three of us—a shared mission to restore order amid the chaos.

Once the artist was back on her feet and her work was secure, she looked at us with newfound appreciation. "I can't thank you both enough! I would've been a complete wreck without your help."

"No problem at all," I said, feeling a sense of satisfaction at having contributed to a moment of joy amidst the frenzy of the festival.

As she moved on, thanking us once more before disappearing into the crowd, I turned to Liam, who was leaning against a booth, arms crossed with an amused expression. "Look at you, being a hero. Who knew you had it in you?"

"Don't get used to it," he replied, his smile broadening. "I prefer my chaos unimpeded."

"Of course you do," I laughed, shaking my head. "The world needs its resident tornado, after all."

Our playful banter resumed, each remark bouncing off the other like colorful balloons in the autumn breeze. But as I glanced at the vibrant tapestry of life unfolding around us—the laughter, the art, the connections—I realized something deeper was happening. This festival was more than just a competition; it was a tapestry of moments, an opportunity to forge unexpected connections. And perhaps, just perhaps, the man I had once viewed as an adversary was about to become something altogether different.

The festival thrummed with life, a vibrant heartbeat that pulsed through the colorful stalls, the lively chatter of artists and patrons mingling with the melodies drifting from a nearby string quartet. Each note danced in the crisp autumn air, creating an enchanting backdrop that stirred something deep within me. I had initially intended to keep my focus solely on my booth, yet here I was, sharing moments with Liam that felt curiously charged, as if the universe were conspiring to draw us together.

"Are you always this captivating, or is it just the festival?" he teased, tilting his head slightly, eyes glimmering with playful mischief.

"Just the festival, I assure you," I shot back, an eyebrow raised. "At least, that's the plan. I'd hate to think my charm is a year-round endeavor."

"Too bad," he said, crossing his arms, feigning disappointment. "I was hoping to catch a glimpse of the great Adalyn Bennett in her natural habitat—mastering the art of pottery and sass."

His casual confidence grated against my carefully curated walls, yet I found myself drawn to him in spite of it. It was maddening, really. I shook my head, forcing myself to focus on my pottery and not on the way his voice seemed to linger in the air long after he spoke.

As the day wore on, I couldn't help but steal glances at his booth, where vibrant canvases danced in the breeze, each one a burst of color and emotion. I could see patrons lingering, their fingers itching to touch the striking pieces. It was hard to admit that Liam's talent was undeniable, even if his presence felt like a continuous challenge.

Suddenly, the bustling festival atmosphere was punctured by a loud commotion. A group of children raced past, their laughter infectious, but their carefree joy was soon overshadowed by a loud crash. I turned just in time to see a cascade of Liam's paintings tumble to the ground, their vibrant colors splashing across the cobblestones like spilled secrets.

"Not again!" he exclaimed, rushing to save them. My heart twisted at the sight of his frustration, and instinctively, I joined him, our competitive spirits momentarily set aside.

"Here, let me help!" I said, kneeling to scoop up one of the fallen canvases, its corner frayed but still beautiful.

Liam glanced at me, surprise flickering in his eyes before he smiled. "I didn't think you'd join the rescue mission. Are you sure you want to be seen helping your rival?"

I rolled my eyes. "Only because I'd hate to see your genius splattered on the ground. It's still competition, remember?"

"Ah, the competitive spirit rears its head," he said, laughter dancing in his voice. "I can respect that."

As we worked side by side, there was an unexpected rhythm to our movements. I handed him a canvas, our fingers brushing briefly, and I felt a jolt of energy course through me. It was a reminder of the tension that had always simmered between us—a mix of rivalry and an undeniable connection that was hard to ignore.

Once the paintings were safely stacked, I leaned back, wiping my hands on my apron, a sense of satisfaction washing over me. "There. No more tragic spills today, I hope."

"Thanks," he said, glancing at me with a sincerity that momentarily disarmed me. "I owe you one. Maybe we could call it a truce for the rest of the festival?"

I feigned contemplation, tapping my chin. "A truce? How noble of you. But I'll need something in return. Let's say... a promise that you won't steal my ideas during the judging process."

He laughed, and it was the kind of laugh that made my heart race. "Deal. But only if you promise not to comment on my 'artistic flair' when the judges come around. I can't have my reputation sullied."

As the playful banter continued, I couldn't help but feel a shift in the atmosphere around us. The laughter of festival-goers faded into a soft hum as our attention drew closer, the spark between us igniting something I hadn't anticipated.

But just as I felt the air thicken with unspoken possibilities, a shadow loomed over us. A tall figure appeared, their presence demanding attention, instantly cutting through the lightheartedness like a knife. I looked up to find a woman in a sleek black coat, her hair slicked back in a tight bun that hinted at both power and poise.

"Liam Callahan," she said, her voice crisp and authoritative. "I need to speak with you."

Liam's smile faltered, replaced by a flicker of concern. "Sabrina? What are you doing here?"

"I came to discuss your contract," she said, glancing between us with an unreadable expression. The atmosphere shifted dramatically, tension crackling like static electricity.

My heart sank as I watched Liam's face cloud with apprehension. "Can't this wait until after the festival? I'm a bit... busy at the moment."

"No, it can't," she replied firmly, her tone leaving no room for negotiation. "You have a serious decision to make, and it needs to be addressed now."

A knot twisted in my stomach. The playful banter between us was abruptly replaced by a heavy silence, and I suddenly felt like an intruder in a world I didn't understand. The glimmer of connection we had just established began to fade, overshadowed by the weight of this woman's presence.

"Okay," Liam said, his voice steadying, yet I could see the tension in his shoulders. "Let's talk."

Before he could turn back to me, Sabrina added, "And Adalyn, if you're smart, you'll step aside. This is a conversation that doesn't concern you."

A chill ran down my spine at her words, and a wave of vulnerability washed over me. I stood frozen, caught between the excitement of the festival and the sudden gravity of the moment. The connection I thought we might be building evaporated like mist under the morning sun, leaving behind an unsettling void.

"Wait," I managed to say, my voice barely above a whisper. "What's going on?"

But before either of them could respond, the ground beneath us trembled slightly, a deep rumble that sent a shiver through the air. Gasps erupted from the crowd, and I instinctively grabbed onto the edge of my booth for support.

"What was that?" I asked, panic rising in my chest.

Liam's eyes widened as he turned back to me, the playful banter replaced by a look of concern. "I don't know, but we need to—"

Suddenly, a loud crack split the air, echoing through the festival grounds like thunder. The ground shook again, this time more violently, sending several booths wobbling precariously. My heart raced as chaos erupted around us, artists scrambling to secure their work, festival-goers shouting in confusion.

"Stay close!" Liam shouted, reaching for my hand. The warmth of his grip sent shockwaves through me, grounding me amidst the chaos, but before I could respond, the tremor intensified.

The crowd surged, and in an instant, everything changed.

Chapter 2: Collisions

The night of the festival pulsated with a vibrant rhythm, a living mosaic of laughter, music, and the intoxicating scent of candied apples mingling with the crisp autumn air. Fairy lights twinkled like stars caught in a net, casting soft glows on the faces of festival-goers who flitted from booth to booth, their cheeks flushed with delight. I had set my heart on this evening, convinced it would be the moment I finally cemented my place among the local artisans, a chance to showcase my handmade jewelry to a crowd that thrummed with energy.

As I arranged my delicate silver pieces, the moon hung high, a luminous overseer to the spirited chaos unfolding beneath it. The intricate designs I had poured my soul into sparkled under the lights, but all at once, the atmosphere shifted. I felt it before I saw him—an electric charge crackling in the air that drew my gaze like a moth to a flame. Liam stood there, tall and brooding, his dark hair tousled by the gentle night breeze. His presence was a cocktail of annoyance and intrigue, a combination that sent my heart racing like a runaway train.

Our eyes met, and in that instant, the world around us faded. I could feel the intensity of his stare, deep enough to drown in, and suddenly my carefully arranged booth felt precarious, like it might topple at any moment. It was infuriatingly clear that this man had a way of unraveling my composure. Just then, a shout cut through the revelry—a piercing sound that sliced through the laughter, drawing our attention to the edge of the square.

A figure burst into view, cloaked in shadow and chaos. The festival's cheerful facade crumbled as gasps and murmurs rippled through the crowd. I squinted, trying to discern what was happening, but the figure was a whirlwind, sending festival-goers scattering like leaves before a storm. Panic erupted, and I instinctively took a step back, heart hammering in my chest.

"Stay close," Liam commanded, his voice a low rumble that resonated deep within me. Before I could respond, he reached for my arm, his grip firm yet reassuring. I could feel the warmth radiating from him, an anchor in the tumult. As we moved together, weaving through the chaos, I could hardly believe that mere moments ago, we had been locked in a silent battle of glances, and now we were bound by the very real threat looming before us.

The crowd surged, a wave of panic that threatened to engulf us. I glanced up at Liam, and in that fleeting moment, the intensity of his expression ignited a spark of bravery within me. We couldn't let fear dictate our night, not now, not when I had come so far to claim my moment. "We need to see what's happening!" I shouted over the din, adrenaline fueling my resolve.

His gaze softened for a heartbeat, as if he were considering my words, then he nodded. Together, we plunged into the fray, his hand still clasped around mine. The heat of his palm sent shivers down my spine, and I had to shake my head to clear the distraction. This was not the time for those kinds of thoughts.

As we pushed forward, the chaotic scene unfolded before us—a man, clad in dark clothing, shouted incoherently, waving his arms like a puppet with broken strings. He looked wild, eyes alight with a frantic energy that could only be described as unhinged. The crowd had retreated, forming a cautious perimeter, but I felt a pull toward the center, curiosity gnawing at me.

"Are you crazy?" Liam hissed as I moved to get a closer look. "Stay back!"

"Someone needs to help him!" I shot back, my heart racing not just from fear but from the thrill of defiance.

With a deep breath, I stepped forward, my pulse thrumming in my ears. "Hey! Are you okay?" I called, my voice slicing through the cacophony. The man turned, and for a moment, our eyes locked. What I saw in his gaze wasn't just chaos; it was desperation.

"Help! They're coming for me!" His voice cracked, the words tumbling out like stones from a crumbling wall. I instinctively knew this was about more than just a night gone awry—it was a plea steeped in urgency, a warning wrapped in madness.

"Who's coming?" I asked, my voice steady despite the shivers dancing down my spine.

Before he could answer, a flash of movement behind him caught my eye. A group of figures emerged from the shadows, their faces obscured but their intentions clear. My instincts screamed for us to run, but I felt rooted in place, the adrenaline surging through me like wildfire.

"Liam!" I shouted, turning to him, my heart racing. "We have to do something!"

But just as I looked back, a sudden surge of energy erupted. Liam stepped forward, his body blocking mine as he positioned himself protectively between me and the oncoming figures. "You need to get out of here!" he barked, his jaw clenched in determination.

I felt the world tilt on its axis, the electric tension between us crackling like a live wire, charged with something deeper than just the chaos surrounding us. But as the figures advanced, fear coiled around my heart, a vice tightening with each heartbeat. "We can't leave him!" I insisted, feeling a surge of conviction.

Liam turned, his expression fierce yet conflicted. "You're not thinking clearly!"

But in that moment, something shifted in me. The night was no longer just about showcasing my jewelry or proving my worth; it was about standing up for someone who was clearly lost in a world of shadows, a world I had no idea existed until this very moment.

"Maybe it's time to rethink what's worth fighting for," I whispered, barely audible over the tension thrumming in the air.

The words hung between us, heavy with the weight of an unspoken understanding. I wasn't just in this for myself anymore; I was in it for him, for us, and whatever the night had in store.

The chaos that unfolded around us felt surreal, a twisted blend of urgency and dread. As the figures emerged from the shadows, their silhouettes sharp against the backdrop of fairy lights, the reality of our situation hit me like a jolt of cold water. The festival, once a riot of joy and excitement, had morphed into a battleground, with my heart pounding in sync with the chaos swirling around us.

"Stay behind me," Liam said, his voice firm yet laced with an edge of something softer—concern, perhaps. I felt a rush of warmth at his protectiveness, but the instinct to push forward surged within me. How could I stand by while someone needed help?

"I won't let you face this alone," I shot back, my determination flaring like a flame against the gust of fear that threatened to extinguish it. "We need to figure out what's happening. This isn't just a random outburst." I glanced back at the frantic man whose plea had ignited my resolve. He was still writhing in the grip of his panic, eyes darting around as if he were cornered prey.

As Liam and I stepped closer, the figures advanced, and I could make out more details—dark clothing, hooded faces, a palpable tension crackling in the air. They were a stark contrast to the jovial festival-goers who had once filled the square with laughter and warmth. My stomach twisted with apprehension, but the thought of retreating was not an option.

"Who are you?" one of the shadowy figures demanded, his voice low and gravelly, slicing through the murmur of fear. "Step aside."

Liam's stance shifted subtly, muscles coiled beneath his shirt, a silent promise to protect me at all costs. "You need to leave him alone," he replied, each word a measured strike against the rising tide of menace. The defiance in his voice drew my admiration, igniting a sense of camaraderie that I hadn't expected to find amidst the chaos.

"Or what?" the figure taunted, stepping forward, his bravado overshadowed by the fear glinting in his eyes. "You think you can stop us?"

"Actually, I do," I interjected, surprising even myself with the strength of my conviction. I had no idea what I was about to unleash, but there was something empowering in standing up against this threat, however absurd it seemed. "You're scaring everyone. You need to back off and let him go."

For a heartbeat, silence reigned, an expectant hush that stretched taut as a drawn bowstring. I could see the gears turning in the figures' minds, weighing the cost of their aggression against the unlikely resolve radiating from us. I stole a glance at Liam, whose eyes held a mixture of surprise and admiration, and it fueled my determination.

"Why don't you take your drama elsewhere?" I added, my voice steady, eyes narrowing in challenge. "I mean, it's not even Halloween yet. You're a little early for all this, don't you think?"

A flicker of amusement crossed Liam's face, and for a fleeting moment, I felt a connection beyond the crisis—a shared sense of absurdity in our circumstances. The tension was palpable, yet in that instant, it felt like we were cocooned in a bubble, impervious to the chaos surrounding us.

But the figures were not amused. The leader, a tall man with a scar slashed across his cheek, stepped closer, his eyes glinting with a mixture of anger and curiosity. "You're brave," he said, a sneer curling his lips. "Or foolish. Either way, this doesn't concern you."

"Oh, I think it does," I replied, straightening my back and summoning every ounce of courage I possessed. "We're not just going to stand by and let you terrorize this festival. This is supposed to be a night of celebration, not a stage for your theatrics."

Liam turned to me, a flicker of surprise lighting his features. "You really have a way with words," he murmured, a hint of admiration threading through his voice.

The scarred man scoffed, his patience waning. "Enough of this nonsense. Move aside, or you'll regret it." He gestured to his companions, who shifted restlessly, eager for action.

"Liam, we need a plan," I whispered, my heart racing as I felt the energy in the air shift once more.

He met my gaze, his expression fierce, eyes glinting with determination. "We'll distract them. You find a way to help him."

Before I could protest, Liam pushed me to the side, stepping into the open, his presence solid and unyielding. "You want a show? Let's give them one."

I felt a surge of pride and fear as I watched him confront the figures. He was a force of nature, and I wanted nothing more than to match his courage. But the frantic man needed me. I turned back to him, urgency flooding my veins. "Listen to me!" I said, my voice urgent. "What do they want? You have to tell me!"

He looked at me, eyes wide and filled with a mix of gratitude and terror. "They're after something... something I took," he stammered, his breath coming in ragged gasps. "I thought I could escape. I didn't know they would come here."

"Okay, okay. We'll figure this out," I assured him, glancing back at Liam, who was buying us time with bravado and bravura. He was doing this for us, for the festival, and perhaps, in some unexpected way, for me.

With a swift motion, I stepped forward, my voice rising above the tension. "You don't have to hurt him!" I cried out, my heart pounding with desperation. "Whatever he has, just take it and go. This isn't the place for this kind of violence!"

The leader turned, a look of disdain mixed with intrigue on his face. "And why should we listen to you? You're just a girl playing hero in a fairy tale."

"Maybe," I replied, my voice steady despite the fear coursing through me. "But every story has a hero, and right now, you look like the villain. And villains rarely win."

The crowd around us had started to gather again, hesitant but drawn in by my boldness. There was power in numbers, and I could sense the tide shifting.

The scarred man narrowed his eyes, momentarily thrown off balance by my audacity. It was the opening I needed. "You want to scare us? Fine. But I won't back down. We will stand together, and if you think you can bully us, you'll find we're stronger than you think."

In that moment, a flicker of hesitation crossed his face. Just as it seemed I might have planted a seed of doubt, the ground beneath us seemed to tremble—a subtle but unmistakable sign of shifting allegiances.

As I stood my ground, Liam moved closer, his presence an unyielding wall of strength beside me. "You heard her," he said, voice low and steady. "You're not welcome here. You can leave, or we'll make you regret sticking around."

The tension in the air grew thick, charged with an unpredictable energy, as the crowd held its breath, waiting for the next move.

Liam's presence beside me felt like a living shield, his body tense and poised as he faced the figures closing in on us. I couldn't help but admire the way he stood there, every muscle defined under the dim glow of the festival lights, embodying a mix of courage and fierce protectiveness. It was a stark contrast to the swirling uncertainty that threatened to envelop me.

"Are you always this dramatic?" I quipped, forcing a laugh that barely masked my own fear. "I didn't sign up for a street brawl when I came to sell jewelry."

"Funny, neither did I," Liam replied, his tone steady but a hint of a smile tugging at his lips, the corners crinkling in a way that made my heart flutter against the backdrop of impending chaos. "But here we are, and it seems we're both very much in it together."

The crowd had thickened, a sea of anxious faces peering through the chaos, tension bubbling just beneath the surface. I could sense their collective anticipation, an energy that swirled like the autumn leaves caught in a gust of wind. The moment was charged, and I couldn't shake the feeling that we were at the eye of a brewing storm.

The scarred man glanced back at his companions, their expressions a mixture of impatience and incredulity. "You think you can protect him?" he spat, his voice dripping with scorn. "You're just a couple of kids playing hero. This isn't a game."

"I may not have a cape," I shot back, feeling a surge of audacity, "but I can definitely be a distraction if that's what you need."

Liam's surprised glance met mine, and a flicker of understanding passed between us—an unspoken acknowledgment that we were in sync, both wanting to break free from the confines of fear. The scarred man seemed momentarily taken aback, uncertainty flickering across his features. It was a crack in the façade, and I knew I had to exploit it.

"Look," I said, raising my hands in a gesture of negotiation. "You want whatever it is he took? Fine. But you're not going to find it here tonight. Let's just talk this through like civilized people."

"Civilized?" The man barked out a laugh, sharp and mocking. "You think this is about civility? You really have no idea what you're dealing with, do you?"

"Then enlighten me," I retorted, refusing to let his bravado intimidate me. "What is this about?"

Suddenly, a shrill scream pierced the night air, cutting through the tension like a knife. I turned instinctively, and the crowd recoiled as another figure—this one smaller, almost fragile—broke free from the throng, her face streaked with tears.

"Maddie!" The frantic cry escaped my lips before I could stop it. It was my younger sister, and seeing her in the middle of this madness sent a jolt of panic through me.

"Get back!" Liam shouted, stepping forward protectively as if to shield me from any impending danger.

"Maddie, what are you doing here?" I called, forcing my voice to remain steady despite the turmoil inside me.

"I was looking for you! I didn't know where you were!" she cried, fear evident in her wide eyes. "I heard the shouting and—"

"Maddie, go back to the booth! Now!" I ordered, my heart racing as the figures turned their attention toward her, the atmosphere suddenly charged with even greater peril.

"Stop right there!" the scarred man barked, pointing a finger at my sister. "You don't belong here, little girl. This isn't a place for you."

"Leave her alone!" I snapped, fury igniting within me as I felt Liam's hand on my arm, grounding me in the maelstrom of emotions.

"Let her go!" Liam's voice thundered, resonating with a deep authority that startled even me. "You want what he has? Then take it from him and leave the innocent out of this!"

The scarred man hesitated, his brow furrowing as he considered Liam's challenge. "Innocent? You think anyone's innocent in this mess?" His eyes flickered to Maddie, then back to me. "You're all tangled up in this, whether you like it or not."

Just then, as if summoned by our mounting tension, the festival lights flickered ominously. The glow dimmed for a heartbeat before bursting back to life, casting the scene in an eerie glow. Gasps filled the air, and the crowd shifted, whispering among themselves, a collective fear gripping them tighter.

"Enough of this," I said, desperation clawing at my throat. "You want the man, take him. You don't need to involve my sister or anyone else."

But the scarred man's gaze was fixed on Maddie, a sinister glimmer lighting up his features. "Maybe I do want something more than what he stole."

"Over my dead body," I shot back, my heart racing as I prepared to lunge toward my sister, ready to protect her at all costs.

"Step aside, girl," the man warned, voice low and dangerous. "You have no idea what you're getting into."

"Trust me, I have an idea," I replied, grounding myself with a fierce determination that bubbled beneath the surface. "You're not scaring us off. You've underestimated us. That's your first mistake."

As if sensing the shift, Liam moved closer, his presence a fortress beside me. "If you think you can intimidate us, you're sorely mistaken," he said, voice low and steady. "We're not going anywhere. You'll have to deal with us both."

The figures shifted, uncertainty rippling through them like a wave. I could see the gears turning in their minds, weighing their options. The crowd had started to rally, murmurs of support echoing through the air.

"Maddie, get back!" I shouted again, this time with a fierce urgency. "Stay behind us!"

But just as my sister turned to comply, a shout erupted from the far side of the square, pulling everyone's attention. "What's going on here?"

A group of local officers had arrived, their badges glinting in the festival lights. They moved swiftly through the throng, the tension in the air shifting once more. I felt a rush of hope, but the scarred man's expression darkened, his eyes narrowing with fury.

"This isn't over," he spat, turning on his heel. "Not by a long shot."

Before I could react, he pushed through the crowd, signaling his companions to follow. The figures melted away into the shadows, their retreat leaving a trail of uncertainty in their wake.

Liam's grip tightened on my arm as he turned to me, breathing heavily, the adrenaline still coursing through him. "Are you okay?"

"I—I think so," I stammered, heart racing from the sudden shift in the air. But then, as the weight of what had just transpired began to settle in, another realization struck me.

"Maddie!" I gasped, turning back to my sister, who stood wide-eyed, trembling slightly but unharmed. Relief washed over me, but before I could embrace her, a piercing scream echoed from the edge of the square.

The officers, alerted by the sudden commotion, rushed forward, and I felt my heart plummet as I caught a glimpse of the scarred man again, standing atop a nearby stage, a menacing figure silhouetted against the night sky.

"Gather your people!" he shouted, his voice booming. "You have no idea what's coming!"

My blood ran cold, the chilling certainty settling in my bones. The night was far from over, and the real danger was just beginning.

Chapter 3: The Whispering Shadows

Days turned into weeks, and the atmosphere of Ashwood began to shift, thickening with an unspoken tension that wrapped around the town like a shroud. The festival incident had ignited a series of unsettling events: mysterious disappearances and hushed conversations whispered under the flickering glow of streetlamps. Each morning brought new tales, some innocuous and others laced with fear, making the air feel electric. Shadows loomed longer, and the once-vibrant streets seemed to hold their breath, waiting for something to break the silence.

Reluctantly, I found myself approaching Liam, the town's enigmatic figure, whose presence had previously only served to fuel my irritation. Our rivalry had been the stuff of gossip—a playful banter that sometimes bordered on sparring. But desperation has a way of shifting perspectives. I stood on the edge of a decision that felt monumental, feeling the weight of the town's history pressing down upon me.

"Liam," I called, my voice surprisingly steady against the cacophony of rustling leaves and distant laughter. He paused, turning toward me with that infuriatingly confident smirk, his dark hair tousled as if he had just emerged from a battle with the wind itself.

"What do you want, Mia?" he asked, a hint of teasing in his tone, though the underlying seriousness of my expression must have registered with him.

I hesitated, the words dancing just out of reach, tangled in the threads of pride and fear. "We need to talk. About the disappearances."

His smile faded, replaced by a look of genuine concern. "You're not suggesting we investigate, are you? Sounds dangerously fun."

"Fun? This is serious, Liam. People are missing."

"Fine, fine. I'll bite," he said, raising his hands in mock surrender. "Lead the way, fearless leader."

As we walked side by side, the air grew cooler, tinged with the scent of damp earth and pine. The sun dipped below the horizon, casting an ethereal glow that flickered through the trees like a warning. I could feel the weight of his presence beside me, a constant reminder of the complexities woven into our rivalry. Each moment spent in his company chipped away at my preconceived notions, revealing glimpses of vulnerability beneath the confident facade.

"Did you ever think about what it might feel like to be the one who disappears?" I asked, glancing at him from the corner of my eye.

He turned his head slightly, as if pondering my question. "It would suck. But you know what? People vanish for a reason. It's not always some grand conspiracy."

"And yet," I pressed, "the town has been on edge. Why is that?"

He shrugged, a flicker of something unreadable crossing his face. "Maybe they know more than they're letting on."

With each step, I found myself piecing together a version of Liam I hadn't recognized before—a complexity that intrigued me more than I was willing to admit. His keen insights hinted at a deeper understanding of our surroundings, a knowledge that belied his seemingly carefree attitude. But just as I was ready to lean into this unexpected connection, a rustle in the underbrush drew our attention.

"What was that?" I whispered, my heart racing as instinct kicked in.

Liam held a finger to his lips, signaling for silence. The shadows danced ominously around us as we strained to listen. The sound came again, this time accompanied by a low growl that sent chills skittering down my spine.

"Let's get out of here," I urged, the urge to flee battling with my curiosity.

But Liam stepped forward, his eyes gleaming with an inexplicable thrill. "No, wait. What if it's something interesting?"

"Interesting? Liam, it sounds like a rabid dog!"

"Or something worse," he countered, stepping cautiously toward the underbrush, a mix of bravery and reckless abandon. My pulse quickened, torn between the adrenaline of adventure and the instinctual urge to run.

Suddenly, the source of the noise leaped into view—a large, disheveled dog with matted fur and wild eyes. Relief washed over me, followed by an unexpected twinge of sympathy. "Poor thing," I murmured, kneeling down, hands outstretched. "Hey there, buddy."

Liam watched, amusement dancing in his eyes. "You're not seriously going to pet it, are you?"

"Why not? It's just scared."

The dog approached cautiously, sniffing at my fingers before allowing me to stroke its coarse fur. It leaned into my touch, letting out a low whine that tugged at my heartstrings. "See? Not everything in the woods is out to get us," I said, casting a triumphant glance at Liam.

"Yeah, but it might bite if you're not careful," he replied, half-joking, though there was a softness in his tone that suggested he, too, felt the pull of empathy.

The moment hung between us, charged with something unspoken. My heart fluttered as I realized how easily our rivalry had shifted into something more nuanced. The fleeting tension was intoxicating, a dance of banter and burgeoning friendship that left me both exhilarated and terrified.

"Do you think it has an owner?" I asked, scratching behind the dog's ears, feeling a warm connection forming.

"Maybe. Or maybe it's another mystery waiting to unfold. Ashwood has a funny way of twisting the ordinary into the extraordinary."

Just then, a distant howl echoed through the trees, sending a shiver through me. I stood, brushing dirt off my knees, my heart still racing. "Okay, maybe we should get moving," I said, glancing toward the darkening path.

"Agreed," Liam said, his playful demeanor returning as we resumed our trek. But as the shadows deepened around us, I couldn't shake the feeling that we were teetering on the edge of something significant—an adventure that promised to change everything.

The night deepened around us, a velvet cloak sprinkled with stars that seemed to watch over our every move. With the dog now trailing behind, its scruffy form blending into the shadows, Liam and I ventured further down the twisting path. The crunch of leaves beneath our feet punctuated the silence, each sound amplifying the palpable tension in the air. The world felt alive, the wind whispering secrets in a language I didn't yet understand.

"So, what's our game plan?" Liam asked, a hint of mischief dancing in his eyes. The playful lightness of his tone seemed at odds with the seriousness of our situation, but I found comfort in it, a reminder that even in darkness, a flicker of humor could light the way.

"Game plan? I thought we were just winging it," I shot back, my heart racing with a mix of fear and excitement. "But seriously, we should probably check in with some of the locals. They might know something."

"Great idea. Let's find the nearest tavern and see if anyone's been dipping into the local moonshine. Nothing draws out secrets quite like a little liquid courage," he replied, his grin widening.

We pushed forward, the faint glow of streetlamps becoming visible in the distance. As we approached, the low murmur of voices spilled out onto the street, mingling with the scent of wood smoke and something savory simmering inside. The tavern stood like an old friend, its weathered façade inviting and warm.

"After you," Liam gestured, bowing slightly as if ushering me into the court of gossip. I rolled my eyes but stepped inside, the familiar creak of the door welcoming me into a world of laughter, clinking glasses, and the rich scent of spiced ale.

A chorus of eyes turned toward us, some curious, others wary. I scanned the room, spotting familiar faces from the festival—old friends and distant acquaintances—all wrapped in conversations that fluttered around like moths to the flame. "I'll grab a table. You go charm the barmaid," I suggested, nudging him with my elbow as we made our way to the back.

"Charm? Is that what we're calling it now?" he replied with a smirk, his brows raised in mock disbelief. "How about I just try not to get us kicked out?"

I laughed, a light sound that felt like a small victory against the weight of the evening's undertones. Settling into a booth, I watched as Liam approached the bar, his easy confidence on display. The barmaid, a fiery redhead with a quick smile, seemed taken by his charm as he leaned in, exchanging playful banter while I tried to ignore the flutter of envy that accompanied it.

He returned moments later, sliding into the seat across from me with a pint in hand. "She said the usual suspects have been talking. Everyone's on edge since the festival. Apparently, there's been more than just disappearances; some folks are claiming they've seen things—figures lurking in the shadows."

"Figures?" I echoed, raising an eyebrow. "What kind of figures? Ghosts? Goblins?"

"Neither, I think. Just people. Or at least that's what the rumor mill is churning out." He took a sip of his drink, eyeing me over the rim. "And you know what they say about rumors."

"They're usually just a bunch of hot air," I replied, rolling my eyes. "But they can lead to something real."

"Exactly," he said, his expression turning serious. "I think we need to dig deeper, start with the people who might know more. Old Mrs. Caldwell at the edge of town—she's seen everything and everyone. If anyone has answers, it'll be her."

The thought of approaching Mrs. Caldwell sent a shiver down my spine. She was notorious for her sharp tongue and sharper gaze, and more than one brave soul had fled her doorstep with a piece of their dignity missing. But I nodded, steeling myself. "Right. The witch of Ashwood. Let's do it."

With a newfound sense of purpose, we finished our drinks and pushed ourselves back into the night, the stars blinking overhead as if encouraging our little expedition. The path to Mrs. Caldwell's cottage wound through a dense thicket, the trees looming like silent sentinels.

"I'll go first," Liam offered, stepping ahead as if to shield me from the encroaching shadows. "Just in case she turns us into toads."

I chuckled, the sound echoing in the stillness. "You'd make a terrible toad."

"Thanks for the vote of confidence," he shot back, glancing over his shoulder with a grin that sparked warmth in my chest.

We arrived at the small, crooked cottage nestled among the trees, its windows glowing with an eerie light. A crooked sign hung from the front porch, swinging slightly in the wind, announcing the presence of "Mrs. Caldwell—Herbs, Remedies, and the Occasional Curse." The humor of the sign masked the dread curling in my stomach.

"Here goes nothing," I said, raising a hand to knock. The sound echoed against the wooden door, and almost immediately, it creaked open, revealing a woman wrapped in layers of shawls, her silver hair framing her face like a halo of storms.

"What do you want?" she asked, her voice sharp as a knife, slicing through the evening's quiet.

"We—um—we're looking for information," Liam started, but Mrs. Caldwell's piercing gaze silenced him.

"Information comes at a price," she replied, her eyes narrowing as if calculating our worth. "And you two look like you have a few secrets of your own."

"Secrets? Us?" I feigned innocence, though my heart raced at her insight.

"Secrets are like shadows. They lurk even when you don't see them," she murmured, stepping aside to let us enter. The scent of dried herbs filled the air, mingling with something earthy and ancient.

The inside of her cottage was a jumble of jars, books, and curiosities that told stories of lives intertwined with the arcane. I felt a rush of energy, as if the very walls pulsed with history and untold tales.

"Sit," she commanded, gesturing to a rickety table cluttered with odd trinkets. "What do you seek, and what are you willing to offer in return?"

The weight of her gaze bore down on us, and I exchanged a glance with Liam. We were entering dangerous territory, but the thrill of the unknown spurred me on. "We want to know about the disappearances," I said, my voice steady despite the tremor in my hands. "And anything else that might be happening in Ashwood."

"Ah, the disappearances." A shadow flickered across her face, one that seemed to mirror the unease settling in my gut. "They are no accident, my dear. The whispers of the woods have grown louder, and they carry warnings of things best left undisturbed."

As she spoke, I felt the very air thrum with an intensity that hinted at deeper currents flowing through Ashwood—currents that threatened to pull us into the depths of a mystery far darker than we had anticipated. I could sense that this was only the beginning, the first brushstroke on a canvas that promised both danger and discovery.

"What do you mean?" Liam pressed, leaning forward as if trying to capture the truth spilling from her lips.

"Something stirs beneath the surface, something that hungers for what you hold dear." Her words danced around us, cloaked in foreboding. "You must tread carefully, for not all shadows are merely a play of light."

The weight of her warning hung in the air, a palpable reminder that our curiosity had unleashed a force we could hardly comprehend. As I met Liam's gaze, the spark of adventure was dimmed by a flicker of fear. We were in deeper than we had anticipated, the whispers of Ashwood beckoning us to unravel a mystery entwined with secrets, shadows, and the promise of danger lurking just out of sight.

The flickering candlelight in Mrs. Caldwell's cottage danced like spirits caught in an eternal waltz, casting shadows that seemed to breathe and pulse with secrets. My heart raced as her words sank in, twisting in my mind like tendrils of smoke. The very essence of Ashwood felt alive, whispering warnings that echoed in the corners of my thoughts.

Liam shifted uncomfortably in his seat, his brow furrowed with concern. "What do you mean, 'something stirs beneath the surface'?" he pressed, his voice steady yet edged with an urgency that resonated with my own.

Mrs. Caldwell leaned closer, her gray eyes piercing through the gloom. "There are forces at work here that you cannot comprehend, young ones. Ashwood holds its breath, teetering on the brink of chaos. The disappearances are just the beginning." Her voice dropped to a conspiratorial whisper, "There are those who wish to harness what lies beneath, and they will stop at nothing to get it."

I exchanged a glance with Liam, a shared understanding forming in the silence. "What does that even mean?" I challenged, frustration bubbling beneath the surface. "What lies beneath Ashwood? Are we talking about some ancient creature, or are you hinting at something more... sinister?"

Her laugh was a gravelly sound, filled with equal parts amusement and menace. "Oh, it's more than a creature, dear. This is a battle of wills, of power and darkness that dates back to before Ashwood was founded. What you seek to uncover could be the very thing that consumes you."

The warning clung to the air like thick fog, saturating my senses. I could feel the weight of it pressing down, almost suffocating in its intensity. "We're not afraid of a little darkness," I declared, though my voice wavered slightly, revealing the truth I was trying to hide.

"Fear is not the enemy," she replied, her tone now somber. "It's ignorance that will destroy you."

Just then, the cottage door creaked open, the gust of wind bringing with it a chill that swept through the room. I turned, half-expecting to see the trees come alive with whispers. Instead, it was just the night, yawning wide with mystery. "We should probably go," I said, glancing at Liam, who looked equally unsettled.

Mrs. Caldwell straightened, her gaze lingering on us like a hawk observing its prey. "Take heed, my dears. The shadows will follow you. Trust in each other, for there are alliances that are more powerful than you can fathom."

With that, we stepped back into the cool night air, the weight of her words lingering like a fog. As we walked away from the cottage, I could feel the tension thrumming between us, a mixture of fear and exhilaration igniting my senses.

"Did that feel like a horror movie to you?" Liam quipped, attempting to break the thick tension hanging in the air. "I half expected her to pull a crystal ball out and start predicting our doom."

"Very funny," I replied, nudging him playfully. "But she was serious. We need to figure out what she meant about the shadows and whatever is hiding beneath Ashwood."

"Right, because nothing says 'fun night' like investigating creepy legends," he replied, rolling his eyes, though a smirk lingered on his lips. "What do you propose? A midnight stakeout?"

"Actually, yes. A stakeout could work. We could check the old quarry. Rumor has it that strange happenings have been reported there, especially during the night."

"Fine, but if we get mauled by a wild animal, I'm holding you responsible," he joked, though I could tell he was intrigued.

The path to the quarry twisted and turned, shrouded in darkness as we navigated through the trees. The silence was punctuated only by the rustle of leaves and the distant call of an owl, making the hairs on the back of my neck stand on end. I felt a blend of fear and excitement coursing through me as we approached the rocky outcrop, the moonlight spilling over the jagged edges like a silvery blanket.

"Alright, this is it," I whispered, my voice barely carrying above the night sounds. "Let's see what's hiding in the shadows."

As we crept closer to the edge of the quarry, I noticed something—a flicker of light emanating from the depths below. It pulsed rhythmically, a beacon calling us into the abyss. My heart raced, a mix of curiosity and trepidation propelling me forward. "Do you see that?" I asked, glancing at Liam.

"Yeah. That's definitely not normal," he replied, his voice steady despite the tension crackling in the air. "Should we go down?"

"Absolutely," I said, my pulse quickening as I took a step closer. "We have to find out what it is."

Descending into the quarry was no easy task; the rocks were uneven and treacherous. With every step, I felt the energy shift, the atmosphere growing thicker, as if we were moving deeper into a living entity that breathed and pulsed beneath our feet. The light flickered, beckoning us closer until I could make out figures—dark silhouettes gathered around an altar of stone.

"What the hell is happening?" Liam murmured, disbelief coloring his tone.

Before I could respond, a chilling howl echoed through the quarry, cutting through the night like a knife. The figures turned toward us, their faces obscured in shadow, yet their eyes glowed with an otherworldly light. Fear surged through me, a primal instinct telling me to turn and run.

But before I could move, one of them stepped forward, raising a hand as if to stop us. "You shouldn't have come here," they warned, their voice layered with an unsettling mix of authority and warning.

"Who are you?" I demanded, my voice trembling slightly.

The figure smiled, a slow, deliberate motion that sent a shiver down my spine. "We are the keepers of what lies beneath. And you've just opened a door that should have remained closed."

The air crackled with tension, the gravity of the situation hitting me like a tidal wave. I glanced at Liam, who looked just as bewildered as I felt. "We need to leave," he whispered urgently.

But before we could retreat, the ground trembled beneath us, the light flickering wildly as if responding to the fear coursing through my veins. The quarry erupted in chaos, the shadows swirling around us, enveloping us in a darkness that felt both alive and hungry.

"Run!" I shouted, grabbing Liam's arm, but before we could escape, the figures surged forward, their eyes glowing fiercely in the night.

A piercing scream echoed in the distance, cutting through the chaos, a sound filled with desperation and despair. The world around us warped and twisted, plunging us into a nightmare we hadn't anticipated. And as I felt the shadows close in, I realized with dawning horror that we might have just stumbled into something far more dangerous than we had ever imagined, something that would change the very fabric of our lives forever.

Chapter 4: Breaking Barriers

The clock on the wall ticked a steady rhythm, the sound mingling with the low hum of the overhead lights. My fingers curled around the chipped handle of a mug that had seen better days, the warmth of the cheap coffee within contrasting sharply with the chill that permeated Liam's studio. I watched as he leaned over a spread of old maps and photographs, his brow furrowed in concentration, the soft light casting shadows across his angular features. Each moment spent with him was a delicate dance between curiosity and apprehension, and I found myself captivated by the way he immersed himself in the mysteries that lay before us.

The scent of roasted beans lingered in the air, mingling with the faint odor of musty paper and the lingering remnants of a half-eaten sandwich from our last marathon session. I shifted in my seat, the worn cushion squeaking beneath me as I leaned forward, drawn into the puzzle we were piecing together. "You know," I said, breaking the silence that had settled like a fog, "if we don't find something soon, I'm going to have to start charging rent for squatting in your studio."

Liam's head snapped up, a playful glint in his eye that made my heart skip a beat. "Is that so? And here I thought you enjoyed being my unpaid intern." His smirk was disarming, the kind that could make anyone forget their troubles for a moment. "Besides, I'm pretty sure the coffee has been your primary source of sustenance for weeks now."

I rolled my eyes, but the corners of my mouth betrayed me, twitching upward in a smile. "You mean that sludge? I think I've had better brew at a gas station." Leaning back, I crossed my arms, feigning indignation. "You really need to invest in some proper coffee-making equipment."

"Oh, so now you're a coffee connoisseur?" His teasing tone softened, revealing a hint of warmth that made the air around us shimmer. "I'll add it to my list of things to improve in my life along with my general social skills and ability to not be utterly consumed by work."

There it was again—his self-deprecating humor, a mask that veiled the shadows lurking just beneath the surface. I had seen glimpses of that shadow, especially on those late nights when he thought I was too absorbed in the task at hand to notice the flicker of pain that crossed his face. The easy banter between us was a double-edged sword, teasing out moments of connection while reminding me of the distance that still lay between us, laden with secrets and fears that threatened to unravel everything.

As I traced my finger along the edge of the table, my mind wandered to the case we were unraveling—the disappearance of a local artist years ago, a mystery that had drawn us together. The more we uncovered, the deeper the entanglements seemed to grow, threading their way through our lives like the roots of a sprawling tree. Each lead we followed peeled back layers of the past, revealing truths that were at once exhilarating and terrifying.

"Okay, let's take a step back," I suggested, my voice steady despite the fluttering in my stomach. "What do we know for sure?"

Liam pulled his chair closer, the wood creaking in protest. "We know that she was last seen here, at the annual arts festival. Her booth was popular, but she vanished without a trace, leaving behind her work and—" he hesitated, the air thick with unspoken implications, "—some rather dubious acquaintances."

"Dubious is a generous term," I countered, leaning in. "We're talking about people who seemed to be more interested in her talent than her as a person."

He nodded, his gaze distant as he toyed with a crumpled photo of the artist. "That's the problem. Everyone had something to gain, but no one seems to care where she went."

A shiver traced my spine at the thought. "What if it's more than just a disappearance? What if it's something darker?"

"Like someone wanting to silence her?" Liam's voice dropped to a conspiratorial whisper, sending a thrill down my back.

"Exactly," I replied, excitement dancing in my chest. "And if that's true, we might be getting too close for comfort."

Liam's eyes locked onto mine, and in that moment, the world outside faded away. "We can't stop now. Not when we're so close."

The tension in the air thickened, my breath catching as I registered the weight of his words. Something flickered between us, an unspoken acknowledgment of the danger we faced and the exhilaration of discovery. But beneath that thrill lay an undercurrent of fear that threatened to wash over me. I wanted to lean into that connection, to embrace the warmth that spread through me when our hands brushed against each other while sorting through the cluttered chaos of his studio. But the memory of the warnings—the ones whispered in hushed tones by those who cared for my safety—pulled me back, reminding me that some barriers were built for a reason.

I took a sip of the coffee, hoping to ground myself, but the bitter taste only heightened my senses. I could see the determination etched on Liam's face, the way his fingers curled around the photograph as if it were a lifeline. "I'm not afraid," I declared, my voice steady but my heart racing. "But if we're going to do this, we need to be smart. We can't let the thrill of the chase blind us to the risks."

Liam leaned back, studying me, and for a moment, I thought I saw a flicker of admiration in his gaze. "You're right. We need a plan."

As we turned our focus back to the evidence sprawled before us, I couldn't shake the feeling that we were standing on the precipice of something monumental. Each word exchanged, every shared glance, felt like a silent promise that this journey was only beginning, and that the barriers we faced—both external and internal—were only waiting to be broken down.

The next few nights passed in a blur of caffeine and late-night brainstorming sessions. Each evening, as the sun dipped below the horizon and shadows draped themselves over the cluttered surfaces of Liam's studio, our conversations flowed deeper, more intimate. The initial thrill of unraveling the mystery began to intertwine with something more personal, an invisible thread drawing me closer to him.

As I scribbled notes in the margins of old newspapers, my thoughts were frequently interrupted by the way his laugh echoed against the walls—a rich, warm sound that made my insides flutter like leaves caught in a gentle breeze. "You know," I said one night, barely looking up from the papers, "if this whole detective thing doesn't pan out, you could always consider a career in stand-up comedy. You've got the timing for it."

"Only if you promise to be my number one fan," he replied, a playful glint in his eye as he leaned back in his chair, stretching his arms overhead like a lazy cat. The motion highlighted the muscles in his arms, and I suddenly felt a rush of heat creeping up my neck, forcing my focus back to the table, where the dim light cast a warm glow over the yellowed pages.

"Only if I get free tickets," I shot back, allowing a smirk to dance on my lips as I resisted the urge to follow the curve of his smile. There was an electric current in the air, one that made my heart race and my palms slightly sweat, and I was becoming increasingly aware of how easy it was to lose myself in him.

"Deal," he said, his voice dropping an octave, filled with mock seriousness that made my heart flutter again. "You'll get a front-row seat to my spectacular failures."

The teasing banter, while lighthearted, acted as a balm to the simmering tension that crept in with every shared glance and accidental brush of our fingers. However, with each moment that brought us closer, a sense of foreboding loomed in the background, threatening to shatter the fragile bubble we had created. I could almost hear the whisper of danger, reminding me of the risk we were taking by probing into matters that were better left undisturbed.

"What if we're not supposed to find anything?" I ventured one evening, my fingers fiddling nervously with the edge of the newspaper. "What if someone doesn't want us to?"

Liam's expression shifted, his playful demeanor falling away, replaced by a more serious, contemplative look. "You think someone's watching us?"

I nodded slowly, trying to articulate the vague anxiety gnawing at my gut. "Maybe not watching, but... aware. The deeper we dig, the more likely it is we'll unearth something that ruffles feathers."

His gaze narrowed thoughtfully. "Or maybe it's just our imaginations getting the better of us."

"Maybe," I conceded, though the hair on the back of my neck prickled at the thought. The last thing I wanted was for our investigation to veer into dangerous territory, and yet, the pull of the unknown was magnetic.

"Let's not overthink it," he said, reaching across the table and placing his hand over mine. The contact sent a jolt through me, a surge of warmth that left me breathless. "We're in this together, right?"

I inhaled sharply, overwhelmed by the weight of his words and the reality that hung between us. "Together," I echoed, willing myself to focus on the reassurance in his voice instead of the tension coiling within.

The following week felt as if it were strung tight like a guitar, ready to snap at the slightest provocation. Every interaction we had was charged, laced with an energy that simmered beneath the surface, begging for release. As we worked tirelessly to piece together the clues, I couldn't help but wonder if the mystery we were uncovering was only half of what lay ahead of us.

One evening, while we sifted through a box of old letters and photographs, I unearthed a faded postcard, the edges tattered and worn. The image depicted a picturesque beach, golden sands glistening under the sun, a stark contrast to the heaviness of our current endeavor. "Look at this," I said, holding it up to the light. "Seems like someone was dreaming of a life far from here."

Liam leaned in, his shoulder brushing against mine, sending a delightful shiver down my spine. "Or maybe it's just a postcard."

"But it's the little things," I insisted, my voice almost reverent as I traced the scene with my finger. "These pieces of a life we're trying to understand. It's more than just a mystery; it's someone's story."

He studied me for a moment, and I could feel the weight of his gaze, as if he were trying to discern the thoughts swirling within me. "You're right," he finally said, his tone thoughtful. "And that story deserves to be told."

As the evening wore on, I couldn't shake the sensation that we were on the brink of something significant. Each clue we unearthed felt like a thread weaving a larger tapestry, connecting us not only to the artist we were seeking but also to each other in ways that frightened and exhilarated me.

But as I left Liam's studio that night, the weight of his words lingered in the air like an unspoken promise. The streets were empty, the moonlight casting long shadows as I walked home, each step echoing in the silence. I couldn't shake the feeling that we were being watched, that someone lurked just out of sight, ready to pounce the moment we got too close to the truth.

The chill of the night wrapped around me, and with it came a shiver of dread. I had stepped into the unknown, and while the excitement was intoxicating, the reality of what we were facing clawed at the edges of my mind. I clutched the postcard tightly, feeling the texture of the paper against my skin, a tangible reminder of the risk that lay ahead. The path we were carving was fraught with danger, but if there was one thing I knew, it was that I wasn't willing to back down—not now, not when we were so close to uncovering the truth, and perhaps discovering something deeper within ourselves along the way.

The following week unfolded like an intricate puzzle, each piece fitting together just enough to spark my curiosity but not enough to reveal the full picture. Each time I stepped into Liam's studio, the air felt charged, brimming with possibilities and lingering questions. The walls, decorated with half-finished canvases and scattered notes, seemed to vibrate with our unspoken tension, whispering secrets that both exhilarated and frightened me.

One night, as we combed through more of the artist's correspondence, I stumbled upon a letter that felt different—a crisp, neatly folded page tucked within a thick folder. The handwriting was elegant, the ink a deep blue that stood out against the yellowed paper. I carefully unfolded it, my heart racing in anticipation of what it might reveal.

"Read it," Liam urged, leaning closer, his breath warm against my ear. The proximity sent a thrill down my spine, igniting a fire that chased away the chill of the evening.

"Dear Sophia," I began, my voice steady as I let the words wash over me. "If you're reading this, it means I've gone away, perhaps forever. Know that I never wanted to leave you…"

I paused, glancing at Liam, whose expression had shifted to one of intense concentration. I continued, "The world outside this little town is dangerous, and I fear that my passion for art will be my undoing. Trust no one. I've seen too much."

"What does that even mean?" Liam asked, his brow furrowed. "What could she have seen that put her in danger?"

ENIGMATIC PROMISE

"I don't know," I replied, my voice barely above a whisper. "But it sounds ominous."

"Maybe it's a clue," he suggested, his eyes brightening with excitement. "If we can trace her steps before she disappeared, perhaps we can find out what she meant."

I nodded, the spark of adventure reigniting the energy between us. "Let's see what else is in that box."

As we sifted through more documents, the pieces began to come together. Each letter painted a portrait of a woman passionate about her art but increasingly aware of the darkness lurking in the corners of her life. Liam and I exchanged glances filled with unspoken promises, each new revelation fueling our determination to uncover the truth.

"Did you know she had a sister?" I said suddenly, pulling out another letter. "It looks like she was trying to reconnect before she vanished."

"Maybe the sister knows something we don't," Liam suggested, his voice filled with resolve. "We should find her."

That night, we plotted our next steps, the walls of the studio closing in around us as the night deepened. The energy between us shifted, becoming almost tangible, electrifying the air.

"Can you believe we're getting this close?" I said, glancing at Liam, who was now leaning back in his chair, a satisfied grin spreading across his face. "We might actually solve this mystery."

"Don't get ahead of yourself," he teased, the familiar glimmer in his eyes. "We're still just two people with a lot of old letters and some very strong coffee."

"Speak for yourself," I shot back, laughing as I leaned closer, emboldened by the moment. "I happen to have a knack for solving puzzles. You're just lucky I'm letting you tag along."

Liam chuckled, the sound rich and warm, and for a heartbeat, I let myself imagine a world where the shadows receded and the thrill of discovery took center stage.

The next day, we set out to find Sophia's sister, tracking down a few leads from the letters we had uncovered. Our search led us to a quaint café on the outskirts of town, a charming little place draped in ivy and brimming with the scent of freshly baked pastries. It felt like a haven, a momentary escape from the weight of our investigation.

As we settled into a corner table, the atmosphere buzzed with the lively chatter of patrons, the clinking of cups providing a comforting backdrop. I fidgeted with the edges of my napkin, feeling a blend of excitement and anxiety as I scanned the room. "So, what's the plan? Do we just ask random strangers if they know her?"

Liam smirked, leaning back in his chair, his eyes dancing with mischief. "I thought we'd play it cool. You know, act like we belong here."

"Right, because that always works in the movies," I retorted, rolling my eyes. "Let's just hope we don't trip over ourselves in the process."

Just then, a woman entered the café, her presence commanding attention. She had dark hair pulled into a sleek bun, a striking contrast to her vibrant red coat. She moved with a grace that hinted at confidence, her eyes scanning the room before landing on us.

"Speak of the devil," Liam murmured, nudging me with his elbow. "That's her, isn't it?"

I leaned forward, my heart racing as the woman approached our table, her expression unreadable. "You're looking for me," she stated, her voice low and smooth.

My breath caught in my throat as I exchanged a glance with Liam, whose eyes widened slightly in surprise. "We, um, might be looking for information about your sister, Sophia," I managed, forcing the words out.

Her gaze hardened, a flicker of something unnameable flashing in her eyes. "You should stop. There are things about Sophia that are better left buried."

Before I could respond, the door swung open again, and the atmosphere shifted dramatically. The café's chatter dimmed, and a chill raced through the air as a tall figure stepped inside, his presence radiating danger. My heart pounded as I turned to look, the sudden tension palpable.

The woman's eyes darted toward the newcomer, panic momentarily flickering across her features. "You shouldn't have come here," she whispered, her voice barely audible over the soft murmur of conversation.

"What do you mean?" I asked, confusion swirling in my mind.

She hesitated, her gaze locked on the stranger, whose piercing eyes scanned the room with an intensity that made the hairs on my arms stand on end. "You don't know what you're getting into," she warned, her voice trembling slightly. "You need to leave now."

Just then, the stranger's gaze landed on our table, a predatory smile breaking across his lips as he strode toward us, each step echoing like a drumbeat in my chest. The air grew thick with tension, and every instinct in my body screamed that we were teetering on the edge of something dangerous and unknown.

"Hello there," he said, his voice smooth and chilling, sending shivers down my spine. "I believe you've been looking for someone."

I froze, the words caught in my throat. As Liam and I exchanged frantic glances, the weight of the moment settled heavily around us, closing in like a vice. In that instant, I realized that the investigation that had begun as a simple quest for truth had spiraled into something far more perilous. And there was no turning back.

Chapter 5: The Heart's Descent

The damp scent of earth and foliage enveloped me as I navigated the winding path through Ashwood, the late afternoon sun filtering through the vibrant canopy overhead. Each footfall crunched against the carpet of fallen leaves, a reminder of the season's relentless march toward winter. I paused, drawing in a deep breath, letting the crisp air fill my lungs, mingling with the underlying tension that had gripped my heart since I had discovered the note tucked away in Liam's jacket. It was scrawled in hurried script, speaking of secret meetings and unspoken pacts that felt like the bitter end of a long, enchanted dream.

My mind raced with possibilities as I replayed the day in my head, the echoes of laughter and warmth from earlier now replaced by a chilling sense of betrayal. I had wanted to trust him; I had wanted to believe that the late-night conversations, the stolen glances, the way he seemed to know me in ways that I hadn't yet uncovered—all of it had meant something. But this? This was a fracture in our fragile connection, one that threatened to splinter my hopes into a million jagged pieces.

As I stepped onto the small bridge that arched over a sleepy brook, the water murmured beneath me, its gentle flow a stark contrast to the tempest brewing inside. I leaned against the weathered railing, gazing into the crystal-clear depths, contemplating the clarity of the water against the murkiness of my thoughts. It felt unfair that something as pure as a stream could exist alongside the murky secrets I was beginning to uncover.

Then I saw him—Liam, leaning against a nearby tree, arms crossed, his expression shadowed by a veil of uncertainty. The sight of him twisted something deep within me, a mingling of desire and dread. How had we arrived at this point? I could see the tension etched into his features, the way his brow furrowed and lips pressed together tightly. He was waiting for me, and in that moment, I knew we were about to either bridge the gap that had widened between us or plunge into an abyss from which we might never return.

"Liam," I called, my voice barely above a whisper, but the sound seemed to hang heavily in the air. He pushed himself off the tree, the muscles in his jaw tensing as he approached. I took a step forward, my heart thundering, adrenaline coursing through my veins as if preparing for battle. "We need to talk."

"About what?" he replied, his tone guarded, as if he had already braced himself for whatever storm I was about to unleash. "You seem... tense."

"Tenser than usual, you mean?" I shot back, a spark of defiance igniting in my chest. "This isn't just about us anymore. It's about everything you've been hiding from me."

His eyes widened, surprise flickering across his face before it morphed into a mask of indignation. "Hiding? What are you talking about?"

"Don't play coy," I snapped, my anger bubbling to the surface. "I found your note. You were talking about meetings in the woods, something about the others. You can't expect me to stand here and pretend I don't know something's off."

A shadow passed over his features, the hurt spilling forth, raw and unguarded. "You shouldn't have gone through my things."

"I shouldn't have? Maybe you shouldn't have been keeping secrets!" The words burst from me like fire, fueled by the hurt I felt. I wanted to yell, to confront him with every ounce of betrayal that coursed through me. But beneath the anger was an unsettling vulnerability, a desperate wish that he would explain, that he would unravel the tangled threads of mystery before me.

Liam ran a hand through his hair, the gesture a sign of his own frustration. "You don't understand. It's not what you think. I was trying to protect you."

"Protect me?" I echoed, incredulity coloring my voice. "From what? The truth?"

"I can't just tell you everything," he said, his tone dropping to a low murmur as he stepped closer, his presence a magnetic pull I found hard to resist. "There are things you don't know, things that could put you in danger."

"Then tell me!" I demanded, my voice rising. "I can handle it, Liam! Just be honest with me for once."

He hesitated, eyes darting away as if searching for the right words. "You really don't understand what's at stake here. This isn't just about us; it's bigger than that."

A flicker of fear danced in the back of my mind, igniting a sense of urgency within me. "Bigger how? What are you involved in?"

"Promise you won't freak out," he said, his voice trembling slightly, a note of uncertainty creeping in.

"Liam, just tell me!"

He sighed, the weight of the world seemingly resting on his shoulders. "There's something happening in Ashwood. Something strange. The town isn't what it seems, and neither are the people in it. I'm part of a group—"

"A group?" I interrupted, feeling the world tilt dangerously on its axis. "What kind of group?"

"Something that monitors the... occurrences," he said, his voice dropping again as if uttering forbidden words. "There are forces at play here that could change everything."

Every word he spoke felt like a shard of glass, cutting through the facade of our relationship. The thrill of adventure I had felt when I first arrived in Ashwood was now tinged with an impending dread that clung to my skin like a chill. As much as I wanted to believe him, to embrace whatever this mystery was, I could feel my heart stutter against the mounting tension.

"But why wouldn't you tell me this before?" I asked, my voice softening, the anger ebbing away, replaced by a gnawing disappointment. "We could have faced this together."

"Because I didn't want to drag you into it," he admitted, a flicker of vulnerability breaking through the bravado. "I thought I could handle it myself, that I could keep you safe."

His sincerity, the way his voice cracked with the weight of his words, tugged at my heart. A part of me wanted to step forward, to close the distance between us and forget the world beyond our own tangled reality. But another part—the one that had stumbled upon that note, the one that had felt the sting of betrayal—held me back.

"Liam, how can I trust you now?" The question hung in the air, heavy and laden with the tension between us, the thread of our connection fraying under the strain.

The silence stretched between us, thick and palpable, as I searched Liam's face for something—an explanation, a flicker of truth, or perhaps a glimpse of the boy I had come to care for. Instead, I found only shadows and uncertainty, each passing moment tightening the grip of doubt around my heart. The sun dipped lower in the sky, casting an ethereal glow that danced off the leaves, but it did little to illuminate the darkness clouding my thoughts. I had never imagined that the person I was falling for could be wrapped up in something so convoluted.

"I know it's hard to understand," he said, his voice a low murmur, almost lost in the gentle rustling of the branches. "But I promise you, everything I did was to keep you safe. If you knew the truth, you might want to run back to where you came from."

"Maybe I would," I shot back, the words escaping before I could temper them with the kindness I desperately wanted to show. "But you can't decide that for me. I deserve to know what I'm dealing with."

"Do you really want to?" His gaze bore into mine, searching, and for a brief moment, I felt the weight of our shared moments pressing down, memories of laughter and late-night confessions swirling like fallen leaves around us. "Once you know, there's no unknowing. It changes everything."

"Are you really that scared of me knowing? Or are you scared of what it might mean for you?" My voice softened, a hint of vulnerability creeping in. Beneath his bravado was a boy who might be just as lost as I was.

"I don't know," he admitted, a tremor in his voice. "Maybe both."

Just then, the air shifted, charged with an electric tension that sent shivers down my spine. A sudden rustle from the underbrush snapped our focus away from each other, and instinct kicked in. I stepped back, my heart racing. Liam moved closer, shielding me with his body, a protective stance that sent conflicting emotions coursing through me.

"Stay behind me," he whispered, scanning the darkening woods with a wary gaze. The transformation in him was startling; the boy I had laughed with only moments ago was now an entirely different creature, tense and alert. The chill of apprehension wrapped around me, merging with the thrill of uncertainty.

"What's out there?" I asked, my voice barely more than a breath, heart pounding as the underbrush shifted again.

"I don't know, but we should move. It might not be safe here." His tone was urgent, and I could see the resolve in his eyes. The last flicker of daylight was fading, shadows stretching ominously around us.

With a nod, I fell into step beside him, my heart racing in rhythm with our hurried breaths. We made our way down the path, and I tried to swallow the growing knot of fear in my stomach. The forest seemed to come alive around us, the sounds of evening creeping in—a symphony of rustling leaves, distant calls of unseen creatures, and the haunting whisper of the wind through the branches. Every sound felt amplified, every shadow seemed to stretch, and my imagination ran wild with the possibilities of what might be lurking just out of sight.

"What do you think it was?" I ventured, glancing sideways at Liam, who kept his gaze fixed ahead.

"Something... unnatural," he replied, his voice steady but low, like a warning bell. "This place is different than it seems. There are things in Ashwood that people don't talk about. The woods, they have a way of keeping secrets."

The words hung heavily in the air, a reminder that I had entered a world where normal rules didn't apply, where shadows hid more than just darkness. "You keep saying that," I pointed out, frustration bubbling beneath my calm facade. "What do you mean by 'things'? Is there a creature out here that's going to jump out and gobble us up?"

He chuckled softly, the sound breaking through the tension momentarily. "Maybe. But it's less about creatures and more about the intentions behind them. There are people here who have their own agendas, and sometimes those agendas are darker than we can imagine."

"Sounds like a plot twist in a bad horror film," I quipped, trying to lighten the mood, though a part of me knew it was anything but funny.

"Maybe it is," he said, a ghost of a smile crossing his lips. "But I'm not making this up. You've seen things, haven't you? The disappearances, the odd behavior of the townsfolk."

"Okay, I'll give you that," I conceded. "But you've been acting like you're part of some secret society, and I'm not sure how I feel about that."

The path twisted ahead of us, and with every step, the unease in my chest expanded. "Are you saying that I'm part of this too?" I asked, my voice wavering slightly. "You've dragged me into whatever this is, haven't you?"

"It wasn't my intention," he replied, the sincerity in his voice palpable. "But now that you're involved, I can't just let you walk away. Not anymore. You need to know what you're up against."

"And what is that exactly?" I pressed, frustration creeping back in. "What are you so afraid of? What does this all mean?"

His jaw tightened, and for a moment, I thought he might clam up again. But then he took a deep breath, as if steeling himself. "It means that there are forces at work in Ashwood that are manipulating things behind the scenes—forces that don't want anyone to find out the truth. If they see you getting too close, they'll do anything to stop you."

"Is that why you've been keeping secrets? To protect me from them?" I questioned, my heart racing with a mixture of anger and confusion. "Because I can't live like that, Liam! I won't let fear dictate my life!"

He stepped closer, his gaze intense, his breath warm against my skin. "This isn't just about fear. It's about survival. If you want to dig deeper, we need to tread carefully. There are things I can't explain now, but I promise I'll tell you everything—just not here, not right now."

An unyielding determination flared within me, fueled by the desire to uncover whatever hidden truths lay beneath the surface. "Fine," I said, a newfound resolve edging into my tone. "But I'm not backing down. If we're in this together, we're doing it my way, and that means no more secrets."

He regarded me for a moment, something shifting in his expression. "You're stubborn, you know that?"

"Stubbornness is one of my many charming qualities," I shot back, raising an eyebrow. "You either embrace it or get left behind. Your choice."

He grinned, the warmth returning to his eyes as if the weight of the world had lightened just a fraction. "Alright, then. Together it is. But I have to warn you, this ride may get a little bumpy."

"Bring it on," I replied, the thrill of the challenge surging through me, a fire igniting in the pit of my stomach. If Ashwood had secrets to unveil, I was ready to peel back the layers, no matter how dangerous or tangled the path might be. In that moment, side by side with Liam, I felt the intoxicating blend of fear and excitement that came with venturing into the unknown. Whatever lay ahead, we would face it together, and maybe—just maybe—I would find my footing in this twisted narrative after all.

The moon hung high in the sky, a silver coin casting its glow over Ashwood like a watchful guardian. Liam and I moved quietly, the soft crunch of leaves beneath our feet punctuating the stillness that surrounded us. Each step felt heavier than the last, laden with the unspoken words swirling in the air between us. As we ventured deeper into the forest, the trees loomed taller, their gnarled branches reaching out like ancient fingers trying to ensnare us in their secrets.

"Where are we going?" I finally asked, breaking the silence that had settled around us like a thick fog. My voice sounded oddly small against the backdrop of rustling leaves, but the question hung in the air, filled with urgency.

"To a place where we can talk without being overheard," he replied, glancing back at me. The shadows danced across his face, hiding some of the vulnerability I had seen earlier, but not all. The intensity in his gaze gave me pause. I could sense the weight of whatever secret he harbored.

"Is it far?" I asked, trying to keep the anxiety from creeping into my tone. "Because I'm not exactly equipped for a midnight hike." My attempt at humor was met with a slight smirk from him, a flicker of warmth that momentarily melted the ice of tension surrounding us.

"Not far, just to the clearing." He gestured ahead, and I followed his lead, my heart racing. The thought of revealing hidden truths filled me with a mix of dread and anticipation.

As we pushed through a thicket of brambles, the forest opened up to reveal a small clearing bathed in moonlight. The air was cooler here, almost crisp, and I took a moment to breathe deeply, hoping to calm the fluttering in my chest. There was a certain tranquility in the space, a contrast to the storm of emotions that churned within me.

Liam turned to face me, his expression serious. "This is where I usually come to think. It feels safer here."

"Safer?" I raised an eyebrow, glancing around as if the trees might suddenly spring to life and eavesdrop. "You mean from whatever it is you're afraid of?"

"Exactly." His gaze hardened. "I told you there are people who don't want this to come to light. If they find out you're asking questions..." He trailed off, the implication hanging ominously between us.

"What are we talking about, Liam?" I urged, desperate to push through the layers of his secrecy. "What do you mean by 'people'? What's at stake?"

He took a deep breath, running a hand through his tousled hair, the weight of his words almost palpable in the air. "There's a group in town, a coalition of sorts, that monitors the strange happenings here. They're trying to control the narrative—keep the rest of us in the dark. The disappearances, the odd behavior from the townsfolk—it's all connected. They want to maintain their power, and anyone who digs too deep becomes a target."

"Target?" The word sent a shiver down my spine, and I stepped closer, needing to close the distance between us. "You can't be serious. Are you saying they might hurt someone?"

"Worse." He looked away, the vulnerability in his eyes now eclipsed by a deeper fear. "They have their methods—intimidation, threats, even worse. I didn't want to involve you in any of this, but…"

"But here we are," I finished for him, frustration bubbling beneath the surface. "You should have trusted me enough to let me decide for myself. I'm not some delicate flower who needs protecting. I can handle myself, you know."

"I do know," he replied, stepping closer, a fierce look of determination crossing his features. "But this isn't just about strength. It's about survival. And I can't let you get caught in the crossfire."

The air thickened with tension as I tried to process his words. "And you think keeping me in the dark is going to protect me? Secrets can be just as dangerous, Liam. I need to know everything if I'm going to stand by your side."

"Alright," he conceded, the resolve in his tone wavering. "But you need to promise me something. Promise you'll be careful. They're watching, always."

"Promise." I met his gaze, my heart racing at the weight of our unspoken pact.

"Good." He stepped back, the distance between us seeming to expand as he braced himself. "There's something I need to show you, something that might help you understand."

"What do you mean?" My curiosity piqued, but a knot of apprehension twisted in my stomach.

Without another word, he turned and walked deeper into the clearing, beckoning for me to follow. The soft rustle of his footsteps seemed to echo, amplifying the growing sense of foreboding. As I stepped closer, the air felt charged, almost alive, as if the forest itself was holding its breath in anticipation.

Liam led me to a gnarled tree that stood apart from the others, its bark twisted and worn. At its base was a shallow indentation, half-hidden beneath a blanket of fallen leaves. He knelt down, brushing aside the debris with a practiced hand, revealing a small, weathered box nestled within the roots.

"This," he said, lifting it out with care, "is something I've been protecting. Something that explains a lot of what's happening in Ashwood."

"What is it?" I leaned in closer, my curiosity piqued. The box was ancient, its surface etched with symbols that looked oddly familiar, a sense of déjà vu washing over me.

"Open it." He handed it to me, his expression a mix of excitement and trepidation.

My fingers trembled as I flipped open the lid, revealing a collection of brittle papers and a tarnished pendant that gleamed softly in the moonlight. As I sifted through the contents, my heart sank, the reality of what I was seeing beginning to crystallize. The papers were filled with notes—sketches of the town, names of residents, dates, and events meticulously documented. It was like peering into the inner workings of a secret society.

"Liam, what is all of this?" I asked, the weight of his past hanging heavy in the air. "Why do you have this?"

"Because," he said, taking a step closer, his voice dropping to a whisper. "It reveals the truth about what happened to those who disappeared. They're not just gone; they were taken. And this—" he gestured to the pendant, "is what they're after. It's powerful, and if they get their hands on it again..."

Before he could finish, a low growl rumbled through the trees, freezing me in place. I turned sharply, instincts kicking in, every nerve in my body screaming that we were no longer alone.

"Did you hear that?" I whispered, dread pooling in my stomach.

"Yes," Liam replied, his voice taut with tension. "We need to go. Now."

As we turned to leave, the growl came again, louder this time, accompanied by the unmistakable sound of snapping twigs and rustling underbrush. Panic surged through me as I caught a glimpse of movement in the shadows.

"Run!" Liam shouted, his hand grabbing mine, pulling me into a sprint.

We dashed through the clearing, the sounds of pursuit echoing behind us. My heart raced, not just from fear but from the rush of adrenaline coursing through my veins. We burst through the thicket, branches clawing at our skin, but we pressed on, driven by a primal need to escape.

Just as we reached the edge of the forest, a figure emerged from the shadows, blocking our path—a tall silhouette, cloaked in darkness, eyes gleaming with an unsettling light.

"Going somewhere?" a smooth voice taunted, sending chills down my spine.

In that moment, I knew we were cornered. The secrets of Ashwood were closing in, and whatever lay ahead was far more dangerous than I had ever imagined.

Chapter 6: Into the Abyss

In the dim glow of twilight, the city exhaled its familiar sigh, a symphony of honking horns, rustling leaves, and the distant laughter of children lingering in the air like a bittersweet memory. Each heartbeat felt like a countdown, a quiet reminder that danger wasn't merely lurking in the corners but was striding through the bustling streets, just waiting for the opportune moment to strike. As I walked along the cobblestone path, a shiver snaked down my spine, ignited not just by the cool breeze but by the prickling sensation of being watched.

I glanced over my shoulder, the hairs on my neck standing at attention, and for a fleeting moment, I thought I caught a glimpse of a shadow retreating behind an oak tree. But in a city teeming with secrets and stories, shadows were part of the scenery, shapeshifting like the characters in our lives. Yet, something about this felt different—too calculated, too deliberate. I quickened my pace, heart pounding like a drum, every footfall echoing a warning.

"Why do you look like you've just seen a ghost?" A voice cut through my anxiety, smooth and teasing, like honey sliding over warm toast. I turned to face the source, and there he was: Jake, the charming rogue who seemed to have an uncanny knack for appearing when I least wanted him to. His grin was lopsided, the kind that could charm the wings off a butterfly, but beneath that easy facade lay a depth that had, against my better judgment, begun to intrigue me.

"Let's just say I'm not in the mood for ghost stories right now," I replied, trying to maintain my composure.

"Ah, so it's a haunted night, is it?" He stepped closer, his eyes glinting with mischief, but I noticed the flicker of concern shadowing his gaze. "Care to share the scare?"

I hesitated, feeling the weight of my worry seep into my words. "It's nothing—just a feeling. You know how it is." But even as I said it, I felt the fissures of my trust in him crack open. How could I share the urgency of my fears with someone whose very presence danced on the precipice of chaos?

"I can assure you," he leaned in, voice dropping to a conspiratorial whisper, "that my charms are effective against ghosts." He straightened, an exaggerated seriousness on his face. "But against the real monsters? Well, that's a different story."

There was something endearing about his bravado, even as it sent another chill down my spine. We both understood the monsters we faced weren't the kind that could be banished with a mere incantation or a lighthearted quip. They were tangible, lurking just beyond the fringes of our lives, making themselves known through chilling warnings that echoed like an ominous drumbeat in the quietest hours of the night.

I crossed my arms, trying to fend off the growing unease. "Jake, you don't understand. I think someone's been watching me. And it's not just my imagination." The confession hung in the air between us, heavy with the weight of truth.

He tilted his head, his expression shifting from playful to concerned, the warmth of his earlier bravado fading slightly. "You're serious?"

"Completely. I've had strange messages, things left for me. It's like someone is playing a twisted game, and I'm the unwitting player." My words tumbled out in a rush, each one laced with the palpable fear that had gripped me for days.

"Messages? What kind of messages?" He stepped even closer, an intensity flickering in his gaze that set my heart racing for reasons beyond mere apprehension.

I pulled out my phone, my hands shaking slightly as I scrolled through my messages. "Like this." I handed it to him, biting my lip as he read the chilling words that had sent me spiraling into a frenzy of paranoia. Each letter felt like a blade, carving into the already fragile armor I had built around myself.

His brow furrowed as he read, the lighthearted demeanor giving way to a grim determination. "This isn't just a prank. This is serious." He returned my phone, his fingers brushing against mine—a spark that sent an unexpected thrill through me, mingling with the tension thickening in the air.

"So what do we do?" I asked, the urgency in my voice revealing the vulnerability I often tried to conceal. The world around us felt suddenly smaller, closing in as if the very shadows were drawing nearer.

Jake's jaw clenched, and for the first time, I could see the lines of worry etched into his usually carefree features. "We need to figure out who's behind this. It's not safe for you to be alone right now."

I swallowed hard, my heart fluttering at the thought of him staying close. "You mean you're going to help me?"

"Of course. I'm not going to let you face this alone. Besides," he added with a flicker of his trademark humor, "who else is going to save you from the ghost stories?"

His attempt at levity cut through my fear, but I could see the determination brewing beneath the surface. "All right, but we have to be smart about this. We can't let whoever this is get the upper hand."

"Agreed," he said, his tone turning serious again. "Let's start by retracing your steps. Maybe we can find something—anything—that leads us to the source."

As we began walking side by side, I couldn't shake the feeling that this was not just about confronting the shadows lurking in the corners of my life. It was about unraveling the tension that had begun to weave itself between us, turning our rivalry into an unexpected alliance—a partnership forged in the fire of danger, where trust felt both exhilarating and terrifying. And perhaps, amidst the chaos, I could learn to lean into that trust, even if it meant risking everything I thought I knew.

The streets felt alive as we navigated through the bustling crowds, the air thick with the scents of roasted chestnuts and the sweet, sticky allure of caramel popcorn. I focused on the kaleidoscope of faces around us—people lost in their own worlds, laughter punctuating conversations, blissful ignorance swirling around my rising anxiety. Jake walked beside me, his presence a comforting anchor amidst the chaos, yet the shadows that clung to my thoughts refused to disperse.

"So, where do we begin?" he asked, his voice a playful lilt against the backdrop of street performers strumming guitars and the distant sound of a saxophonist pouring his heart into a soulful melody. I could hear the underlying seriousness in his tone, though he wore that devil-may-care smile like armor.

"We could start at the coffee shop," I suggested, my instincts pulling me back to the familiar—a place where I felt safe, where I could gather my thoughts away from the prying eyes that seemed to watch me from every corner. "That's where I first got the message."

"Perfect. Nothing screams danger like a frothy cappuccino," he quipped, feigning a dramatic shudder. I chuckled despite myself, grateful for the momentary distraction as we made our way toward the quaint café tucked between two towering buildings. Its warm glow beckoned like a lighthouse, offering respite from the storm brewing inside me.

As we pushed through the glass door, the familiar chime announced our arrival, wrapping us in the comforting aroma of fresh coffee and baked goods. The barista, a cheerful woman with a cascade of colorful hair, greeted us with a smile that softened the edges of my growing unease.

"Two coffees, please," Jake said, flashing a grin as if we were simply here for a casual afternoon break rather than strategizing against an unseen threat. I leaned against the counter, feeling the warmth radiate through the cool air.

"Do you always order coffee like it's a life-or-death situation?" I teased, trying to keep the mood light.

"Only when the stakes are high, my dear Watson," he replied, his eyes dancing with mischief. The banter felt like a balm, momentarily easing the tension that had become a constant companion.

"Espresso for the detective, and a caramel macchiato for the lady," the barista announced, placing our drinks on the counter with a flourish. Jake picked them up, expertly balancing both cups as we navigated to a corner table bathed in the warm, golden light of a hanging lamp.

I took a sip of my drink, savoring the sweetness as I let the rich flavors wash over me. "Okay, back to the matter at hand," I said, setting my cup down with a determined clink. "I need to retrace my steps from the day I received the first message."

"Lead the way, Sherlock," he said, gesturing with a dramatic sweep of his hand, a hint of playful sarcasm underlining his enthusiasm.

We mapped out my day, my memories weaving together like the intricate patterns of a tapestry. I recalled the moment I had received the first message—a single text that sent shivers down my spine. The words were simple, almost innocuous: "I see you." But the chill in my bones and the way my heart raced had turned it into something sinister.

"I went to work, then stopped by the park for lunch before heading here," I recounted, glancing up to see Jake studying me intently, as if he were trying to decode a puzzle. "Nothing unusual. Just a normal day until that text. But then..." I hesitated, the fear creeping back in like a shadow stretching across my thoughts.

"But then what?" Jake prompted, leaning forward with genuine curiosity.

"I don't know. I thought I saw someone watching me at the park. Just a flash of a face among the trees. But I didn't think much of it until later." I swallowed hard, the memory sharp and vivid. "And then the messages kept coming—each one more threatening than the last."

Jake's expression shifted, a blend of concern and determination lighting up his features. "We need to go to that park. If someone is watching you, we might be able to find some clues."

"Or we could get ourselves into even more trouble," I warned, a pang of trepidation slicing through my resolve. But deep down, I recognized that hiding would only allow the shadows to grow bolder.

"Trouble is my middle name," he said with a wink, and for a moment, the weight of our situation lightened. "But in all seriousness, we can't let fear dictate our moves. Let's get to the park and see what we can find."

I nodded, finishing the last sip of my drink, the warmth settling in my stomach a small comfort against the uncertainty that lay ahead. As we stepped back out into the world, the sun dipped lower in the sky, casting elongated shadows that danced at our feet, mingling with the growing tension that wrapped around us like a second skin.

The park loomed ahead, its entrance flanked by gnarled trees that whispered secrets to the wind. I felt a rush of apprehension wash over me as we walked beneath their arching branches, the once-inviting atmosphere now suffocating, each rustle of leaves sounding like a warning.

"Stick close," Jake said, his voice low, eyes scanning the perimeter with the vigilance of a seasoned detective. I felt the weight of his gaze and the comfort of his presence anchoring me, even as the shadows seemed to thicken with each step.

We wandered along the path I remembered, the vivid colors of autumn leaves painting the ground in fiery hues. The chatter of children playing nearby filled the air, but beneath that, a tension crackled, an electricity that made my skin prickle.

"Over there," I pointed toward a bench, my heart racing. "That's where I sat when I saw him."

Jake moved closer, his demeanor shifting as he examined the area, his brows furrowed in concentration. "What did he look like?"

"I don't know. Just a flash of a figure in a dark jacket," I admitted, frustration creeping into my voice. "It all happened so fast."

He crouched down, inspecting the ground around the bench. "Look for anything unusual—anything that feels out of place."

I nodded, scanning the grass and scattered leaves, my heart pounding like a drum. My gaze caught on something glinting just beneath a fallen branch. "Wait!" I exclaimed, rushing forward. I reached down and pulled out a small, silver locket, the clasp slightly tarnished but the surface still gleaming.

"Is that what I think it is?" Jake asked, his tone shifting to something more serious.

"Not a clue," I replied, turning it over in my palm. As I examined the delicate engravings, I felt a sense of unease wash over me. It was beautiful yet haunting, and suddenly, it felt like a key to a door I had no intention of opening.

"Let's find out," he urged, leaning closer to inspect it as if it held the answers we desperately sought.

But the moment stretched between us, thick with unspoken words and the weight of the locket, and for an instant, the shadows receded just a little. Here, with him, standing in the fading light of day, I felt a flicker of hope amid the chaos, the promise that maybe, just maybe, we could unravel the threads that bound us to this growing darkness.

The locket dangled in my hand like a pendulum, the silver glinting in the soft light filtering through the trees. A wave of uncertainty washed over me, a reminder that every choice made had led us here, to this moment fraught with possibility and danger. "What do you think it means?" I asked, my voice barely a whisper as I stared into the intricate design etched into the metal.

Jake took the locket from me, his expression serious, his fingers brushing against mine in a fleeting touch that sent a jolt through my chest. "Could be a clue. Or it might just be a piece of jewelry left behind by someone who sat here. Let's see if there's anything inside." He flipped the locket open with a practiced motion, and I leaned in closer, curiosity piquing as the clasp clicked softly.

Inside, nestled in the worn velvet lining, was a photograph—a faded image of a couple with wide smiles, faces I didn't recognize. The woman's hair caught the light like spun gold, and the man had an easy charm, a sparkle in his eye that drew you in. They looked so blissfully happy, a stark contrast to the turmoil that had enveloped us.

"This looks like it's from ages ago," I said, my voice tinged with disappointment. "Not exactly the sinister trophy I was hoping for."

"Or maybe it's just the cover story," Jake suggested, his tone a mix of playfulness and seriousness. "Let's not underestimate the power of nostalgia in a good mystery."

"Right. Because what screams 'danger' more than an antique locket?" I rolled my eyes but felt a sliver of hope. "But really, Jake, if someone is watching me, why leave a locket? It feels more like a love story than a horror film."

"Could be a love story gone wrong," he replied, a hint of a smile playing at the corners of his mouth. "Or a warning from beyond the grave."

I laughed, but the sound felt hollow as the shadows stretched around us, creeping closer like a living entity. "Now you're just being ridiculous."

"Am I?" He raised an eyebrow, the glimmer of mischief in his gaze. "What if this couple had a connection to whoever is after you? Or what if they were—dare I say it—ghosts? Spooky stuff!" He chuckled, lightening the mood, yet a part of me sensed his serious undertones.

"Just stop before I start checking over my shoulder for spectral lovers," I retorted, though I couldn't help but smile back at him.

Just as I felt the tension begin to lift, the world around us shifted. The air grew heavy, thick with an unshakeable sense of foreboding. I turned my head slightly, catching movement from the corner of my eye—too swift, too deliberate. My heart raced, the playful banter falling away as dread pooled in my stomach.

"Jake," I whispered, my voice quaking slightly as I gripped the locket tightly. "Did you see that?"

"See what?" he asked, a frown creasing his brow as he followed my gaze.

"There's someone... I think they're watching us." My instincts flared, adrenaline surging through me like fire, and I scanned the area, every nerve ending alert.

"Where?" he asked, his tone shifting from lighthearted to serious in a heartbeat, eyes narrowing as he took on a protective stance.

"There—by the trees!" I pointed, heart pounding. The figure I'd glimpsed was now obscured, blending into the shadows as if it had melted into the very fabric of the park. I could feel my breath quickening, each inhale laced with fear.

Jake moved instinctively closer, the atmosphere charged between us. "Stay behind me," he commanded softly, the playful bravado stripped away, replaced by a focus I hadn't seen before. "Let's find out who it is."

I couldn't argue; he had become my shield against the unknown, my anchor in this storm. But as we stepped forward cautiously, a chilling thought prickled at my mind: what if it wasn't just someone passing by? What if this was the moment the shadows emerged, taking form, becoming more than just whispers in the dark?

Suddenly, a loud crack echoed through the stillness, like the snap of a twig underfoot. I froze, glancing up at Jake, who had gone still, his expression taut. The sound had come from behind the thick trunk of a nearby tree, and it resonated in the silence that followed, pulling me further into the abyss of uncertainty.

"Stay here," he whispered, stepping toward the sound. His silhouette framed by the fading light seemed more imposing than before, a warrior bracing for battle.

I wanted to protest, to yell that we shouldn't split up, but the words lodged in my throat. Instead, I watched as he moved stealthily, tension radiating from his every pore, an intensity that pulled me along even as fear coursed through me.

"Jake," I called softly, the unease rising like bile. "Be careful."

"Always am," he shot back, but I could hear the tightness in his voice. The vulnerability beneath his bravado reminded me that he was human, too—fallible, just like me.

In a heartbeat, he disappeared behind the tree, leaving me alone with the unsettling quiet. I stood frozen, every instinct screaming at me to turn and run, yet my feet were anchored to the ground, paralyzed by fear and an inexplicable need to know.

Time stretched, each second feeling like an eternity. I could hear the faint rustling of leaves and the distant laughter from the children at the playground, but it felt like a world away. Then, from behind the tree, a figure emerged—dark, shrouded in a hoodie that obscured their features.

My breath hitched as I took a step back, ready to call out to Jake, but before I could find my voice, the figure turned toward me. The air seemed to still, and in that fleeting moment, I could see the glint of something metallic in their hand.

"Who are you?" I managed to choke out, my voice shaking.

But the figure didn't answer. Instead, they raised the object—something that shimmered in the dim light—and the realization hit me like a cold wave: a knife, its blade catching the fading rays of sunlight, a reflection of the peril that had been stalking me from the shadows.

"Get down!" I heard Jake shout from behind the tree, but I was already moving, instincts driving me as I ducked and rolled behind a nearby bush. The air filled with adrenaline as chaos erupted, the world spinning into a frenzy as I scrambled for cover.

The figure lunged toward where I had been standing, but I wasn't there anymore. I could hear Jake's footsteps pounding as he raced toward me, and in that moment, my heart thudded with a desperate hope—he would save me. But as the adrenaline surged, an unfamiliar sense of dread seeped into the air, thickening the atmosphere around us.

"Run!" he yelled, urgency lacing his words as I glanced back, adrenaline flooding my veins. But even as I made to obey, I caught the glint of a second figure emerging from the opposite side, blocking our escape, sealing us in a trap of shadows and peril.

And in that horrifying instant, I realized—this was no longer just about messages in the dark. We were caught in a web far more intricate than I had imagined, a chilling game where trust could quickly unravel, and the stakes were higher than ever.

Chapter 7: The Fire Within

Rain hammered against the windows, each drop a relentless reminder of the tempest raging outside. The dim light of the single lamp in the corner flickered as if mirroring the tumult in my heart. I tucked my knees beneath my chin, wrapping my arms around them, trying to ward off the chill that seeped into the very bones of this old house. The walls, once a soothing cream, now felt like they were closing in on me, cloaked in shadows that danced with the flickering light. Outside, the storm roared, a symphony of chaos that seemed to echo my inner turmoil.

Liam sat across the room, his eyes drawn to the window, brow furrowed with concern. A flicker of lightening cast his features in sharp relief, highlighting the way his dark hair fell across his forehead, and for a brief moment, I forgot the storm. There was something magnetic about him, a pull that tethered me to this moment in ways I couldn't yet understand. As the wind howled like a wounded animal, I felt a shift in the air, a crackle that had nothing to do with the weather.

"You think it's ever going to let up?" His voice was a low rumble, cutting through the oppressive silence, but I could hear the worry etched in every syllable.

I shrugged, forcing a casual tone despite the knot in my stomach. "It's just a storm. They come and go. What's life without a little drama, right?" I attempted a smile, but it felt forced, as if the storm had stolen my light.

Liam turned to me, his gaze piercing, and I could feel the intensity between us like a static charge in the air. "Yeah, well, some storms are more than just weather. They change everything." His eyes softened for a moment, and I caught a glimpse of something deeper—a shared understanding of the chaos swirling around us, both outside and within.

It was a night that begged for honesty, for the kind of vulnerability that could easily be drowned in the din of the storm. I bit my lip, feeling the urge to confess my fears, my hopes, all tangled together like the branches of the trees outside, swaying violently in the wind. But as soon as I opened my mouth, the words tangled up in my throat, wrapped in uncertainty.

Suddenly, a deafening clap of thunder shook the room, the lights flickered once more, then went out entirely, plunging us into darkness. For a heartbeat, the world outside roared, and in that instant, the vulnerability of the moment felt overwhelming. I could feel my pulse quicken, the darkness amplifying the tension between us.

"Great," I muttered, letting out a shaky breath. "Nothing like a little atmospheric pressure to lighten the mood."

Liam chuckled, a warm sound in the dark, and it sent a ripple of warmth through me, igniting something deep within. "I'd say it's pretty dramatic. But if we're going to survive this storm, we might as well find some light."

"Do you have a flashlight or something?"

"I think I saw one in the kitchen."

As he stood to search, the silence of the room enveloped me, and I realized how acutely I was aware of his presence—the way his movements were fluid, the scent of rain-soaked earth clinging to him, mingling with something distinctly him, a blend of warmth and adventure.

When he returned, the small beam of light sliced through the darkness, illuminating the contours of his face, highlighting the way his lips curled into a half-smile, and my breath hitched. It felt surreal, as if time had paused just for us.

"Here we go," he said, sitting back down, the light bouncing off the walls like a heartbeat.

The shadows cast around us felt charged, alive, and with every glance, I could sense a burgeoning connection that thrummed just beneath the surface. The storm outside raged on, but here, in this intimate cocoon of flickering light and heavy shadows, everything else faded away.

"What if we never get out of here?" I whispered, my voice barely above the crackle of the storm. "What if we're stuck like this forever?"

Liam's eyes locked onto mine, an intensity that sent a shiver down my spine. "Then I guess we make the best of it," he said softly, his voice low and inviting. "And maybe we share a few secrets while we're at it."

A heartbeat passed, and then he leaned closer, the light casting his features in soft relief. My pulse raced, anticipation thrumming in the air like a live wire. "What do you think, Liz?"

"What if I told you I'm terrified of the dark?" I replied, half-joking, but the truth of my words hung in the air.

"I think everyone is a little afraid of the dark," he said, his voice dropping to a conspiratorial whisper. "But sometimes, it's in the dark where we find our true selves."

His gaze held mine, a magnetic force that drew me in closer, and for a fleeting moment, I forgot the storm, forgot everything except the warmth pooling in my chest and the fluttering of my heart.

The walls seemed to dissolve, the space between us charged with unspoken words and shared fears. My breath caught as he shifted even closer, the soft light creating a halo around him, and I could feel every heartbeat echoing in the silence.

"I—"

Before I could finish, a flash of lightning illuminated the room, and in that split second, our lips met, a tentative brush that ignited something fierce within me. The kiss was electric, a collision of fear and longing that sent shockwaves through my body. The taste of him—warm, sweet, and intoxicating—swirled around us, wrapping me in a cocoon of desire that was both thrilling and terrifying.

Time seemed to stand still, and as we pulled back, breathless and wide-eyed, I realized I'd stepped into uncharted territory—a world where the storm outside faded into insignificance, overshadowed by the fire ignited between us.

"Wow," I breathed, still reeling from the kiss, feeling an unexpected thrill dance through my veins. "That was... intense."

"Just a taste of what's to come," Liam replied, a teasing smile playing on his lips.

I couldn't help but laugh, a sound that mingled with the storm, and just like that, I was swept into a world both chaotic and exhilarating, a whirlwind where love and danger intertwined like the darkened branches outside, swaying in the tempest.

The kiss lingered in the air like a fragile promise, a tether pulling us closer together even as the storm outside continued its ferocious dance. My heart raced, each beat drumming a rhythm of uncertainty and desire as I caught my breath, still caught in the whirlwind of our unexpected moment. The remnants of his warmth clung to me like a cherished secret, igniting a rush of feelings I'd been trying to contain.

"What was that?" I asked, my voice a blend of curiosity and disbelief. It felt surreal, like the entire world had faded away, leaving just us in this cocoon of light and shadow.

Liam chuckled softly, his eyes glinting with a mix of mischief and sincerity. "Just testing the waters. We've got a lot of storm to weather, right?"

"More like a hurricane," I quipped, crossing my arms in a mock defensive posture, though my heart betrayed my bravado. "You know, metaphorically speaking."

He raised an eyebrow, that playful smirk returning to his lips. "Oh, I thought it was a hurricane of passion."

"Flattery will get you everywhere," I shot back, unable to suppress a smile. The atmosphere around us had shifted, the earlier tension replaced by something lighter, more buoyant. "But if we're getting swept away by passion, I hope you can swim."

"Drowning in passion isn't so bad," he countered, leaning back slightly, the beam of the flashlight illuminating the rugged contours of his face. "Unless you forget to come up for air."

We both laughed, and in that moment, the world outside ceased to exist. The wind howled in the distance, but inside this small room, it was just us—two souls entwined in a dance of playful banter and newfound attraction.

But as the laughter faded, I felt a shadow creep back in, the weight of reality pressing against my chest. "What happens when the storm passes?" I asked, my voice softer now, laced with a vulnerability I could no longer hide.

Liam's expression shifted, the playfulness giving way to something more serious. "We face what's on the other side. Together." The sincerity in his tone wrapped around me like a comforting blanket, and I found myself leaning into that warmth.

The storm had become a metaphor for so many things—my fears, my doubts, the chaos of my life that had been spiraling out of control for so long. Could I really trust this connection? Could I lean into this fire burning between us, or was it destined to fizzle out as quickly as it had ignited?

The weight of those questions hung in the air, but Liam seemed to sense my turmoil. "Hey," he said gently, breaking the silence that had settled around us like a thick fog. "Let's distract ourselves. How about a game?"

"A game? Like what?" I asked, tilting my head in curiosity.

"Truth or dare," he said, a twinkle in his eye. "But with a twist. We can only choose things we actually want to know about each other."

"Ah, so it's a game of secrets then?"

"More like a game of revelations," he replied, grinning. "I'll go first. Truth or dare?"

"Truth," I answered, the competitive spark igniting within me.

"Okay. What's something you've never told anyone?"

I paused, my mind racing through the labyrinth of my thoughts. There were secrets, of course, things I had hidden even from myself, but something urged me to be bold, to take a leap. "I've always wanted to travel the world," I admitted, my voice steady despite the vulnerability of the confession. "But I've never had the guts to leave. It seems so... overwhelming."

"Why not?" Liam leaned in, genuinely interested. "What holds you back?"

"The idea of leaving everything behind," I admitted, feeling the knot in my stomach loosen slightly as I shared this piece of myself. "And what if I get lost?"

"Lost can be an adventure," he replied, and for a brief moment, I felt as if he were reaching through the chaos to pull me closer to him, closer to the life I yearned for but had always kept at arm's length.

"Your turn," I said, deflecting, eager to keep the momentum going.

"Dare," he said, a mischievous glint in his eye.

"I dare you to... share your biggest regret."

He hesitated for a moment, the light from the flashlight catching the uncertainty in his expression. "Alright, but only because you dared me." He ran a hand through his hair, the gesture both anxious and endearing. "My biggest regret? Not taking more chances when I had the opportunity. There were moments in my life where I let fear hold me back, and I wish I could go back and change that."

I met his gaze, the air between us thickening as his words sunk in. It felt like we were peeling back layers, exposing our fears and desires, raw and unfiltered. "What would you change?" I asked, genuinely curious.

"I'd have traveled more, explored the world beyond my hometown." He smiled wistfully. "And maybe not waited so long to tell someone I care about them."

Heat rushed to my cheeks, the intimacy of the moment wrapping around us like a gentle embrace. "Oh really?" I teased, trying to mask the tremor in my voice. "And who would that someone be?"

"Now that's a question for another round," he replied, his grin infectious. The playful banter had rekindled the spark in the room, and I found myself grateful for the distraction.

"Okay, my turn again," I said, heart racing as I formulated my next question. "Truth or dare?"

"Truth," he replied, leaning closer, his voice low and inviting.

"Do you believe in love at first sight?" I asked, the question slipping out before I could catch it.

Liam regarded me thoughtfully, his expression serious. "I believe in connections that happen in an instant, where everything aligns just right," he replied slowly. "But love? That takes time. It's the little moments that build up, like the raindrops outside, creating a storm of their own."

I couldn't help but admire his perspective, feeling as if he was peeling back the layers of his heart, just as I had done. "And what if those moments lead to something more?"

He leaned back, a contemplative look on his face. "Then I guess we'd have to navigate that storm together."

The intensity of his gaze sent a thrill through me, and for a moment, the world outside faded into insignificance. It was just the two of us, lost in this game, this moment, in the fragile cocoon we had woven together amidst the chaos.

As the thunder rumbled in the distance, I realized that the storm was just the backdrop to a far more significant shift—the fire within us was only just beginning to ignite, and I felt ready to embrace the heat.

The laughter from our game still hung in the air, a fragile thread binding us together in the intimate cocoon we had woven against the storm's chaos. I could feel the warmth radiating between us, an electric connection that crackled with each passing moment. The glow from the flashlight flickered, creating a play of shadows on the walls that seemed to echo our thoughts, reflecting the unpredictable nature of what was unfolding.

Liam leaned closer, the space between us shrinking as if drawn by an unseen force. The tension hung thick in the air, vibrating with unspoken words. "So, what's next?" he asked, a grin tugging at the corners of his mouth. "Another round of truth or dare, or should we skip to the good part?"

I raised an eyebrow, half-amused and half-flustered. "And what exactly is the 'good part' in your mind? I mean, are we talking about deep philosophical discussions, or are you implying something more... adventurous?"

His eyes sparkled with mischief. "How about both? But first, I dare you to tell me one secret you've never shared with anyone."

My heart raced at the thought of revealing something so personal. A rush of vulnerability washed over me. "Okay, here goes. I used to write poetry when I was a kid. I'd lock myself in my room for hours, scribbling my thoughts into an old notebook. I thought it was just a silly phase, but I still have it, hidden under a pile of old clothes."

"Poetry?" He leaned back, feigning shock. "So you're a romantic at heart, hiding in plain sight. I would have guessed you for a thrill-seeker."

"Thrill-seeker? Please. I'm more like a professional over-thinker." I chuckled, grateful for the laughter that had become our safety net. "And I still have that notebook, just in case I ever feel inspired again."

"Maybe we could start a poetry club," he teased. "Just the two of us. I could share my sonnets about the beauty of rain."

"Only if you agree to perform them with interpretive dance," I shot back, laughing.

Liam rolled his eyes dramatically. "I'll work on my choreography."

As the playful banter continued, a sudden gust of wind rattled the window, interrupting our moment. The lights flickered again, this time casting the room into darkness for a heartbeat longer than before. The storm outside felt more imposing, as if it were pressing against the walls, desperate to breach our sanctuary.

"Okay, enough games," I said, my voice trembling slightly as I steeled myself. "Let's talk about something real. The storm is intensifying, and I can't shake the feeling that we're not safe here."

"Are you afraid?" he asked, his expression shifting to one of seriousness.

"It's not fear, really. It's a sense of dread," I admitted, wrapping my arms around myself as the wind howled outside. "I don't know what's coming next, and it terrifies me. This—" I gestured between us, "is exhilarating, but what happens when the storm calms down?"

Liam moved closer, the light illuminating the concern etched on his face. "We can't control the storm, but we can control how we respond to it. And right now, I'm here with you. That counts for something, doesn't it?"

"Sure, it counts. But what if the storm is just a metaphor for something worse?" I felt the heaviness of my words linger in the air, the gravity of the situation pressing down on me like the oppressive humidity before a summer downpour.

"Then we'll face it together," he replied, his voice steady, a lifeline in the tumult. "No more holding back."

Just as I opened my mouth to respond, a thunderous crack shook the room, and the power abruptly cut out. The flashlight flickered out, plunging us into darkness. My heart pounded, and for a brief moment, I could barely hear anything over the roar of the storm and the thunderous beating of my pulse.

"Liam?" I called, trying to sound braver than I felt.

"I'm right here," he assured me, his voice close and grounding. I could feel his presence, a solid anchor amidst the swirling chaos.

"I can't see anything!" I exclaimed, my voice rising in panic. "What if the roof caves in? Or—"

"Calm down. It's just a power outage." He reached out, his fingers brushing against my arm, a touch that sent a jolt of electricity through me. "We'll figure this out."

His touch was reassuring, but the anxiety clawing at my insides refused to be quelled. "What do we do now? It feels like we're in some sort of horror movie."

"Then let's turn it into a comedy," he suggested, his voice laced with warmth. "I'll be the brave hero, and you can be my sidekick."

"Right, because nothing says bravery like pretending to be in a movie while a storm is trying to tear our lives apart."

"I think it says something about the human spirit. Or maybe just how well I can improvise."

I couldn't help but laugh at his ridiculousness, the sound slicing through the tension like a knife. "If we survive this, I'm definitely putting that on your resume."

"Please do. 'Brave hero, skilled improvisor.'"

"Don't forget about my stunning dance moves," I quipped, forcing myself to stay lighthearted despite the weight of the situation.

But as we sat together in the darkness, the laughter began to fade, replaced by an uncomfortable silence that settled between us. The storm's fury outside continued unabated, and the darkness felt thick and suffocating, as if it were alive and reaching for us.

"Liam?" I whispered, unsure why the sudden unease clawed at my chest.

"Yeah?" His voice was low, almost a murmur, but there was a note of tension in it that made my heart race.

"I think we should check the windows. If it gets any worse, we might need to leave."

"Agreed." His hand found mine in the dark, fingers intertwining as we made our way cautiously across the room. The wind howled outside like a banshee, and I could feel my nerves tightening with every step.

Together, we approached the window, the sound of rain slamming against the glass like an urgent warning. With trembling hands, I pulled the curtain aside, peering out into the chaos. The world outside had become a swirling vortex of rain and wind, trees bending under the strain, their branches clawing at the sky as if seeking salvation.

"This is really bad," I breathed, the words escaping before I could contain them.

"Stay close," Liam said, his voice steady, but I could feel the tension in his grip. We stared out together, our breath fogging up the window as we watched the storm rage, a feral beast refusing to relent.

Suddenly, a flash of lightning illuminated the street, and in that brief moment of brilliance, I saw something move beyond the trees—something dark and unyielding creeping toward us. My heart dropped into my stomach, a wave of cold dread washing over me.

"What was that?" I stammered, pulling back instinctively, our hands breaking apart.

"I don't know," Liam replied, his expression sharpening. "But I think we need to—"

A deafening crash interrupted him, the sound reverberating through the house as if the very foundations were shaking. The walls rattled, and I could feel the floor beneath us tremble. The power flickered back on for a brief moment, illuminating the room, but just as quickly, the lights went out again, plunging us into darkness once more.

The realization hit me like a punch to the gut. Something was happening beyond the storm, something that threatened to tear apart the fragile world we had begun to build together.

"Liam!" I cried, feeling the panic rise within me. "What do we do? What's happening?"

His hand found mine again, gripping it tightly as we stood together, bracing for whatever was coming. The storm outside raged on, and in that moment, I knew we were on the brink of something—something terrifying and inevitable. And as I stood there, my heart pounding in my chest, I realized I was more afraid of what lay ahead than the storm itself.

Chapter 8: The Reckoning

The air crackled with tension, thick and heavy like the humid breath of summer lingering past twilight. I stood at the edge of the forest, a sentry in my own heart, where shadows tangled with the last light of day. The trees loomed tall and ancient, their bark rough against the delicate skin of my fingertips as I braced myself for the confrontation that felt like it had been brewing forever. My heart thudded against my ribs, a relentless drum echoing the turmoil inside me. Just beyond the line of trees, the clearing awaited, shrouded in an expectant silence that felt almost mocking.

Beneath the vibrant hues of a fading sunset, memories of laughter and stolen kisses flooded my mind. I could almost hear his voice—rich and warm, a comforting balm against the chaos that was threatening to swallow us whole. But with that warmth came the bitter chill of uncertainty, a reminder of the secrets we had buried beneath layers of affection and unspoken fears. Did love truly conquer all, or was that just a fairy tale we told ourselves to survive the darker moments?

A sudden rustle in the underbrush startled me, and I straightened, squaring my shoulders. It was now or never. With every step I took toward the clearing, my resolve solidified. I had to face him—the one who had turned my world upside down, weaving himself into my thoughts and dreams in ways I could no longer ignore. But in the back of my mind, I could already feel the darkness that accompanied him, curling around our shared moments like a malevolent vine.

"Is this how it ends?" I whispered into the stillness, more to myself than to the encroaching shadows. The weight of uncertainty pressed down on me, making each breath feel like a conscious effort. I took a deep breath, inhaling the earthy scent of damp soil and moss, and stepped into the clearing.

He stood there, silhouetted against the dying light, an enigma wrapped in shadow. The strong lines of his jaw were barely visible, but I could feel the intensity of his gaze as it locked onto mine. His presence filled the space between us, charging the air with an electric hum that made my skin tingle. "You came," he said, his voice low and gravelly, resonating deep within me.

"Of course, I came," I replied, my tone sharper than intended, as if I could slice through the tension with words alone. "But you need to explain what's going on. This... this mess we're in—it can't just be brushed aside."

He shifted, the movement subtle yet deliberate, as if he were trying to contain a storm. "You don't understand the dangers at play here."

I bristled at his attempt to shield me from the truth. "Then make me understand. I'm not some delicate flower you need to protect. If we're going to face this together, I need to know everything."

A moment of silence hung between us, heavy with unspoken thoughts. Finally, he stepped closer, the shadow of his past reflected in the depths of his eyes. "You're right. You deserve to know. But once you do, there's no turning back."

"Trust me," I said, my heart racing with a mix of fear and determination. "I've already stepped into this mess. I refuse to back down now."

With a reluctant nod, he ran a hand through his hair, a gesture that spoke volumes about the weight he bore. "Fine. But remember, this isn't just about us anymore."

The words rolled off his tongue like a bitter pill, and I felt a chill creep down my spine. "What do you mean?"

"There are people involved. Dangerous people. My past... it's more tangled than I let on. I didn't just fall into this; I chose it. And now it's threatening everything—everyone I care about, including you."

I took a step back, the revelation hitting me harder than I anticipated. "You made choices that put me in danger? Why didn't you tell me?"

His eyes darkened, filled with a mixture of regret and resolve. "Because I wanted to protect you from the fallout. I thought I could handle it alone."

"Handle it alone?" I echoed, incredulous. "You think you can just shoulder this burden while I sit back and watch? I'm not a bystander in this. I care about you—about us."

He stepped forward, closing the gap between us, his voice a fierce whisper. "Caring about me could get you killed. You don't understand the stakes."

"Then help me understand! We can't be kept in the dark, not anymore. If we're going to fight, we do it together."

Our gazes locked, a silent battle of wills unfolding in the space that pulsed with the weight of our shared fears. The shadows of the forest encroached, but I felt a warmth spreading through me—an ember igniting against the cold grip of fear.

As he began to speak, the tension thickened like the fog rolling in from the sea, shrouding us in mystery. "There's a group, a network of people who want to control everything. They've been watching me for a long time, waiting for the right moment to strike. I got involved thinking I could bring them down, but they're more dangerous than I imagined."

"Why didn't you come to me?" I pressed, my heart aching at the thought of him facing this alone. "We could've figured this out together."

"Because I couldn't bear the thought of you getting caught in the crossfire. I thought I could end it without involving you. But now..." His voice trailed off, the weight of his regret palpable.

"Now you realize that protecting me by shutting me out was the wrong choice," I said softly, feeling the truth settle between us like a fragile truce.

He nodded, the lines of tension in his shoulders easing slightly as if the weight of the world were beginning to lift, even just a little. "I should have trusted you, should have known you'd want to fight by my side."

"Always," I breathed, my heart pounding with a mix of fear and fierce determination. The stakes had never felt higher, and yet I knew we were stronger together, even if the path ahead was fraught with uncertainty.

With a shared understanding and a newfound resolve, we stood on the precipice of what lay ahead, ready to confront the shadows that sought to pull us apart. In that moment, under the fading light and the watchful eyes of the forest, I realized that our love was a force unlike any other—a force that could illuminate even the darkest of paths.

The tension in the clearing felt almost alive, an electric charge that surged between us as the sun dipped below the horizon, casting long shadows that reached toward the trees like grasping fingers. I could hear the soft whisper of leaves rustling in the gentle breeze, an eerie contrast to the storm brewing in my heart. Just as I was about to speak again, the unmistakable sound of footsteps echoed behind me, a reminder that we were not alone in this tangled web of secrets and danger.

I turned, my instincts flaring as a figure emerged from the thicket, tall and imposing. The shadows masked his features, but I could feel the weight of his gaze as he stepped into the fading light. My heart raced, adrenaline pulsing through my veins, setting every nerve alight with anticipation. This was not just a confrontation with the man I cared about; it was the potential spark that could ignite the entire situation, sending us hurtling toward a fiery climax.

"Stay behind me," he said, his voice a low growl, protective yet laced with urgency.

"Not a chance," I shot back, stepping forward, my resolve solidifying. "We're in this together, remember? I won't hide while you face whatever this is alone."

His eyes flared with surprise and something akin to admiration, but before he could respond, the newcomer spoke, a sardonic edge in his tone that cut through the tension like a knife. "Ah, the brave heroine ready to charge into battle. How charming."

"What do you want?" I demanded, shifting my stance defiantly, the weight of his words hanging in the air like a dark cloud threatening rain.

He chuckled, a sound devoid of warmth. "Isn't it obvious? I'm here to deliver a message. You've both gotten too close to the truth, and now it's time to put an end to your little adventure."

A chill ran down my spine, and I instinctively moved closer to him, feeling the strength radiate from his body. It was strange, but in that moment, the fear didn't overshadow the fierce determination blossoming within me. "You think you can scare us away? We're not backing down."

His laughter echoed through the clearing, mocking and sharp, sending a shiver through the trees. "Ah, such spirit. But it's misplaced. You see, lovebirds, the game you're playing isn't just dangerous; it's lethal. And you've already lost."

The realization hit me hard, like a punch to the gut. The stakes were higher than I'd imagined, and our naïve bravado might have painted a target on our backs. But as I looked at him, his eyes burning with a mixture of anger and determination, I knew we couldn't let fear dictate our choices. "What do you know about us?" I demanded, feeling the heat of my own words invigorating me.

The figure leaned closer, shadows playing across his face. "I know enough to know you should be afraid. But fear isn't what keeps you alive in this world; it's cunning."

"Cunning?" he echoed, a hint of a challenge in his voice. "Maybe that's the problem. You're underestimating us. We're more than you think."

"Prove it," the intruder shot back, his voice a sneer. "You have no idea what you're up against. But if you want a taste of the darkness lurking just out of sight, I can arrange that."

"I don't need a taste of anything," I replied, my voice steady despite the tremor in my hands. "You can keep your threats. We're not afraid of the dark; we're ready to confront it."

With a flick of his wrist, he pulled a small object from his pocket, catching the last rays of sunlight—a glint of steel. I sucked in a breath as he brandished a knife, its blade gleaming ominously. "Brave words for a foolish girl. But bravery can be a fatal flaw."

"Enough!" he shouted, his voice booming in the quiet evening air, and I flinched at the intensity. "Put that away. We're not here to fight—at least not yet."

"Then what are you here for?" I shot back, my heart pounding as the reality of the situation settled in. This was no idle threat; we were standing on the edge of something precarious, and one wrong move could send us tumbling into the abyss.

The man shrugged, feigning disinterest, but his eyes betrayed him—calculating, assessing. "I'm here to offer you a choice. You can either walk away from this, leave the shadows behind, or plunge deeper into the abyss. But know this: you cannot walk both paths. It's one or the other."

I exchanged a glance with him, and in that fleeting moment, we shared an understanding that transcended words. We had both known the stakes were high, but hearing it laid out so starkly sent a tremor of doubt coursing through me. Could we truly turn back now?

"Let me get this straight," I said, my voice steady. "You're offering us a way out? Just like that?"

"Consider it an invitation," he replied, amusement dancing in his eyes. "But make no mistake—it's a trap disguised as a choice. Choose wisely, because the clock is ticking, and you'll soon realize that time is not on your side."

His words hung in the air, a heavy fog that clouded my thoughts. I felt the rush of urgency pulse through my veins, driving me to act. I couldn't let fear or indecision dictate our fate. "You think you can intimidate us into submission? That's where you're wrong. We'll face whatever it is together."

"Together," he echoed, his gaze steady and fierce, grounding me amidst the chaos. "We've come this far; we're not going to stop now."

"Good luck with that," the intruder scoffed, flicking the knife dismissively before sliding it back into his pocket. "But mark my words; you'll regret this choice."

With that, he turned and melted back into the shadows, leaving us in a whirlpool of confusion and uncertainty. As the last echoes of his footsteps faded into the distance, I felt a rush of adrenaline mingling with the remnants of fear that still clung to the air.

"Do you think he meant it?" I asked, my voice barely above a whisper, the gravity of the situation pressing down on me.

"Honestly?" he said, a flicker of doubt crossing his features. "Yeah, I do. But we can't let his words shake us. We're stronger than this, and whatever they're planning, we'll meet it head-on."

"Head-on, huh?" I quipped, attempting to lighten the mood. "So, like two freight trains barreling toward a collision?"

"Exactly," he replied, a hint of a smile tugging at the corners of his mouth. "And you know what? I've always liked a good crash."

His attempt at humor broke through the tension, a reminder that beneath the fear and uncertainty lay the bond we had forged—a bond that could withstand even the darkest of nights. In that moment, as the stars began to twinkle above us like distant beacons of hope, I knew that whatever lay ahead, we would face it together, refusing to be consumed by the shadows that sought to pull us apart.

The silence that followed the intruder's departure felt more profound than the rumble of thunder in a storm. I stood there, breathless, as the echoes of his taunts lingered in the air like the scent of rain-soaked earth. The world around us had shifted, a pivoting point where shadows danced just beyond the edges of the clearing, whispering secrets that were no longer safe to ignore.

"What do we do now?" I asked, glancing up at him, searching his face for answers. He looked as determined as ever, but I could see the strain in his eyes, the weight of a thousand unspoken fears clawing at his resolve.

"We prepare," he said firmly, his voice low, yet laced with an intensity that pulled me closer. "We can't allow ourselves to be caught off guard again. We need a plan, a way to confront whatever comes next."

"Sounds like a solid plan," I replied, trying to inject a bit of levity into the suffocating tension. "But do we have a secret lair where we can plot our superhero moves? Maybe a rooftop with a view?"

He laughed, the sound breaking through the haze of anxiety. "Unfortunately, I can't offer you a view like that. But I do know a place—an old cabin I inherited. It's isolated, hidden. We can strategize there without anyone eavesdropping."

"An isolated cabin? Are we going full survival mode?" I teased, trying to lighten the mood. "Should I pack a bear trap and some canned beans?"

"Canned beans sound great, actually," he said, a smirk playing on his lips. "But don't worry. I'll make sure the only bears we encounter are the metaphorical kind."

His humor momentarily lifted the oppressive weight of the situation, but as we made our way back through the forest, I felt the shadows closing in, their presence a constant reminder of the danger that lurked just beyond our reach. Each step I took echoed in the stillness, as if the very ground beneath us was holding its breath, waiting for something to happen.

By the time we reached the cabin, the sky had draped itself in a heavy cloak of indigo, the stars emerging like distant sentinels. The cabin stood sturdy and unyielding, its wooden walls cloaked in ivy and secrets, a relic of the past that somehow felt alive with possibilities. The door creaked as we pushed it open, revealing a dimly lit space that smelled of aged wood and dust—a forgotten sanctuary.

"Welcome to my humble abode," he said, gesturing dramatically as if unveiling a grand palace. "Not quite what you expected, huh?"

"More rustic than I imagined," I admitted, stepping inside. "But it has character. And you can't argue with that fireplace."

As I moved around the room, I noticed the remnants of a life once lived—faded photographs hanging crooked on the walls, mismatched furniture that somehow worked together in a symphony of nostalgia, and a small kitchen with an old stove that looked like it had cooked a million meals. The atmosphere wrapped around me like a warm embrace, but the weight of our reality hung heavily in the air.

"Let's get to work," he said, breaking my reverie as he moved toward a small table cluttered with maps and notes. "We need to figure out what we're dealing with and how to combat it."

"Right, the grand plan," I replied, joining him at the table, curiosity piqued. I could see his mind whirring, each thought a cog in the intricate machinery of strategy. "But before we dive into that, we need snacks. A proper plan requires sustenance."

"Snacks, huh? I should have stocked up better," he said, chuckling. "But I think I have some granola bars somewhere. Better than nothing, right?"

"Granola bars will fuel our fight against the forces of evil," I quipped, rummaging through the cupboards as I imagined us battling unseen foes with the power of fiber and whole grains.

While he gathered the supplies, I leaned over the maps spread before us, tracing my fingers along the lines that marked our town. I could feel the pulse of it—the roads winding like veins, connecting us all. My heart raced at the thought of how easily those connections could be severed, the delicate balance of our lives upended by the shadows we had yet to fully understand.

"Okay, here's what we know," he began, pulling me back into focus. "The group we're up against is well organized. They operate in secrecy, and they're ruthless. We need to uncover their weaknesses, find their leaders. Only then can we turn the tables."

"What about the guy we just encountered?" I asked, a flicker of doubt gnawing at me. "He seemed confident, almost cocky. That can't be a good sign."

"Confidence can be a weakness," he countered, his voice steady. "If we can bait them, lead them into a false sense of security, we can gain the upper hand. We just need to play our cards right."

"Great, let's get our poker faces ready then," I said, forcing a grin. "I've always fancied myself a card shark."

He laughed again, and for a moment, the tension faded, leaving only the warm glow of camaraderie between us. But as the laughter echoed in the small cabin, the shadows outside seemed to shift, almost as if they were listening, waiting for the right moment to pounce.

As the night deepened, we poured over the maps, scribbling notes and strategies, the flickering candlelight casting playful shadows that danced across the walls. I could feel the sense of purpose building between us, a fragile thread woven from shared determination and unspoken fears.

"Okay," he said, glancing up from the papers. "We'll need to gather more information—find out who else is involved in this."

"Let's make a list of contacts," I suggested, tapping my finger on the table. "People who might have insight or connections. We'll need allies."

"Good idea. But we must be careful," he warned. "Anyone we reach out to could be a potential threat. Trust is a luxury we can't afford."

The gravity of his words settled over us like a shroud, reminding me of the fragile line we walked. Every decision, every word carried weight, and the wrong move could tip the balance in the wrong direction.

Just as we were getting lost in our strategizing, the cabin door creaked open, sending a gust of cool air swirling around us. I froze, heart racing as I instinctively reached for his arm. "Did you leave that open?"

He shook his head, eyes narrowing. "No. I locked it."

A chill ran down my spine, the implications heavy and suffocating. We weren't alone. The shadows had found us.

"Stay behind me," he whispered, moving toward the door, his stance tense and ready.

Before I could protest, he pushed the door open wider, revealing nothing but darkness beyond the threshold. The trees loomed like silent sentinels, their branches swaying gently, but I felt the unmistakable sense of being watched.

"Is anyone there?" he called out, voice steady, but I could hear the undercurrent of tension.

Silence answered him, thick and suffocating, but then came a low chuckle from the darkness, rich with malice. "Did you really think you could hide from us?"

The voice sent a jolt of fear through me, and as I stepped closer, a figure emerged from the shadows, cloaked in darkness, face obscured. My breath caught in my throat as I recognized the twisted grin.

"Well, well, well. Look who decided to play hero."

"Who are you?" I demanded, my voice shaking, heart hammering against my ribcage.

The figure stepped closer, the moonlight revealing glints of silver, a knife reflecting the light ominously in his hand. "You're in over your heads. But don't worry; I'm here to help. Or perhaps to ensure you never leave this place."

I exchanged a panicked glance with him, the weight of danger thick in the air as the figure loomed closer, the shadows swirling like a storm ready to break.

And just like that, we stood at the precipice of chaos, the choices we'd made hanging by a thread, poised to unravel in ways we could never have imagined.

Chapter 9: The Hidden Truth

The scent of aged paper filled the musty air of the attic, a blend of dust and hidden memories swirling around us as I opened the first letter. The attic had long been a forgotten space in the Ashwood estate, cluttered with cobwebs and relics of a bygone era. I could hear the faint creak of the floorboards beneath my feet, a reminder that this house held its breath, waiting for the past to be unveiled. My fingers trembled slightly as I held the fragile sheet, the ornate handwriting like a delicate lacework of secrets begging to be revealed.

"Another one?" Liam asked, leaning over my shoulder, his breath warm against my neck. I felt an electric thrill at the proximity, but the intensity of our investigation kept my focus sharp. He was a steadfast presence, grounding me amid the storm of emotions and revelations swirling around us. Each letter we uncovered drew us deeper into a narrative of jealousy and vengeance that echoed through the generations of the Ashwood lineage.

"Let's see," I whispered, my heart racing as I began to read aloud. The letter spoke of a forbidden romance, a scandal that set two families against each other, their animosities festering like an untreated wound. "It says here that Evelyn Ashwood was in love with a man from the Westons, a family our ancestors despised. They were torn apart by their families' grudges." The words hung in the air, heavy with the weight of history. "How could something so beautiful be crushed under the weight of hatred?"

Liam's brow furrowed, his dark hair falling into his eyes as he mulled over the implications. "This could be why strange things have been happening. The unresolved bitterness may have manifested somehow. People around here believe the past lingers. Maybe they're right."

I nodded, absorbing his words while scanning the page for more clues. It was as if the very house echoed our sentiments, the walls vibrating with unsaid truths. "The final entry is more ominous," I said, swallowing hard. "It mentions a 'cursed inheritance' that would bring only pain to the Ashwoods if not addressed."

Liam's gaze sharpened, a mixture of concern and determination flashing across his features. "If there's a curse, then we need to figure out how to break it. Maybe that's why things have escalated in the town lately. People are feeling the effects of old grudges." His intensity drew me closer to him, a thread of camaraderie weaving our fates tighter.

As I placed the letter down, I caught a glimpse of a dust-covered trunk tucked in the corner, half-hidden beneath an old, moth-eaten quilt. "What do you think is in there?" I asked, nodding toward the trunk. Curiosity tinged my voice with excitement, a distraction from the gravity of our findings.

"Only one way to find out," Liam replied, his eyes sparkling with mischief. Together, we approached the trunk, our footsteps muffled by the thick carpet of dust. With a gentle tug, I pulled the lid open, the hinges creaking like a ghost's whisper. Inside lay a collection of items, each with a story etched into their surfaces—a tarnished locket, yellowing photographs, and an intricately carved wooden box.

"Let's see what we've got," I murmured, reaching for the locket first. I unclasped it, revealing a tiny portrait of a woman with hauntingly beautiful features, her gaze both fierce and sorrowful. "She looks just like you," Liam teased, leaning closer, the warmth of his body brushing against mine, igniting a spark I had tried to ignore.

I shot him a playful glare, heat creeping to my cheeks. "Only if I'm dressed in the fashion of the 1800s," I quipped, but his comment lingered, igniting a flicker of something between us—a connection that was both thrilling and terrifying.

With a gentle nudge, Liam reached for the carved box. "Let's hope this holds more than just dust." He opened it slowly, revealing an array of delicate trinkets—a diary bound in cracked leather, a set of ornate keys, and a map, the edges frayed and yellowed.

The map drew my attention immediately, a meticulous representation of Ashwood and its surrounding lands, with one spot circled in red ink. "This must be important," I said, tracing the ink with my finger, my heart racing as the realization set in. "We need to go there. Whatever's hidden could unravel the truth behind the curse."

Liam nodded, his expression serious yet excited. "We should do it now. Who knows what we'll find if we wait? The sooner we uncover this mystery, the better."

His enthusiasm was contagious, and as we descended the rickety stairs of the attic, I felt a sense of adventure swelling within me. The atmosphere thickened with anticipation, every creak of the floorboards a reminder of the steps we were taking to confront the shadows of our past.

Outside, the air was crisp, the leaves rustling underfoot like whispers of ancient secrets. The light was beginning to fade, casting a golden hue over everything, but I felt emboldened. This was our moment—Liam and I, united against the echoes of history.

As we reached the edge of the estate, I paused, taking in the sprawling grounds of Ashwood. "You know," I said, casting a sideways glance at Liam, "if we don't survive this, at least we'll have a good story to tell in the afterlife."

"True," he replied with a smirk, his eyes dancing with mischief. "But I plan to stick around for a few more chapters. I'd like to see how this love story unfolds."

The banter between us felt like a lifeline, pulling me back from the precipice of fear. Together, we stepped toward the unknown, ready to face whatever lay ahead, drawn by the promise of adventure and the thrill of unearthing the secrets that had bound our families for generations.

The woods stretched before us like an ancient tapestry, threads of shadows weaving through the gnarled trees that stood sentinel along the path. With every step, I felt the earth sink softly beneath my feet, a subtle reminder of the weight of history pressing down upon us. Sunlight filtered through the leaves, casting dappled patterns on the ground, illuminating the trail we followed. Liam walked beside me, his presence a steady force that banished any remnants of doubt swirling in my mind.

"What if the cursed inheritance is something ridiculous, like a collection of bad poetry or a hideous vase?" I mused, attempting to defuse the tension coiling tightly around us. The very notion of stumbling upon something absurd amid our serious quest made me chuckle, and Liam turned to me, his expression a mix of amusement and earnestness.

"I'd take a hideous vase over family feuds and dark curses any day," he replied, grinning. "At least it wouldn't threaten our sanity. Besides, I've always believed there's a certain charm in ugly decor."

We shared a laugh, a fleeting moment of levity that brightened the growing heaviness of our undertaking. Yet beneath the humor lay an undercurrent of anticipation, a palpable energy that hummed in the air as we approached the location marked on the map. It was a small clearing, bordered by thick brambles and towering trees, their roots twisting like fingers grasping for something long lost.

The map had led us to a flat stone that jutted out from the earth, its surface covered in moss and lichen. "Looks like we found it," I said, my voice barely above a whisper. I knelt beside the stone, brushing away the damp moss to reveal an inscription barely legible through the grime.

"What does it say?" Liam leaned in closer, his shoulder brushing against mine, and I felt a rush of warmth that surged through me, mingling with the chill of the gathering dusk.

"It's faint, but it mentions a 'key to the past,'" I read, frowning at the cryptic words. "And something about a secret passage." I glanced up at Liam, our eyes locking in a moment charged with possibility. "A secret passage? Sounds like we've stumbled into a treasure hunt straight out of a storybook."

"I'm all for a little adventure," he said, his tone light, but his gaze was serious. "Just keep in mind that sometimes, treasure hunts come with traps."

I laughed softly, trying to shake off the unease creeping back in. "Like falling into a pit filled with snakes? Or maybe a puzzle that will turn us to stone if we get it wrong?"

"Both sound equally terrifying. Let's hope it's more of a whimsical riddle than a life-threatening challenge," he replied, his smirk both reassuring and daring.

Kneeling before the stone, I felt a sudden tug of energy as if the ground beneath us was alive. I pressed my hands against the cool surface, searching for a hidden mechanism, a latch, anything that could lead us deeper into the mystery. After a moment, I noticed a small indentation, barely noticeable unless one knew to look.

"Liam, over here!" I called, excitement bubbling within me. He knelt beside me, curiosity dancing in his eyes as I pressed the indentation. With a low rumble, the stone shifted slightly, revealing a narrow gap that led into darkness.

"Brilliant!" he exclaimed, his enthusiasm contagious. "I suppose we should have brought flashlights."

"I suppose we should have," I admitted, but as the last rays of sunlight slipped away, an unshakeable determination settled in my chest. I took a deep breath, steeling myself for whatever lay beyond. "Ready to face the unknown?"

"With you? Always," he said, and there was a sincerity in his tone that sent a thrill through me.

Together, we crawled through the narrow opening, the cool air enveloping us as we emerged into a hidden chamber, the faint glow of bioluminescent fungi lining the damp walls casting an ethereal light. The space was larger than I'd anticipated, the air heavy with the scent of earth and something distinctly floral, as if nature had claimed this secret realm as its own.

"Wow," I breathed, taking in the sight of intricate carvings etched into the stone walls—figures of people in the throes of celebration and sorrow, a history captured in stone. "This is incredible."

Liam stepped deeper into the chamber, his eyes wide with wonder. "It's like a forgotten gallery. Each carving tells a story." He traced a finger along one of the reliefs, depicting a couple locked in an embrace, their expressions a mixture of joy and despair. "I wonder if they were part of the Ashwood family."

"Or perhaps part of the Weston family," I suggested, feeling the tension of our families' histories looming overhead. "This could be a testament to their entangled fates."

As we explored the chamber, I spotted something gleaming in a shadowed alcove. I made my way over, my heart racing as I reached for it—a locket, intricately designed, nestled between two stones. It felt familiar, echoing the one I had found earlier.

"Look at this!" I called to Liam, holding it up to the dim light. "I think it's a match."

He joined me, his expression shifting from curiosity to something deeper. "Let's see if it holds any secrets."

As I opened the locket, a brittle piece of paper slipped out, fluttering to the ground like a fallen leaf. Liam and I exchanged glances, a sense of urgency swirling between us as I picked it up. The words were hastily scrawled, the ink smudged in places as if the writer had been racing against time.

"'The truth lies in the shadows. Beware those who seek to keep it hidden,'" I read aloud, my voice faltering slightly. "What does that even mean?"

Liam's brows furrowed in thought, his expression serious. "It means we're not the only ones interested in this."

A chill skittered down my spine as we stood in that dim chamber, surrounded by the echoes of a history we had only just begun to unearth. Whatever secrets lay ahead, it was clear that the past was determined to keep its hold on us, and the threads of our lives were tangled in a web spun from generations of sorrow and regret.

The air in the chamber grew thick with anticipation, the flickering glow of bioluminescent fungi casting eerie shadows that danced across the stone walls. The locket lay heavy in my palm, its significance pressing down on me like the weight of an unspoken truth. I glanced at Liam, his brow furrowed as he studied the paper that had fallen from the locket, his expression a mixture of intrigue and concern.

"Do you think this means someone's watching us?" I asked, my voice barely a whisper. The thought sent a ripple of unease through me, as if the very walls were eavesdropping on our every word. "What if we're not alone in this?"

"Could be," Liam replied, his tone low and serious. "But it could also mean that the truth is more dangerous than we realize. The kind of truth that can shatter lives." He paused, running a hand through his hair, which tousled in the soft glow. "We have to stay vigilant."

I nodded, my heart racing as I processed the implications of our discovery. We had stepped into a world of shadows, where secrets lurked in every corner and the past refused to be silenced. "So, what do we do now? Do we keep exploring or retreat?"

"Exploring, definitely," Liam said, the glimmer of excitement in his eyes outweighing his caution. "We can't turn back now. The truth is here, waiting for us."

With a deep breath, I took a step further into the chamber, drawn to the intricate carvings that lined the walls like an ancient storybook. Each figure seemed to tell a tale of love and betrayal, a vivid tapestry of emotions that transcended time. I traced my fingers along one carving—a woman with flowing hair, her hand outstretched, as if reaching for something just out of reach.

"What do you think she's trying to grasp?" Liam asked, stepping beside me, his voice barely above a murmur.

"Maybe it's hope," I replied, my heart stirring at the thought. "Or perhaps freedom. She looks like she's yearning for something beyond her grasp."

"Sounds like all of us at some point," he said, a hint of humor in his tone. "Still, it makes me wonder how many people have come through here, searching for the same answers we are."

As I moved deeper into the chamber, I noticed a slight depression in the stone floor, almost hidden beneath a layer of dust. I knelt down, brushing the surface away to reveal what looked like a small opening, just large enough for a hand to reach in. "Liam, check this out!"

He leaned closer, his eyes narrowing in concentration. "What do you think is inside?"

"Only one way to find out." My heart raced as I slipped my hand into the opening, fingers brushing against something cold and metallic. I pulled it out slowly, revealing a tarnished key, its ornate design glinting in the bioluminescent light. "This could be it! The key to the hidden passage!"

Liam's expression shifted to excitement, his eyes sparkling as he held the key between us. "Looks like we're in business. But what does it unlock?"

"Only one way to find out," I echoed, the thrill of adventure surging through me. "Let's keep looking."

As we navigated through the chamber, we stumbled upon a set of old crates, their wood splintered and worn. Each crate was sealed with heavy iron locks, the rusted metal hinting at secrets long buried. "Do you think any of these could hold more clues?" I asked, curiosity piquing.

"Only one way to find out," he repeated, a mischievous glint in his eye. "Why does that sound familiar?"

With a chuckle, I grabbed the key and tried it in the first lock. It fit perfectly, and with a satisfying click, I opened the crate. Inside lay a collection of yellowed scrolls, each bound with a faded ribbon. I gently unfurled one, revealing a map of the Ashwood estate and its surrounding lands, similar to the one we had found earlier, but marked with additional locations—some of which were unfamiliar to me.

"Look at this!" I exclaimed, showing him the map. "These places aren't on the other map. They could be significant."

Liam leaned in closer, his eyes scanning the details. "What if these are other sites connected to the feud? Maybe there's more to uncover."

I felt a surge of adrenaline as the enormity of our discovery settled in. "We could be onto something big. What if we're not just piecing together a family history, but unraveling the very foundation of this town's past?"

The thought sent shivers down my spine, yet a strange exhilaration accompanied it. The past was alive here, pulsating with energy and unspoken truths.

As we explored further, we unearthed more scrolls, each containing snippets of stories, betrayals, and the intertwined fates of the Ashwoods and Westons. "It's like they were fated to collide," I mused aloud, the weight of their choices hanging heavy in the air.

"Fated or cursed?" Liam countered, his tone suddenly serious. "Every choice they made led to this moment. And now we're here, trying to decipher the chaos."

Our conversation was abruptly interrupted by a low rumble that reverberated through the chamber, shaking the ground beneath us. I exchanged a worried glance with Liam, my heart racing. "What was that?"

"Maybe the spirits of the past are unhappy with us poking around," he joked, though the tension in his voice betrayed his unease.

The rumble intensified, a deep growl that echoed around us, followed by a sudden crack—like the sound of thunder in a clear sky. The walls trembled, dust raining down from the ceiling.

"Liam, we need to get out of here!" I shouted, my voice rising above the din.

Before we could move, a section of the wall slid open, revealing a dark tunnel that seemed to beckon us deeper into the unknown. I hesitated, my instincts screaming to flee, but curiosity held me in place.

"What if this leads to the heart of the mystery?" Liam urged, eyes wide with excitement.

"Or to our doom," I replied, glancing back at the entrance. But there was no time to ponder. The ground trembled again, and with a determined nod, I took a step forward into the tunnel, the darkness swallowing us whole.

The passage was narrow and damp, the air heavy with an earthy scent. I could hear the rush of water somewhere in the distance, mingling with the sound of our footsteps echoing off the stone walls. My heart raced with a mix of fear and anticipation, the thrill of the unknown propelling me onward.

Suddenly, the tunnel opened up into a vast cavern, illuminated by an otherworldly glow emanating from a pool of water at its center.

The sight was breathtaking—a shimmering expanse reflecting the light like a thousand stars captured beneath the surface.

"Look at that," Liam whispered, awe coloring his tone.

But before I could respond, a sudden, chilling realization washed over me. From the corner of my eye, I spotted movement—figures emerging from the shadows, cloaked and silent, their presence as eerie as the glow of the water.

"Liam..." I breathed, panic gripping my heart.

He turned, the smile fading from his face as we stood together, frozen in a moment of uncertainty, surrounded by the echoes of the past and the weight of the hidden truths we had yet to uncover. The air crackled with tension, and as the figures approached, I knew with a certainty that this was only the beginning of our reckoning.

Chapter 10: Shadows of the Past

The air was crisp, carrying with it the scent of damp earth and the rustle of leaves that whispered secrets in the night. As Liam and I walked hand in hand through the park, I felt the chill seep into my bones, but his presence provided an unexpected warmth. It was as if we were wrapped in a cocoon of shared breaths and unspoken promises, our laughter echoing softly against the twilight. The path, lined with flickering lampposts, seemed to beckon us toward the ancient oak that had borne witness to our first kiss—a moment so sweet it felt suspended in time, like a secret captured in amber.

The moon hung high, a silver coin tossed into a deep blue sky, illuminating our surroundings with a mystical glow. The oak tree stood sentinel, its gnarled branches stretching out like the arms of an old friend. I could almost hear it sighing, reminiscing about the lovers who had come before us. We settled beneath its wide, protective boughs, and I glanced at Liam, hoping to read the thoughts flickering behind his emerald eyes. They were usually so bright, but tonight they seemed clouded with shadows from a past he rarely shared.

"Do you ever wonder what this place has seen?" I asked, my voice barely a whisper, afraid that even the wind would carry my curiosity away.

Liam turned to me, a slight smile playing at the corners of his mouth. "You mean the park or the tree?"

"Both, I suppose. It must hold stories of love and heartache—like ours," I said, giving his hand a gentle squeeze, but my heart raced at the thought of exposing my own scars.

He chuckled, a sound that resonated through the quiet. "You know, I think the tree's seen enough to write a bestseller. Young lovers sneaking kisses, old couples reminiscing, and maybe even a few heartbreaks." His eyes darkened for a moment, the laughter fading into something more solemn. "But you don't want to hear about the sad stuff, do you?"

"I do, actually," I said, my curiosity piqued. "You've mentioned your past before, but I'd like to know what's shaped you into the man sitting beside me now."

Liam hesitated, the light from the moon catching the contours of his face, making him look even more compelling. "It's not the easiest story to tell."

"Then it must be worth telling," I replied, hoping to coax the words out of him.

Taking a deep breath, he leaned back against the trunk of the tree, his gaze drifting up to the leaves that fluttered gently in the breeze. "Alright, but I can't promise a fairy tale. It's more like one of those gritty dramas that leaves you with more questions than answers."

I shifted closer, resting my head against his shoulder, the warmth radiating from him steadying my own unease. "I can handle gritty. Just tell me about it."

He began slowly, each word careful, as if he were shaping delicate glass. "When I was seventeen, I lost my mother. She was everything to me—my biggest supporter, my confidant. I remember the day vividly. I was supposed to have a soccer game, but she never showed up to pick me up. It turned out she'd collapsed at home. The doctors said it was sudden, that I'd never see her again."

My heart sank, the weight of his pain settling heavily in the air between us. "I'm so sorry," I murmured, feeling the sting of tears prick my eyes.

"It was a long time ago, but the scars linger," he continued, his voice a little steadier now. "After that, everything changed. My father was there, but he was lost in his own grief. I learned how to fend for myself, to find solace in solitude. I didn't really have friends; I pushed everyone away. I thought if I didn't let anyone in, I couldn't get hurt again."

His words hung in the air, and I wanted to reach out, to pull him back from the memories that seemed to claw at him, but I held back, allowing him the space to unearth the truth.

"And then there's the other part," he added, a grimace crossing his face. "After my mother's funeral, I found an old box in the attic. Letters and photographs. They told stories of a life I had never known—of my mother before she was a mom. I learned things that made me question who she really was and what she kept hidden from me. That's when I realized I didn't know her as well as I thought."

The shadows around us deepened, their fingers creeping closer, and I sensed the palpable tension crackling in the air. "What do you mean?" I asked, heart racing with the implications.

"She had a life before me. Friends, passions, dreams that faded into the background when I was born. It felt like I'd lost her all over again, not just to death but to this stranger I never met." His voice grew softer, almost a whisper. "That's when I understood the importance of honesty—how the shadows of our past can shape our present in ways we can't always see."

I shivered, not from the cold, but from the sudden realization of how deeply entwined our stories were, how the shadows of his past were now creeping into our shared moments. "You don't have to carry that weight alone, Liam. I want to help you carry it."

He looked down at me, surprise flickering across his face before it melted into something tender. "You already do, you know? Just being here makes it easier."

Suddenly, a flicker of movement caught my eye, a shadow shifting at the edge of the park. My heart raced as a chill ran down my spine, the lightness of our conversation dissipating into a sense of foreboding. "Did you see that?" I whispered, gripping his hand tighter.

Liam's posture shifted, his body tense as he turned his head toward the darkness. "What do you mean?" he asked, his voice low, alert.

"I thought I saw something move. In the shadows."

He scanned the area, his eyes narrowing. The laughter of other park-goers faded, and the world around us seemed to hold its breath, the night suddenly feeling less safe, more menacing. "Stay close," he instructed, his tone firm yet calm, grounding me as the sense of danger grew palpable.

With my heart hammering in my chest, I moved closer to him, our fingers intertwined, the warmth between us flickering like a candle flame in the wind. The air felt charged, as if the shadows themselves were waiting, watching, ready to unfold secrets better left buried.

The tension hung thick in the air, wrapping around us like an invisible shroud. My senses sharpened, every rustle of leaves and distant sound amplifying in the stillness of the night. Liam's grip tightened on my hand, his warm palm a stark contrast to the growing chill that permeated the park. I leaned into him, seeking comfort in his presence while my heart raced, a wild rabbit caught in the headlights of something unknown.

"Maybe it's just a raccoon," I whispered, trying to inject some levity into the moment, but my voice wavered slightly, betraying the unease bubbling beneath the surface.

He chuckled softly, but it didn't quite reach his eyes. "Raccoons don't usually lurk in the shadows like they're auditioning for a horror movie." His gaze remained fixed on the darkness that surrounded us, his brow furrowed in concern.

The flicker of movement returned, more pronounced this time, a flash of something—an outline, perhaps—disappearing just beyond the tree line. "I think we should go," I suggested, my voice low but firm. The desire to flee clashed with my instinct to stay close to him, to reassure myself that we were safe in this shared bubble, even as danger loomed nearby.

"Not yet," he replied, a protective determination in his tone. "I need to know what it is."

Before I could argue, he stood, pulling me up with him. The warmth of his hand felt like a lifeline as we crept closer to the edge of the park. My heart thudded in my chest, each pulse a reminder of the uncertainty surrounding us. With each step, I scanned the area, desperately hoping to find nothing but shadows and whispers.

"Liam, we really don't have to do this," I urged, glancing at him. "You're not Batman, and I'm definitely not Catwoman. I can't promise I'll look good in spandex if we get into trouble."

He smirked, the tension easing slightly. "If anything, you'd make a stunning Catwoman. I'd be proud to have you by my side."

I couldn't help but laugh, the sound cutting through the unease. But it was short-lived as we rounded the trunk of the oak, peering into the darkness where the movement had originated. The moonlight barely penetrated the dense thicket, creating pockets of blackness that seemed to pulse with secrets.

"See anything?" I whispered, though I could barely make out the contours of the ground, let alone the potential threats lurking within it.

"Just shadows," he replied, his voice low and cautious. "But I—"

Before he could finish, a figure emerged from the darkness, stumbling into the moonlight. My heart dropped as I took in the disheveled appearance of a woman. Her hair was wild, a tangled halo around her face, and her clothes hung loosely, giving the impression of someone lost in a storm.

"Help me," she gasped, her eyes wide with fear.

I instinctively stepped back, but Liam stepped forward, his instincts as protective as ever. "What's wrong?" he asked, his voice steady despite the chaos of emotions swirling in me.

"I—I'm being followed. I don't know who it is, but they're coming for me," she stammered, her breath quickening as if the weight of her fear was too much to bear. "I saw them in the alley. I thought I lost them, but I didn't know where else to go."

My stomach twisted at the notion of danger inching closer, and yet something about her plea tugged at my heartstrings. "Liam, maybe we should call the police," I suggested, glancing up at him. "She needs help."

He nodded, pulling out his phone, but the woman's eyes widened even further. "No, please! I can't go back there. They'll find me! You don't understand!"

The desperation in her voice sent a chill through me, and I felt an irrational urge to protect her, to draw her into our cocoon of safety. "What happened?" I asked, stepping closer, hoping to bring her some comfort amid her panic. "We can help you. Just tell us what's going on."

She hesitated, glancing over her shoulder as if the shadows themselves were listening. "I can't say too much here, but I was trying to get away from someone. A man—he's dangerous. He doesn't take no for an answer."

Liam's hand found mine again, and I could feel the tension rolling off him in waves. "Where did you last see him?" he asked, his voice firm but calm.

"In the alley behind the coffee shop," she said, glancing nervously toward the exit of the park. "I thought I was being followed, so I ran, but I didn't think he'd actually follow me here."

"Let's go back to the coffee shop," Liam suggested, his tone decisive. "We can find a place to wait for the police. You'll be safe there."

"No!" she cried, her eyes darting around as if the shadows themselves were alive. "If he sees me, I'm finished! Please, you don't know what he's capable of. I just need to hide. I can't go back."

The panic in her voice turned my heart to ice, and I exchanged a worried glance with Liam. "What do you want us to do?" I asked, trying to keep my voice steady, though my mind raced with possibilities.

"Just—please, let me stay with you for a while. I swear, I'll explain everything. Just don't let him find me."

For a moment, I felt the weight of the world pressing down on my shoulders. I wanted to help her, to keep her safe, but I also felt the gnawing fear that this might pull us into something far darker than I could fathom. Liam squeezed my hand tighter, grounding me in this chaotic moment.

"Alright," he said finally, his voice unwavering. "You can stay with us for now, but we need to find a safe spot."

As we led her back toward the heart of the park, I could feel the shadows lurking behind us, a reminder that danger was never far away. I glanced at Liam, his jaw set with determination, and I felt an odd mix of fear and exhilaration coursing through me. In that moment, I realized our lives had shifted, intertwining with a stranger's in a way I had never anticipated. The night had become an unpredictable tapestry woven with threads of danger, secrets, and the promise of something deeper—a journey we hadn't yet begun to understand.

With a mix of anxiety and resolve, we maneuvered through the park, the glow of the streetlights flickering like distant stars trying to cut through the darkness. The woman walked beside us, her steps hurried and uneven, as if she were still half-turned toward the shadows she feared. I couldn't help but notice how the light illuminated her face, revealing the paleness of her skin and the dark circles under her eyes—signs of someone who hadn't slept well in days, perhaps longer.

"Do you have a name?" I asked, striving to anchor her to this moment, to make her feel seen amid her panic.

"Jenna," she replied, glancing nervously at Liam. "Thank you for helping me. I—I didn't know who else to turn to."

Liam offered her a reassuring smile, though his eyes remained watchful, scanning the park with a vigilance that could only come from someone who had faced his share of shadows. "You're safe with us, Jenna. Just stay close."

We reached the center of the park, where a small gazebo stood, its wooden structure adorned with creeping vines and soft fairy lights that twinkled like stars. It felt like a sanctuary in the midst of chaos. I gestured for her to step inside, and she hesitated, glancing back over her shoulder as if expecting a phantom to emerge from the darkness.

"It's okay," I encouraged, stepping in first. "You can breathe here. We'll figure this out."

As she stepped into the gazebo, I closed the door behind us, feeling the weight of the night pressing against the thin wooden walls. The atmosphere shifted; the dim light felt almost ethereal, casting long shadows that danced along the floor. I leaned against one of the posts, crossing my arms in an attempt to appear calm, though my mind was racing.

"Now, can you tell us what happened?" Liam prompted gently, his voice a soothing balm against the tension in the air.

Jenna took a shaky breath, her fingers nervously twisting the frayed hem of her shirt. "It started a few weeks ago," she began, her voice trembling. "I was working at a diner downtown. A regular came in, someone I thought was harmless. At first, he was just a lonely guy looking for company. He'd sit at the counter, chat about his day, nothing too alarming. But then he started getting... intense."

"Intense how?" I pressed, my heart racing with each word she spoke.

She glanced at Liam, as if seeking reassurance. "He began asking personal questions—about my life, my family. I didn't think much of it until one day, he showed up at the diner with flowers. It was sweet at first, but it quickly escalated."

"Escalated how?" Liam asked, his tone shifting to something more serious.

"He started showing up at my apartment," she said, her voice barely above a whisper. "I had no idea how he found out where I lived. He would just stand there, watching from the street. I told him to leave me alone, but he didn't listen. It got worse after that."

A cold shiver ran down my spine, the weight of her words settling heavily in the space around us. "Did you tell anyone? Did you report him?"

"I tried, but they didn't take me seriously. Just some guy with a crush, they said. I thought I could handle it," she said, the frustration and fear in her voice palpable. "But last night, he cornered me after my shift. He was angry—shouting, saying I'd made him look foolish. That's when I knew I had to run."

A silence enveloped us, heavy and fraught with the danger that lingered in the air. I exchanged a glance with Liam, whose expression mirrored my own concern.

"Have you called the police?" he asked gently.

She shook her head. "I can't. If he finds out I'm talking to them, it'll only make things worse."

The tension in the gazebo thickened as Jenna's words hung like a dark cloud over us. "You need to protect yourself," I insisted. "You can't face this alone."

"I know," she replied, her eyes wide with fear. "But I can't go back. I can't let him find me. He'll hurt me."

Just then, a sound broke through the stillness, a low rustle coming from the shadows outside the gazebo. My heart raced as I leaned closer to the edge, peering into the darkness, trying to discern the source.

"What was that?" Jenna whispered, her voice quaking.

"Stay back," Liam instructed, his voice steady as he moved to shield her from view.

The rustling grew louder, accompanied by the crunch of gravel underfoot. I held my breath, straining to see through the dark, my heart hammering against my ribcage. A figure stepped into the light, and I felt my breath hitch in my throat.

It was a man, tall and imposing, with a face that seemed to flicker like a shadow in the low light. His eyes, dark and cold, scanned the area before locking onto our gazebo. Time froze, and I could hear the pounding of my heartbeat echoing in my ears.

"Jenna," he called, a twisted grin spreading across his face. "I know you're in there. Don't be scared; I just want to talk."

Panic surged through me as I turned to Jenna, whose face had drained of color. "Is that him?" I asked, my voice barely a whisper.

She nodded, a single tear escaping down her cheek.

"Liam, we need to go," I urged, fear gripping me like a vice.

But he stood firm, his jaw set in defiance. "No. We can't let him take her. Jenna, stay behind us."

The man took a step forward, his demeanor shifting from friendly to predatory. "You don't need to hide, Jenna. You know how much I care about you. Let's just end this silly game."

The air crackled with tension, the line between safety and danger narrowing with each passing second. I could feel the threat radiating off him like a storm cloud about to burst.

"Liam..." I whispered, feeling the weight of desperation settling heavily in my chest.

"Trust me," he replied, his voice calm but firm.

Just then, the man lunged forward, and instinct kicked in. I grabbed Jenna's arm, pulling her back, while Liam stepped into the fray, his stance unwavering. "Get back!" he shouted, the urgency in his voice slicing through the air.

As I felt Jenna's grip tighten on my hand, the world around us began to spiral, the shadows closing in as fear took hold.

The man's laughter echoed through the park, a chilling sound that sent shivers down my spine. "You think you can protect her? You have no idea what you're up against."

In that moment, I realized that our lives were no longer just entwined; we were caught in a web of darkness, the shadows of our pasts crashing together with an intensity that threatened to consume us all.

And as the figure loomed closer, I braced myself for the fight ahead, knowing that the night was far from over—and that nothing would ever be the same again.

Chapter 11: The Price of Love

The city thrummed with a pulse all its own, a restless energy that mingled with the bitter-sweet scent of impending rain. I watched from the café window, steam curling lazily from my cup, as dark clouds rolled in like an army on the march, promising to drench the streets in their relentless downpour. Each drop that landed on the window felt like a heartbeat echoing the anxiety in my chest. It was a peculiar moment—this blend of nature's fury and my own inner turmoil—as I weighed the gravity of my feelings for Liam against the encroaching shadows threatening to engulf us both.

Our encounters had started innocently enough, each conversation igniting sparks of laughter that danced between us like fireflies in the dusk. But now, every shared smile was tinged with a taste of fear, each tender glance weighed down by the sinister presence lurking just beyond the edges of our sanctuary. The café was a haven, with its worn wooden tables and the comforting aroma of coffee, yet even here, the specter of our reality seeped through the walls. I could almost hear the echoes of their whispers, taunting us with knowledge of our pasts, our fears, our insecurities.

"Do you think they know?" I asked Liam, my voice barely rising above the hum of chatter and clinking cups. I studied him, the way his brow furrowed, creating a storm of thoughts behind those captivating hazel eyes. His hair fell in disarray, framing his face, and I wanted nothing more than to reach out, tuck a loose strand behind his ear, and forget the world for a while.

He leaned back, crossing his arms as if to shield himself from the truth that clung to us like a heavy fog. "If they do, it only makes them more dangerous. We can't let them scare us, Jess." His voice held a steadiness I envied, a calm I desperately craved to emulate. Yet, beneath that bravado lay the unmistakable tremor of concern, an unspoken acknowledgment of the storm brewing beyond the café's glass façade.

"I know," I replied, though doubt laced my words. "But these messages—they're more than just threats. They're taunts. They know us." I gestured towards the corner where a newspaper lay, its headline bold and accusatory, a mirror reflecting our own tangled lives. "Look at that."

Liam's gaze followed mine, and the tension between us thickened, palpable and charged. "We can't let fear dictate our lives," he said, though his attempt at reassurance felt brittle, like glass ready to shatter at any moment. "Let's not give them the satisfaction."

Yet, the words rang hollow in the confines of my heart. Each message left at our favorite spots was a reminder that we were being watched, that our lives were no longer our own. My mind wandered to the note found in the park where we shared our first kiss, the ink scrawled in jagged letters, "You'll regret this." The memory sent a shiver down my spine, the fear creeping in like a thief in the night.

"Let's go somewhere," I suggested, suddenly craving the thrill of spontaneity to distract from the shadows that loomed over us. "Just us. No café, no park—somewhere they wouldn't expect."

His eyes sparked with intrigue, a glimmer of adventure replacing the tension. "You mean a real escape?"

"Exactly. A place where we can breathe, away from prying eyes." I could see his mind racing, calculating the risks as he weighed my suggestion. A moment stretched between us, filled with unspoken promises and the raw electricity of possibility.

"Alright," he finally said, his voice a low, determined whisper. "Just tell me where."

As we slipped out into the street, the first drops of rain fell, splattering against the pavement and mingling with the restless energy that thrummed beneath our feet. We walked side by side, the world around us blurring into a watercolor wash of grays and blues, the damp air heavy with the scent of impending storms. Each step felt like a declaration, a rebellion against the darkness threatening to encroach upon our fragile connection.

I led him to an old bookstore nestled between two towering buildings, its façade charmingly worn, a hidden gem waiting to be discovered. The bell above the door jingled softly as we entered, a welcoming sound that enveloped us in warmth. The musty smell of aged paper wrapped around us like a comforting hug, and I took a deep breath, the atmosphere easing some of the tension clinging to my heart.

"Do you think they'll find us here?" Liam asked, scanning the dimly lit aisles.

"Only if they're really determined," I replied, a playful smile tugging at my lips. "But who would expect a couple of lovesick fools to hide out in a dusty bookstore?"

His laughter rang out, rich and infectious, dispelling some of the shadows that had settled between us. "Well, we are nothing if not lovesick fools."

I found a cozy nook in the back, a small alcove lined with shelves filled with forgotten tales. I settled onto a battered armchair, its fabric soft and inviting, and Liam joined me, our shoulders brushing as we leaned into the warmth of the moment. The rain outside began to fall in earnest, creating a soothing symphony against the windows, a gentle reminder of the chaos beyond our sanctuary.

"Tell me a story," I urged, leaning closer, my heart swelling with affection. "Something that has nothing to do with threats or fears."

He paused, his gaze drifting as he searched for a tale buried deep within his thoughts. "Once upon a time," he began, his voice low and melodic, "there was a girl who loved to explore. She sought adventure in the most ordinary places, turning mundane moments into extraordinary memories."

"Is she a lovesick fool, too?" I interjected, my eyes sparkling with mischief.

"Perhaps," he chuckled, a hint of a smile playing at the corners of his mouth. "But one day, she stumbled upon a treasure map hidden within the pages of an old book. It promised a great fortune, but also peril, leading her through dark forests and treacherous cliffs."

"Did she take the risk?" I asked, entranced by the story.

"Of course," he replied, his expression earnest. "Because sometimes the greatest treasures lie in the journey itself, not just the destination."

As he spoke, the weight of the world slipped away, replaced by the warmth of shared dreams and laughter. In that quiet corner of the bookstore, with rain drumming a comforting rhythm outside, I found solace in Liam's presence. The lingering threat faded into the background, overshadowed by the bond we were forging, fragile yet undeniably strong. In that moment, I believed in the promise of our adventure—a journey filled with uncertainties, yes, but also with love, laughter, and an unquenchable spirit that could weather any storm.

The rain continued its steady rhythm, drumming against the windowpanes like an impatient lover seeking attention. Each drop was a reminder of the world outside, of the chaos lurking beyond the comforting confines of our bookstore refuge. As Liam spun his tale, the shadows of doubt and fear danced at the edges of my mind, but I pushed them away, focusing instead on the soft cadence of his voice and the way the dim light flickered off the spines of the old books that surrounded us.

"Anyway," he continued, leaning forward, the intrigue of his story pulling me in deeper, "the girl ventured into the depths of the forest, armed with nothing but her courage and a vague sense of direction. Every twist and turn brought her closer to the treasure, yet it also led her into the unknown, into places that echoed with whispers of past explorers who had failed."

I raised an eyebrow, teasingly skeptical. "You're not suggesting that she was also being watched, are you? Because that sounds all too familiar."

"Ah, but that's the beauty of stories," he said with a sly grin. "They let us explore our fears in a safe space. She knew that danger lurked around every corner, but her heart urged her forward."

His gaze locked onto mine, and I felt the unspoken connection between us deepen, like the roots of an ancient tree intertwining beneath the surface. "What if the real treasure isn't just gold or jewels?" I mused, my heart racing slightly. "What if it's the courage to face what scares us?"

"Very poetic," he said, his smile warm and genuine. "Maybe she was searching for something far more valuable than mere riches."

Just then, the bookstore's bell chimed again, signaling the arrival of a newcomer. I turned, a flutter of unease settling in my stomach, expecting another innocent patron lost in the world of books. Instead, I found myself staring into the face of someone I hadn't anticipated—Gwen, a former coworker from the agency I had left behind when I chose a different path.

"Jess! Fancy seeing you here!" she exclaimed, her voice a cheery chime that clashed with the heaviness in the air. "And you must be Liam!" She extended her hand toward him with a friendliness that seemed a touch too eager, her eyes scanning us both as if assessing the situation.

"Uh, yeah," Liam replied, confusion flickering in his expression. "Nice to meet you."

I couldn't help but notice the tension that crept into his posture, the way he leaned slightly away from her, as if she were an unwelcome gust of wind that could blow our carefully built sanctuary apart.

"What brings you to this corner of the world?" I asked, forcing a smile that felt more like a mask than genuine warmth.

"Oh, just picking up a few things for a project," Gwen replied, waving her hand dismissively. "You know how it is—there's always something to do. But I didn't expect to find you here, looking all cozy with a handsome stranger. Didn't know you had moved on so quickly."

The words hung in the air, sharp and tinged with an edge I hadn't anticipated. My heart raced as I caught Liam's sideways glance—his jaw tightened, eyes narrowing slightly at the implications of her comment. "It's not what it looks like," I blurted out, feeling defensive.

Gwen raised an eyebrow, a smirk playing at the corners of her lips. "Isn't it?"

Before I could formulate a response, she continued, her tone shifting to one of playful curiosity. "You're lucky to have found someone who looks like he could handle all your... baggage."

"Baggage?" I echoed, my heart pounding, but it was Liam who responded first, his voice steady and low. "Jess is handling her life just fine, thanks."

The tension escalated, filling the small space between us, thick and almost tangible. I could feel the warmth radiating from Liam, a protective barrier that both comforted and startled me. He was a force, unwavering against the waves of doubt and uncertainty that had threatened to pull me under. But Gwen didn't back down.

"Just looking out for you, Jess. You know how quickly things can change. You'd be surprised what people will do when they think they're safe," she said, her tone more serious now, a glint of something dark flashing in her eyes.

"Everything's fine," I insisted, my voice stronger this time, though uncertainty clawed at the edges of my resolve. "Right, Liam?"

"Right," he confirmed, though I sensed a subtle hesitation lingering beneath his words. His eyes darted toward the entrance, and I could almost hear the gears turning in his mind, calculating the potential threat lurking outside.

Gwen studied him, and the air crackled with unspoken tension. "Just be careful, both of you. There are eyes everywhere," she warned, her expression a mix of concern and something else—perhaps jealousy?

With that cryptic farewell, she turned and left, the bell jingling softly as the door closed behind her.

Liam and I sat in silence, the weight of her words hanging between us like a dark cloud ready to unleash a torrent. "What do you think she meant by that?" I asked, my voice barely above a whisper.

"I think she's projecting her own fears," he replied, though his expression was clouded with thought. "But she's right about one thing—there are eyes everywhere, and we need to stay vigilant."

The café's warmth felt distant now, the comfort it had provided suddenly eclipsed by the reality of our situation. I could see the gears of his mind turning, his protective instincts on high alert, and the thought both comforted and unsettled me.

"I don't want to feel afraid, Liam," I admitted, my voice trembling slightly. "I want to focus on us, on what we have."

"I do too," he said, reaching across the small space between us, his hand enveloping mine, grounding me in the moment. "But we can't ignore the danger. We need to be smart about this."

Our fingers intertwined, the warmth of his skin against mine sparking a flicker of hope amidst the uncertainty. I leaned closer, allowing the familiarity of his presence to wash over me. "Then let's be smart together," I murmured, my heart racing. "Let's figure this out."

A faint smile broke across his face, one that softened the edges of worry etched there. "Together," he echoed, and in that single word, I found a renewed strength.

As the rain pattered against the glass, I realized that amidst the threats and shadows, we were forging a bond that felt indestructible, an alliance against the chaos that sought to pull us apart. The mystery that enveloped us was daunting, but within it lay the potential for something beautiful—something worth fighting for.

The rain continued to drench the streets outside, each drop creating small rivers that twisted and turned on the pavement like a chaotic maze. The sound was both soothing and unsettling, a relentless reminder that the world beyond our sanctuary was in turmoil. I leaned against the worn armchair, trying to shake off the weight of Gwen's ominous words. With every passing moment, the tension between us felt like a tightly coiled spring, ready to snap at the slightest disturbance.

"Should we go after her?" Liam asked, his brow furrowing slightly as he considered the door through which Gwen had just exited. "She seemed... concerned."

"Or nosy," I shot back, the words escaping my lips before I could filter them. "Gwen always did have a flair for the dramatic."

He chuckled, but his laughter was tinged with unease. "Maybe we need a little drama right now, considering our situation."

I shook my head, my fingers tightening around his. "What we need is to stay focused. She's not the enemy, but she's definitely not helping."

His eyes softened as he regarded me, and I could feel the flicker of reassurance in the depths of his gaze. "Let's not let her ruin this," he said, his thumb brushing over my knuckles in a tender gesture that ignited a warmth within me. "We're in this together, remember?"

The world outside had taken on an almost surreal quality, the raindrops creating a mesmerizing dance against the glass. I took a deep breath, willing myself to embrace the moment, to shut out the shadows that seemed intent on intruding. "You're right," I replied, forcing a smile. "Let's focus on what's in front of us."

With that, I shifted the conversation back to lighter topics, sharing stories from my time at the agency that had sparked our initial connection. Laughter bubbled between us like champagne, effervescent and alive. But beneath the laughter, I couldn't shake the feeling that we were mere moments away from a confrontation with whatever threat lurked in the dark corners of our lives.

As we exchanged playful jabs about our mutual misadventures, my phone buzzed on the table, shattering the atmosphere we had created. I reached for it, a sense of dread creeping into my stomach as I glanced at the screen. It was a text message from an unknown number.

"Not everything is as it seems. I'm watching."

A chill raced down my spine, and I could feel the blood drain from my face. "Liam," I whispered, my voice barely audible as I handed him my phone, my heart racing.

His expression changed instantly, the warmth in his eyes replaced by a steely focus. "Who is it?"

"I have no idea," I replied, panic rising in my throat like bile. "But it sounds threatening."

"Didn't Gwen just mention that there are eyes everywhere?" he asked, his tone grave as he studied the message. "This isn't a coincidence."

"What do we do?" I felt helpless, the walls of our little haven suddenly closing in on me.

"We have to stay smart and keep our heads down," he said, glancing toward the entrance as if expecting an uninvited guest to walk through the door. "But we can't hide forever."

I nodded, my mind racing with possibilities, each darker than the last. "Maybe we should report this to the police?"

Liam hesitated, his fingers still gripping my phone. "And tell them what? That we're being stalked by someone who sends cryptic texts? It would sound ridiculous."

My heart sank at his words. "So what then? We just wait for them to make their move?"

"No." His jaw tightened, and I saw the determination flicker in his eyes once again. "We need to take control. We can't let fear paralyze us."

I felt a rush of adrenaline surge through me, a fierce desire to fight back. "What if we set a trap? Make them reveal themselves?"

"Now that's a plan I can get behind," he said, his voice low but filled with energy. "We need to draw them out—get them to come to us."

The notion sent a thrill down my spine, igniting a spark of rebellion in my chest. "But how? We can't just sit here and wait."

"Let's use what we know," Liam suggested, his eyes lighting up with possibility. "There are a few spots where we've found those messages. If we return to one of those places, we might lure them in. We can lay a little bait."

I took a moment to process his idea, the gears of my mind whirring. "You mean like... make it look like we're vulnerable?"

"Exactly," he said, the tension between us shifting from fear to anticipation. "We'll make it seem like we're back in our usual haunts, relaxed and unsuspecting. That might just coax them out of hiding."

The prospect of confronting the unknown sent a shiver of exhilaration through me. "Alright," I said, my heart racing. "But we have to be careful. This could backfire spectacularly."

"I wouldn't want it any other way," he replied, his grin infectious. "But we're in this together, remember?"

Together, we concocted a plan, each idea flowing into the next as the thrill of defiance pulsed between us. We decided to return to the park where we had found the first note, the place that felt like the beginning of our troubles. It was both terrifying and exhilarating, the prospect of stepping into the jaws of uncertainty hand in hand.

As the rain eased outside, we gathered our things, adrenaline buzzing in our veins. The warm light of the bookstore flickered behind us as we stepped into the cool evening air, the streets glistening with the remnants of the storm.

I took a deep breath, the smell of wet asphalt mingling with the sharp scent of pine from the nearby trees. "Are you ready for this?" I asked, casting a sideways glance at Liam.

He smiled, a mix of mischief and determination that sent my heart racing. "More than ever."

As we made our way through the park, the shadows deepened, the night wrapping around us like a cloak. We positioned ourselves strategically on a bench, trying to appear nonchalant, our hearts pounding in unison.

"Just act natural," Liam whispered, glancing around the dimly lit area. "We're just two people enjoying a quiet evening."

"Right," I said, though my voice trembled with anticipation. "Nothing suspicious here."

We exchanged knowing glances, the thrill of the unknown igniting our spirits as we settled into our roles. But as the minutes passed, an unsettling stillness settled over the park, the silence amplifying the thumping of our hearts.

And then, just as I began to question our plan, a figure emerged from the shadows at the far end of the path, the dim light catching the glint of something metallic in their hand.

My breath caught in my throat as the figure moved closer, a sense of dread coiling in my stomach. I could feel Liam's tension next to me, the energy between us shifting into something sharp and electric.

"Jess," he murmured, his voice barely above a whisper, "stay close."

The figure stepped into the light, and my heart plummeted as recognition hit me like a freight train, the familiar face sending shockwaves of disbelief coursing through my veins.

It was someone I thought I had left behind—someone I had never expected to see again.

Chapter 12: The Heart's Resistance

The scent of freshly baked bread wafted through the air, mingling with the faint tang of anticipation that lingered in the town hall. It was an unusual blend, like an odd cocktail that somehow felt just right for Ashwood on this particular evening. As the sun dipped below the horizon, casting a warm glow through the stained glass windows, I could hear the chatter of the townsfolk, their voices rising and falling like the tide. Each sound added to the palpable tension, creating a symphony of nerves that thrummed beneath my skin.

I leaned against the wooden podium, my heart racing in time with the murmurs of the crowd. I could see familiar faces scattered throughout the hall: Mrs. Henderson, with her ever-watchful gaze, knitting needles poised as if to stab any dissenting opinion; Mr. Cole, whose eyebrows knitted in a perpetual frown, his gnarled hands clutching the edge of his seat as if it were a lifeline; and of course, Liam, his dark hair tousled, standing at the back with his arms crossed, a shield against whatever storm was brewing.

In that moment, the world narrowed until it was just Liam and me, our eyes locked in a silent conversation. I could feel the warmth of his concern wrapping around me like a safety blanket, even from across the room. His brows knitted in that way that made my stomach flutter, a combination of protectiveness and frustration. He was the knight in my increasingly chaotic fairytale, and I couldn't help but smile at the thought, even as the reality of the evening's stakes settled over me like a thick fog.

"Are you ready?" came a voice from my right, breaking the spell. It was Clara, her face flushed with excitement and fear. Her golden curls bounced as she shifted from foot to foot, the light dancing off her energetic aura. "You've got this. Just remember, the truth will set us free, right?" She winked, but I could see the worry lurking behind her bravado.

"Right," I replied, my voice steadier than I felt. "Just like a warm cup of cocoa on a chilly night." I chuckled, but it felt hollow. The truth had a way of stirring the pot in Ashwood, and I was about to ladle out a hefty portion.

As the clock struck seven, Mayor Thompson stepped up to the podium, his presence commanding instant attention. With his broad shoulders and booming voice, he exuded an air of authority that made even the most seasoned residents sit up a little straighter. He welcomed everyone, his speech a well-rehearsed melody that brushed over the surface of the gathering, but I could see the undercurrents of anxiety flickering in his eyes.

After a few minutes of pleasantries, he turned the stage over to me. "Now, we have a special presentation from our very own Miss Delaney." His tone was laced with a hint of skepticism, but I brushed it aside. I climbed the steps to the podium, my pulse pounding in my ears as I took a deep breath, focusing on the paper in my hands.

I scanned the room, taking in the faces of my neighbors, my friends, even my enemies. "Thank you all for being here tonight," I began, my voice trembling slightly before finding its rhythm. "We've gathered to discuss the strange occurrences in Ashwood, the things we can't quite explain but know are there, lurking just beneath the surface."

Liam's gaze bore into me, a reminder of the late-night conversations we'd shared, piecing together the fragments of mysteries that had unfolded over the past few months. Each revelation had brought us closer, yet the threat of the unknown still loomed like a storm cloud over our heads.

As I delved into our findings—whispers of long-buried secrets, unexplainable events, and the chilling connection to the old mill—an audible murmur swept through the crowd. Eyes widened in disbelief, and I could feel the atmosphere shift, thickening with tension. Some leaned forward, eager for more, while others recoiled as if my words were a tangible threat.

"Why are we digging up old ghosts?" a voice called from the back, slicing through the tension. It was Mr. Cole, the town's unofficial historian, his tone dripping with skepticism. "What do you expect to find that hasn't already been buried?"

My stomach twisted, but I held my ground. "We expect to find the truth," I shot back, my voice stronger than I felt. "The truth about the land we call home. If we don't confront the shadows, they'll consume us whole."

The murmurs intensified, a tide of conflicting opinions crashing against each other. Liam's expression shifted, concern flickering across his features as he stepped forward, eyes blazing. "Delaney is right. We can't ignore what's happening. The past is rising, and it demands to be heard."

In that moment, the air crackled with electricity. My heart raced as I locked eyes with him, a rush of gratitude mixing with the apprehension swirling in my gut. With his support, I felt emboldened. "We've all felt the tremors beneath our feet, the whispers in the wind. If we stay silent, we risk losing everything we hold dear."

As the room simmered with unease, the unexpected twist of an old rivalry bubbled to the surface. Clara, emboldened by my words, raised her hand. "I've seen things too—things that can't be explained by logic or reason. My grandmother spoke of the old ways, of protections and warnings. We can't just brush those aside."

The crowd hushed, the weight of her words settling in the air. The balance shifted; curiosity mixed with apprehension, leaving an opening for something profound to emerge. In that shared silence, we all felt it—a collective heartbeat, a unifying thread weaving through our disparate lives, pulling us closer to the edge of revelation.

As I continued to speak, passion igniting each word, I knew that whatever came next—whatever shadows we unearthed—Liam and I would face it together. Together, we could confront the past and navigate the uncertain path ahead, our destinies intertwined in a dance of resistance and hope.

The murmurs in the town hall swelled, undulating like the waves of a restless sea, crashing against the rocky shores of old grudges and buried secrets. I forged ahead, pouring every ounce of conviction into my words. "We owe it to ourselves to dig deeper. Ashwood has always been more than just a dot on the map; it's a tapestry woven with stories—some glorious, some haunting." The flickering lights above caught the glint of curiosity in the crowd, and for a brief moment, hope danced in the air like a firefly.

Clara leaned in closer, her excitement palpable. "You tell them, Delaney! If we don't act now, we'll just be adding another chapter to the book of regrets!" She raised her fist in mock rebellion, drawing chuckles from the audience, which momentarily lightened the mood.

But the laughter was cut short when Mrs. Henderson cleared her throat, her voice sharp enough to slice through the lingering tension. "And what about the legends? The stories about the cursed mill? You want to awaken those spirits?" Her eyes darted around, as if expecting phantoms to materialize in the flickering shadows.

I took a steadying breath, my mind racing. The legends of Ashwood were a double-edged sword, and I could feel their weight hanging in the air, heavy and foreboding. "Maybe the spirits aren't what we should be afraid of," I countered, a tinge of defiance coloring my tone. "Maybe it's the silence that allows them to thrive."

At that moment, the hall seemed to exhale. It was a collective release, as if everyone had been holding their breath, caught in the web of history that ensnared them. I glanced at Liam, who stood resolute, his jaw clenched and eyes fixed on me with a mixture of admiration and concern. I couldn't tell if he was ready to dive into the depths with me or if he wanted to pull me back to the surface, away from the murky waters.

I pressed on, the cadence of my voice growing stronger. "The strange occurrences, the accidents that have plagued our town—they're not mere coincidences. They are a call to action. To understand what's been hidden, we must confront it head-on." The fervor in my heart ignited a fire in my belly, propelling me forward.

From the back, a new voice rang out—James, a local who had always prided himself on his skepticism. "And what if you're wrong? What if this investigation leads us to something we're better off without? It's like poking a sleeping bear." His words hung in the air, thick with doubt.

I offered him a wry smile, fully aware of the risks involved. "And what if the bear is just hungry for the truth? Sometimes, it takes a little prodding to wake up the beasts." The room erupted into laughter, and I felt a flicker of triumph.

Yet beneath the surface of humor, I sensed a disquieting tension, a looming shadow that threatened to cast a pall over our momentum. I could feel Liam's gaze, hot and steady, urging me to continue even as his worry tugged at my heartstrings.

Suddenly, the doors swung open with a creak that echoed like a gunshot, drawing everyone's attention. A figure stepped inside—Maggie, the town's unofficial oracle, known for her cryptic insights and startlingly accurate predictions. Dressed in flowing layers of earth-toned fabrics, she seemed to glide across the room, her presence commanding silence.

"Miss Delaney," she called, her voice smooth yet tinged with urgency. "You tread on sacred ground. The truth you seek may not only bring enlightenment but also peril." Her words were like a soft breeze that stirred the embers of anxiety already glowing in the hearts of the townsfolk.

I squared my shoulders, determined not to back down. "I understand the risks, Maggie. But what's a little peril when faced with the possibility of understanding ourselves better?"

A flicker of surprise crossed her features, quickly masked by a knowing smile. "Ah, youth and its fearless heart. Just be careful where you step, my dear. Not all paths are meant to be walked."

Her cryptic warning hung in the air, mingling with the scent of the baked goods cooling on a nearby table, where Mrs. Gibbons had set up a display of cookies and pastries. My stomach grumbled in protest, an awkward reminder that hunger still lingered even amidst the gathering storm.

"Are we really going to listen to the town's resident fortune-teller?" Mr. Cole scoffed, crossing his arms. "What does she know about facts and figures?"

Before I could respond, Clara interjected, "What's wrong with a little intuition? If we're diving into the unknown, wouldn't it help to have a compass—something to guide us?"

The crowd shifted again, uncertainty weaving through the fabric of their conviction. I could see the gears turning in their minds, some contemplating Maggie's words, others reluctant to embrace the unexplainable. I felt the tide of the room shifting, the battle of wills teetering on a precarious edge.

I raised my voice, filled with the intensity of our shared purpose. "We've spent too long fearing the whispers of the past. Let's turn those whispers into a chorus of voices demanding to be heard!"

Cheers erupted, echoing off the walls like thunder, but I caught a glimpse of Liam's expression—a mix of admiration and concern. I knew he was worried that we were poking that metaphorical bear, and I couldn't blame him. But beneath that worry, I sensed something else: a flicker of belief that maybe, just maybe, I was onto something.

As the evening unfolded, the discussions morphed from skepticism to intrigue, the townspeople sharing their own stories of the mill, of shadows dancing in the moonlight, and strange noises that had kept them awake at night. The more we spoke, the more the weight of silence lifted, revealing the shared fabric of our fears and hopes.

By the time I finished my presentation, the atmosphere had shifted entirely. It was no longer a town divided; it felt like we were standing on the brink of discovery, bound together by the desire to uncover what had been hidden for too long. But deep down, I knew the journey ahead wouldn't be easy.

I caught Liam's eye again, and this time his smile was more than just supportive; it was a silent promise that we would navigate the tumultuous waters together. As we left the hall that night, the air crackled with possibility, and beneath it all, I sensed the heartbeat of Ashwood, pulsing with the energy of a town ready to confront its past.

The evening air outside was thick with the scent of damp earth, the kind of rich aroma that clung to your skin and whispered secrets of rain-soaked pasts. As we stepped into the chill, the glow of the town hall receded behind us, but the energy inside lingered like a shiver, leaving a trail of anticipation. I took a deep breath, relishing the coolness as it filled my lungs, refreshing and sharp. It was a welcome contrast to the heated debates that had unfurled within those walls.

"Not bad for a first time in the spotlight," Clara remarked, nudging me playfully as we walked. Her bright smile reflected the flickering streetlights that lined the path, illuminating the corners of her freckled cheeks. "I think you might have convinced a few skeptics tonight. Even Mr. Cole looked like he was about to crack a smile."

"Cracking a smile is one thing; actually believing what I said is another." I laughed, shaking my head. "But I'll take it. Tonight was just the beginning."

"Speaking of beginnings," Liam interjected, his voice low and serious, "there's still a lot we don't know about the mill and what's been happening in town. We might have stirred the pot, but we also have to be prepared for what bubbles up to the surface." His dark eyes were intense, glinting with an earnestness that both comforted and unsettled me.

"Yeah, and I'm sure there's more than one bear sleeping out there," I replied, trying to lighten the mood, but the truth hung heavily between us. The events surrounding the old mill had cast a long shadow, and I could sense the weight of uncertainty pressing down on both of us.

Just then, Clara pointed down the street. "Look, there's the old café! We should celebrate tonight's little victory. I could use some hot chocolate and maybe one of Mrs. Dwyer's famous pastries."

Her enthusiasm was infectious, and despite the gnawing anxiety about our next steps, I found myself smiling. "You always know how to motivate a girl," I said, turning toward the inviting glow of the café, its windows fogged with warmth.

As we approached, the chatter and laughter from within wrapped around us like a familiar embrace. The cozy atmosphere was a welcome respite from the intensity of the evening. We stepped inside, the bell above the door jingling softly as we entered, announcing our arrival. The café was bustling, with a mix of familiar faces gathered around tables, sharing stories over steaming mugs and plates piled high with confections.

We made our way to the counter, where Mrs. Dwyer, her hair pulled back in a messy bun, greeted us with her trademark smile. "Well, if it isn't my favorite trio! What can I get for you?" Her hands danced nimbly over the register, and the scent of cinnamon and chocolate filled the air.

"I'll have the hot chocolate with a mountain of whipped cream, and one of those gooey brownies, please!" Clara chirped, her eyes sparkling at the display of treats.

"Make it two of those brownies," I added, feeling a twinge of indulgence surge through me. The tension of the evening needed to be offset with something sweet, and nothing in Ashwood could compete with Mrs. Dwyer's desserts.

"Coming right up!" she called, bustling back to prepare our orders. As we waited, I leaned against the counter, watching the warmth of camaraderie envelop the café. Laughter rang out like music, a stark contrast to the anxiety still echoing in my mind.

Liam stood beside me, looking thoughtful. "You really think we're ready for whatever's coming? I mean, after tonight, things might not just settle back down."

I turned to face him, my resolve hardening. "We have to be. Ignoring the problem won't make it go away, Liam. We're in this together, remember? We've already stirred the pot. Now, we need to see what simmers to the top."

Just then, Clara appeared with our drinks, her eyes wide with excitement. "The mayor's son is here! I just saw him over there with a few of his friends." She gestured toward a table in the corner, and I instinctively turned to look. Sure enough, there was Mark Thompson, laughing with a group of friends, a carefree smile plastered across his face.

"Didn't you guys date in high school?" Clara asked, her tone mischievous.

"Hardly," I replied, rolling my eyes. "We went out once, and it was... awkward, to say the least. It didn't help that he spent most of our date talking about his family's political legacy."

"Sounds thrilling," Liam said, his tone dry as he sipped his hot chocolate.

"Right? Just what a girl dreams of. Anyway, let's focus on more important things than my high school crush." I took a sip of my drink, feeling the warmth spread through me.

But the moment was shattered as the door swung open again, a gust of wind swirling through the café. A man stumbled in, his clothes ragged and eyes wild with a frenzied urgency. "Help! You have to help me!" he gasped, collapsing against the doorframe, breathless and pale.

The laughter died instantly, replaced by a hushed stillness. All eyes turned to him as he struggled to catch his breath, his voice trembling. "There's something out there... in the woods by the mill. You have to believe me! It's not just a story... it's real!"

The atmosphere shifted, a palpable fear snaking through the room. I exchanged glances with Liam and Clara, the weight of uncertainty settling in once more. This was the kind of moment we had feared, the unraveling of a mystery now becoming all too real.

"Please!" the man pleaded, desperation etched across his features. "You have to warn everyone. It's coming back, and we're not safe!"

My heart raced as the room erupted into chaos, the chatter of disbelief mingling with fear. I felt Liam's grip tighten on my arm, his eyes reflecting a blend of concern and determination.

"What do we do?" I asked, my voice barely above a whisper, fear creeping in as shadows loomed larger.

"Stay close," he replied, and as he stepped forward, the weight of our journey felt heavier than ever. We had stirred the pot, but now we had to face whatever was boiling beneath the surface, and I couldn't shake the feeling that we were standing on the edge of something monumental.

In that moment, the café felt both small and vast, a cocoon where the outside world could seep in like poison. Whatever was coming would not just change Ashwood; it would change us all. As the man's warning echoed in my mind, I realized we had only just begun to peel back the layers of a mystery that threatened to consume everything we held dear. And with that realization, I felt the ground shift beneath us, the darkness encroaching, ready to swallow us whole.

Chapter 13: The Gathering Storm

The sun hung low in the sky, casting an orange glow that kissed the edges of the clouds, each one a soft brushstroke against the vast canvas of evening. I followed Liam, my heart thumping in rhythm with the shifting shadows. The streets of Ashwood seemed to echo our apprehension, every corner we turned revealing a furtive glance or a hushed whisper that trailed us like a specter. It felt as though the town itself held its breath, waiting for the inevitable storm that had settled like a weight upon our shoulders.

As we approached the weathered door of his studio, a familiar sense of calm washed over me. The threshold was a barrier against the outside world, the cacophony of anxious murmurs fading into the background. Liam turned the knob, the creak of the hinges a welcoming sigh amidst the tension. Inside, the air was thick with the rich scents of oil paint and turpentine, mingling like old friends lost in deep conversation. I breathed it in, allowing the familiarity to soothe my frayed nerves.

Liam was already moving about the studio, his movements fluid as he set aside brushes and leaned toward a large canvas that dominated the room. The light caught the edges of the artwork, revealing a striking depiction of stormy seas, tumultuous waves crashing against jagged rocks. In the center, a lone figure stood, their face obscured but their stance unwavering, as if bracing against the wrath of the elements. It felt strangely personal, a reflection of our own battles with uncertainty and fear.

"This one's different," he murmured, his voice low, barely above the whisper of the wind outside. "I wanted to capture the chaos—the feeling of being on the edge of something monumental."

I stepped closer, entranced by the turmoil rendered in hues of blue and gray. "You've succeeded," I said, my fingers itching to reach out and touch the paint, to feel the texture of his emotions woven into every brushstroke. "It's breathtaking and terrifying all at once."

"Much like life," he replied, a hint of a smile playing at the corners of his mouth. "You know, it's funny how we try to pretend everything is fine, yet inside, we're often just a tempest waiting to break free."

I nodded, the weight of his words settling over me like a shroud. "It feels like the storm is coming, doesn't it?"

"Definitely," he said, his gaze steady on mine. "But maybe we can ride it out together."

With that, the tension that had coiled tightly in my chest began to unfurl, slowly replaced by a flicker of hope. The intimacy of the studio wrapped around us like a warm embrace, shielding us from the chill creeping in from outside. I gestured toward the canvas, and he stepped aside, allowing me to take it all in.

"Do you ever worry that your art exposes too much?" I asked, glancing at him from the corner of my eye. "Like, what if people see the real you through your work?"

His laugh was rich and unguarded, breaking the somber atmosphere with an unexpected levity. "Oh, I hope they do. I want them to feel something, to connect with whatever I'm trying to say. If my art reveals my soul, then I've done my job."

A thrill surged through me. "Then we're both in the same boat," I replied, a mischievous grin dancing on my lips. "I can't remember the last time I felt fully seen. It's like I'm a ghost wandering through life, haunting everyone but myself."

"Then let's make you a masterpiece," he challenged, his eyes sparkling with playful determination. "You could be my muse."

"Me? Hardly," I protested, laughing at the absurdity of the idea. "I'm not exactly the stuff of great art. My life is more like a chaotic sketch than a polished painting."

"Exactly!" he exclaimed, his enthusiasm infectious. "That's the beauty of it. Chaos can be mesmerizing. Look at that canvas. It's not perfect, but it captures a feeling—a moment of truth."

I pondered his words, feeling a shift within me. Maybe chaos was where I thrived, too. The unpredictability of emotions, the tangled web of relationships, the fight against the lurking dread—perhaps they were the colors that could paint my life anew.

Suddenly, the wind howled outside, rattling the windows, and I jumped, my heart racing. The chill that swept through the studio felt different now, charged with an energy that promised change. "Do you think it's just a storm?" I asked, more to steady my own nerves than anything else.

Liam stepped to the window, peering out as the first drops of rain began to tap against the glass like an impatient visitor. "I think it's a lot more than that," he said, turning back to me, the weight of his gaze igniting something deep within. "It's the beginning of something—something we can't ignore."

In that moment, the air thickened between us, charged with an electric possibility that sent a shiver racing down my spine. The storm outside might have been brewing, but the one inside our hearts was roaring to life, daring us to confront the truths we had hidden away for far too long. As I stood there, breathless and alive, I knew this was just the beginning—a threshold not just to a storm, but to everything we had yet to discover.

The rain fell in sheets, transforming the familiar landscape of Ashwood into a watercolor masterpiece, each droplet blurring the lines of reality. Inside the studio, the storm created a rhythm that pulsed against the windows, a backdrop to the moment that felt suspended in time. The scent of wet earth mingled with the rich, pungent aroma of paint, and I closed my eyes for a heartbeat, allowing the sounds and smells to envelop me.

Liam leaned against the wall, his arms crossed, watching me with an intensity that made my pulse quicken. "What do you see?" he asked, breaking the silence that had settled like dust between us.

I opened my eyes, focusing on the chaos of the canvas. "I see a battle," I said, my voice steady. "A fight against the elements, against ourselves. It's as if you're daring the storm to come."

His lips curved into a smile, a hint of pride shining in his eyes. "That's exactly it. It's a dance, you know? A beautiful, chaotic dance."

"Not all dances are beautiful," I quipped, trying to lighten the mood. "Some are more like flailing around while trying not to trip over your own feet."

"True," he chuckled, the sound warm and genuine. "But sometimes the flailing is the best part. It's raw and real."

Our banter flowed effortlessly, a testament to the bond we'd built amid the chaos. As we stood together, the outside world faded into a mere whisper of wind and rain, and in that cocoon of intimacy, I felt a strange liberation. I stepped back, needing space to breathe, to think, but my gaze remained fixed on the tempest he'd conjured.

"What if we're not just battling a storm?" I pondered aloud. "What if it's something deeper? What if it's all of us—everyone in this town?"

His brow furrowed as he considered my words, the flicker of a candle illuminating the depth of his thoughts. "You think it's more than just a physical storm?"

"Maybe it's the culmination of everything we've ignored," I replied, feeling the weight of my own convictions. "The secrets, the unspoken truths, all bubbling beneath the surface, ready to spill over."

The silence that followed was thick with contemplation. Liam's expression shifted, the lightness from earlier fading as he absorbed the gravity of what I'd suggested. "Then it's not just us who need to confront this chaos. It's the entire town."

I could sense the tension building, the unease of the night creeping back in like an unwelcome guest. "What if no one is ready for that? What if they prefer the quiet?"

"Quiet has never solved anything," he said, determination etching lines on his face. "And sometimes storms are necessary to clear the air."

The air between us crackled, a blend of fear and resolve. We were teetering on the edge of something monumental, and as the storm outside raged on, I realized the tempest within us was just as fierce.

"I can't just stand by and let it happen," I said, the words tumbling out before I could censor them. "I need to be part of the change. But how do we even start?"

Liam stepped closer, a spark of energy igniting in his eyes. "We start by gathering the people who care. We create a dialogue—a way to confront what we've all been dodging. Together."

"Together," I repeated, feeling the power of the word wash over me. "But we can't do it alone. We need allies."

He nodded, a newfound enthusiasm lighting up his features. "Then let's rally the troops. I know a few who will stand with us."

My heart swelled at the thought, hope intertwining with the adrenaline coursing through my veins. "Who do you have in mind?"

He paced the room, considering. "First, there's Clara. She's been itching for change. You know how she's always organizing community events?"

"Clara's definitely passionate," I agreed. "She'll be on board."

"And then there's Marco," he added, glancing at me with a hint of mischief. "He loves stirring the pot—always looking for a cause."

"Ah, the master of dramatics," I laughed, picturing Marco's flair for the theatrical. "He'll add just the right amount of chaos to our efforts."

"And we can't forget about your sister, Lucy," he said, his tone shifting slightly. "She's always been a voice of reason, and with her connections, we could really get things moving."

I hesitated, my excitement faltering for a moment. Lucy had always walked a different path, one that often veered far from mine. "Are you sure she'd be interested? She's busy with her own life."

"She might surprise you," Liam replied, his confidence unwavering. "You know how passionate she can be when something matters to her."

"True," I conceded, my mind racing. "But it's going to take more than just a few of us. If we want to spark real change, we need a crowd."

"Then we'll create a gathering," Liam declared, a grin spreading across his face. "An event that brings everyone together—like a storm cloud gathering before the rain."

"Maybe a town hall meeting?" I suggested, my mind churning with possibilities. "Something that invites everyone to share their thoughts and fears."

"Exactly! We'll set a date and promote it. Posters, flyers, social media. We'll make it impossible for anyone to ignore."

The thrill of planning surged through me, a buoyant energy that chased away the remnants of doubt. Together, we could not only weather the storm but perhaps even harness its fury to ignite change. I smiled, feeling a flicker of excitement.

"Okay, then. Let's do this," I said, determination infusing my voice.

He reached for my hand, and in that moment, as our fingers entwined, I felt a connection deeper than I could articulate—a promise of collaboration, of fighting for something greater than ourselves. The storm outside raged on, but together, we were ready to face whatever awaited us on the horizon.

The promise of impending change hung thick in the air, and as we began sketching out our plans, the warmth of the studio felt like a fortress against the storm. Liam's enthusiasm sparked an unexpected fire within me, igniting ideas that leaped like flames in a hearth. "We'll need a catchy name for the event," I said, pacing back and forth, the wooden floor creaking underfoot. "Something that captures the essence of what we're trying to do."

"'Rally for the Real'?" Liam suggested, his eyes glinting with mischief.

"Sounds like a support group for reality TV show addicts," I shot back, laughing. "How about 'Voices of Ashwood'?"

"Much better! It gives a sense of unity," he agreed, nodding approvingly. "And it's got a nice ring to it."

We fell into a rhythm, brainstorming ideas as the rain pattered against the window like an impatient audience. The world outside was a cacophony of sound—nature's drumroll preparing us for the unveiling of something significant. I could feel the anticipation bubbling inside me, an electric current sparking the ideas swirling in my mind.

"What do we want to accomplish?" I asked, pausing to catch his eye. "It's more than just a gathering, isn't it?"

"Definitely," he said, his voice low and serious. "We want to challenge the status quo. Encourage people to share their stories, to confront what they've been ignoring."

I nodded, feeling the gravity of our mission settle over us. "And we need to make it feel safe for them to do that. Maybe we could offer some refreshments? Comfort food always helps break the ice."

"Hot cocoa and cookies," he replied with a grin. "Who can resist that? But we might want to add something stronger—just in case the discussion gets too heated."

"Now you're talking my language," I said, raising an eyebrow playfully. "A little liquid courage could go a long way."

With every idea, our excitement grew. We filled the whiteboard with notes, drawings, and half-baked thoughts that felt like stepping stones toward a larger goal. We were building something beautiful from the chaos, shaping the storm into a force for good.

Just as I was about to propose an icebreaker game—something lighthearted to coax our neighbors out of their shells—Liam's phone buzzed on the table. He glanced at the screen, a shadow crossing his face.

"Everything okay?" I asked, concern rippling through me.

"It's Clara," he said, his brow furrowing. "She says she has news."

My heart raced, anticipation mixing with anxiety. Clara had a flair for the dramatic, but her instincts were usually spot-on. "Is it about the event?"

"Not exactly," he replied, his voice tense. "She said it's urgent and we need to meet her."

"Now?"

"Yeah, she's at the old coffee shop near the town square."

I felt a twinge of apprehension as the dark clouds rolled outside, reflecting the storm brewing in my chest. "What could be so urgent?"

"Only one way to find out," Liam said, standing and moving toward the door with an air of determination.

"Right. Lead the way," I said, but as I followed him outside, a chill ran down my spine that had nothing to do with the weather. The rain had intensified, drenching the streets and transforming them into a slick, treacherous expanse. The world felt both vibrant and ominous, each shadow holding secrets I wasn't yet ready to confront.

We hurried down the cobbled street, the glow from the streetlamps illuminating our path like guiding stars. Each step echoed in the silence of the evening, punctuated only by the distant rumble of thunder. As we reached the coffee shop, its windows fogged with steam, I felt an uneasy flutter in my stomach.

The shop was almost empty, with only a few patrons huddled at tables, their conversations drowned out by the patter of rain. Clara was seated in the corner, her figure a stark silhouette against the dim light. She looked up as we entered, her expression serious, her fingers tapping nervously against her cup.

"What's going on?" I asked, sliding into the seat across from her.

"I'm glad you're here," she said, her voice a hushed whisper. "I overheard something at the last town meeting, and it's not good."

"What did you hear?" Liam leaned forward, his brows knitted together.

"There's a proposal to develop the land near the old mill into a shopping center. They want to push it through without any community input."

My stomach dropped. The old mill was a piece of our town's heart, a relic of our history, and the thought of it being turned into a soulless shopping center sent a wave of nausea crashing over me. "Who's behind this?"

"Councilman Jakes," Clara said, her eyes wide with urgency. "He's been talking to developers, and they plan to present it next week. If we don't act fast, it could be a done deal."

"What about the Voices of Ashwood?" Liam asked, his voice steady. "This is exactly the kind of thing we need to rally against."

"Exactly," Clara agreed, her tone resolute. "But we need more than just a meeting. We need a movement."

The enormity of what we were facing settled heavily on my shoulders. A simple gathering of voices had turned into a full-blown battle for our town's soul. "We can't let this happen," I said, my resolve hardening. "What's the plan?"

As Clara outlined her thoughts, a rush of adrenaline coursed through me, and the storm outside echoed the turmoil brewing in my mind. It was time to take action, to push back against the tide of apathy that had swallowed Ashwood for too long.

But just as I felt that spark of determination flare to life, the door swung open, and a gust of wind howled into the shop, extinguishing the warmth and comfort we'd built. A figure stood silhouetted against the downpour, drenched and unsteady.

"Help!" they shouted, voice cracking against the roar of the storm. "You have to listen!"

My heart raced as I recognized the newcomer—a familiar face from our town, eyes wild with panic. Something in their expression sent a shiver down my spine, a feeling that this was only the beginning of the storm. As I glanced at Liam and Clara, I could see their expressions mirrored my concern, the tension thickening in the air as we braced for whatever revelation lay ahead.

"What is it?" I called out, but even as the words left my lips, I knew we were already too late. The storm had arrived, and with it, the promise of chaos.

Chapter 14: Into the Abyss

The hidden cellar beneath the old library was a realm untouched by time, where dust danced in the beams of our flashlight like lost souls yearning for release. I stepped cautiously over crumbling stones, each footfall echoing in the silence, the air heavy with the scent of mildew and secrets waiting to be unearthed. My heart pounded in my chest, a relentless drumbeat that seemed to resonate with the very walls of this long-forgotten space. Liam followed closely, his presence a mix of comfort and anxiety, the flicker of our light revealing glimpses of what lay ahead.

"Who knew our charming little town harbored such dark shadows?" I murmured, brushing a hand against the spine of an ancient book, its leather cover cracked and weary. The thought of the ghost stories that had haunted my childhood surfaced, and I couldn't help but chuckle nervously. "Guess the local folklore wasn't just for entertainment after all."

Liam raised an eyebrow, a smirk teasing the corners of his mouth. "Or maybe we're just living in a horror novel. You know, the kind where the protagonists make all the wrong choices." His voice held a teasing lilt, but I detected an undercurrent of seriousness that sent a shiver down my spine.

As we pressed deeper into the cellar, the oppressive weight of the air shifted, thickening with each passing moment. The shadows seemed to reach out, curling around us like tendrils eager to ensnare the unwary. I felt a pull, an unexplainable urge to uncover what lay hidden within the tattered journals scattered across a wooden table, their pages yellowed and frayed.

"Let's see what the past has to say about our lovely town," I suggested, my fingers trembling slightly as I lifted the nearest journal. The cover bore no title, just an intricate design that seemed to swirl and shift beneath my fingertips, almost alive. The first entry was scrawled in hurried, frantic handwriting, the ink barely dry.

"The spirit of Ashwood is restless. It awakens with each blood moon, feeding on the fear of those who dare to remember." I read aloud, the words tumbling from my lips like a curse. My voice echoed in the confined space, punctuated by the soft rustle of pages turning. I exchanged a wary glance with Liam, whose eyes had gone wide, a mixture of fascination and fear etched across his face.

"This isn't just folklore," he whispered, leaning closer. "This is history, the kind that sends chills down your spine."

I turned the pages, the soft sound reminiscent of whispers echoing through the dark. Each entry revealed layers of despair, tales of betrayal and vengeance intertwined with the town's fate. A sense of dread settled over me as I read of a woman wronged, her spirit bound to the very heart of Ashwood, her rage fueling a cycle of chaos that had persisted for generations.

"What do you think it means?" Liam asked, his voice low and tentative.

I hesitated, the weight of the journal pressing heavily against my chest. "It means we're in deeper than we thought. This isn't just a ghost story; it's a warning."

Just then, an icy gust of air swept through the cellar, carrying with it a whisper, barely discernible but unmistakably present. "Leave... while you still can..."

My breath hitched, the hair on the back of my neck standing on end. I turned to face Liam, who looked as startled as I felt. "Did you hear that?"

"Yeah," he replied, his voice barely above a whisper. "What was that?"

Before I could answer, the faintest flicker of movement caught my eye from the corner of the room. I trained my flashlight in that direction, and there it was—an old portrait hanging crookedly on the wall, its colors faded but unmistakably haunting. The woman in the painting had dark hair cascading around her shoulders, her eyes filled with a fury that seemed to penetrate through the canvas.

"Who is she?" I breathed, stepping closer, compelled by a force I couldn't name.

"Maybe the woman from the journal?" Liam suggested, taking a tentative step beside me. "You think she's the one haunting Ashwood?"

As I stared at her, I felt an inexplicable connection, an echo of my own unease resonating within me. "Maybe she's looking for something... or someone," I said slowly, the realization dawning on me that the town's secrets were not just buried but actively waiting for us to unearth them.

Just then, a cold breath wafted against my neck, a distinct chill that sent my heart racing. I turned sharply, eyes wide, expecting to find Liam beside me, but instead, he was frozen, staring at the portrait with a mix of awe and terror. "Did you feel that?" I asked, my voice quaking.

"Feel what?" he murmured, entranced.

"The... the cold. It was right here." I gestured at the empty space beside me, where an invisible presence seemed to linger.

He shook his head, but there was a flicker of uncertainty in his gaze. "You're not imagining it. There's something here."

Just then, the journal slipped from my fingers, falling to the ground with a dull thud, and I gasped as the air crackled with electricity, vibrating with an energy I couldn't comprehend. The shadows around us shifted, deepening, and suddenly, the portrait's eyes seemed to glow with an unearthly light.

"Get out!" a voice boomed, reverberating through the cellar, and the shadows coalesced, threatening to swallow us whole.

Before I could react, Liam grabbed my wrist, pulling me back as we raced toward the staircase. The weight of the past was heavy on our shoulders, but the present felt infinitely more threatening. We had ventured into the abyss, and now it was time to claw our way back to the surface before it was too late.

We bolted up the staircase, hearts pounding like war drums in our chests, the haunting echo of the disembodied voice still ringing in my ears. The air grew heavy with an unsettling mix of fear and adrenaline as we stumbled into the light filtering through the dust motes above. I barely registered the comforting familiarity of the library's wooden shelves, now looming like giants in the aftermath of our descent into darkness.

"Did we just lose our minds?" Liam panted, glancing over his shoulder as if expecting a ghostly figure to emerge from the shadows. The boyish grin that usually danced on his lips was replaced by a seriousness that made my stomach twist.

"Honestly? I'm beginning to think the stories were right," I admitted, my voice barely above a whisper. "What if the spirit is really connected to that woman in the portrait? We have to find out more."

"Or we could just pretend we never saw anything," he shot back, an eyebrow raised in a playful challenge, yet I could see the flicker of intrigue in his eyes. "You know, live our lives blissfully unaware. Sounds great, right?"

I laughed, though the sound was tinged with nervous energy. "And let the spirit continue wreaking havoc? I think not. We might not get another chance."

The library was eerily quiet, the silence amplifying the weight of our discovery. As we returned to the main area, the sunlight streamed through the tall windows, casting a warm glow on the scattered books and reading nooks. I was acutely aware of how normal everything looked, how easily one could forget the darkness lurking beneath.

I grabbed my bag from the nearby table, shoving the journal deep inside. "Let's regroup. We need to find out what happened to her and how it all ties into Ashwood."

Liam nodded, and his resolve seemed to strengthen. "Right. But first, I need coffee. Like, serious fuel for this deep dive into the town's creepy history."

"Good call," I agreed, feeling a wave of gratitude wash over me for his lightheartedness. "It's like caffeine will ward off the spirits. Or at least keep us awake while we dig through more ghostly accounts."

We made our way to the café across the street, the familiar aroma of freshly brewed coffee wrapping around us like a comforting blanket. The place was bustling, filled with townsfolk sipping lattes and engaging in animated conversations, blissfully unaware of the darkness brewing beneath their feet.

As we settled into a corner booth, I couldn't shake the feeling that we were sitting on the precipice of something monumental. "What do you think the journals said about her?" I asked, stirring sugar into my coffee absentmindedly.

Liam leaned back, tapping his fingers against the table. "The spirit? Maybe she's not angry but just... trapped? It could be that she's looking for something or someone, like you said."

"Or seeking revenge," I added, the thought unsettling me. "What if the wrongs done to her are still alive in the town? What if we're unwittingly part of this cycle?"

"Great, now I'm second-guessing our decision to delve into the cellar," he said, a half-smile playing on his lips. "We're probably going to be haunted for life. Maybe I should look into getting a sage smudge stick."

"Definitely! And we can sell it as a ghost-busting starter kit," I shot back, the humor easing the tension that had gripped my chest. "All the haunted townsfolk will flock to us."

His laughter echoed, a welcome sound that reminded me why I'd roped him into this investigation in the first place. We made a good team—an unlikely duo determined to uncover the truth, even if it meant facing our fears.

After our caffeine fix, we ventured to the local archives, a quaint room tucked away in the back of the library filled with aging files and the musty scent of paper that held stories of yesteryears. Dust motes floated lazily in the sunbeams that filtered through the small windows, illuminating our path.

I dove into the records, flipping through yellowing newspapers, hoping to find anything related to the woman in the portrait. "Here! Look at this," I exclaimed, pointing to a faded headline. "Mysterious Disappearances in Ashwood! It happened decades ago, all linked to that blood moon phenomenon mentioned in the journal."

Liam leaned in closer, his eyes narrowing as he read the small print. "It says here that multiple residents vanished without a trace. This feels connected."

I scanned the page, a chill settling deep in my bones. "And if the spirit is tied to those events, we could be walking right into the heart of her anger. We have to be careful."

He looked thoughtful, fingers drumming against the table as he pondered the implications. "Or we could be exactly what she needs to find peace."

The thought sent a shiver down my spine, and I took a moment to consider the weight of our task. What if we were indeed meant to break this cycle of vengeance? Yet, as I absorbed the information, a nagging question remained—could we do it without succumbing to the very darkness we sought to understand?

"Liam, what if we're not strong enough for this?" I confessed, my voice barely a whisper. "What if we end up just like those people?"

His gaze softened, and he reached across the table, placing his hand over mine. "We're not alone in this. We have each other. And whatever happens, we face it together. Besides, if it comes down to it, I'll take on the vengeful spirit with my bare hands."

I couldn't help but smile at his bravado, though anxiety still coiled in my gut. "You think your wrestling skills will come in handy against an angry ghost?"

"Hey, you never know," he retorted with a cheeky grin, the warmth of his presence a balm against the fears swirling within me.

We dove back into our research, the shadows of the past surrounding us as we sifted through records and clippings, piecing together the fragments of a town's haunted legacy. Each revelation felt like a step further into the abyss, pulling us deeper into the tangled web of Ashwood's history. And with each discovery, I realized that the truth we sought was not just about the spirit lurking in the shadows, but about uncovering the courage within ourselves to confront the darkness together.

We left the archives with a treasure trove of eerie tales and a sense of urgency that pulsed through my veins like a second heartbeat. Each tale we unearthed pulled me deeper into Ashwood's history, a twisted tapestry of despair and retribution. Outside, the sun hung low in the sky, casting long shadows across the cobblestones, transforming the town into a chiaroscuro masterpiece.

"I feel like we're living in a ghost story," Liam said, his hands stuffed in his pockets as we strolled down the quiet street. "One where we're the unwitting heroes who will probably get ourselves killed."

"Or worse, stuck in an endless loop of bad decisions," I replied, smirking at him. "You know, like in those horror movies where the characters ignore all the red flags."

"Great. Let's just make sure to avoid the creepy cabin in the woods, shall we?"

We shared a laugh, the tension easing slightly as we walked past familiar shops and homes that suddenly seemed more sinister under the weight of what we had discovered. I couldn't shake the feeling that every glance from the townsfolk held a secret, every smile hid a warning.

"Okay, we need to devise a plan," I said, pulling out the journal from my bag as we reached the park, a green oasis amidst the looming shadows. I spread it open on a nearby bench, eager to revisit the entries that had fueled our investigation. "If the spirit is tied to these disappearances, we need to figure out how to break that connection."

Liam leaned over, studying the pages with an intensity that made my heart flutter. "What if it's as simple as finding out who she was? Maybe her story hasn't been told, and that's why she's still angry."

"Maybe," I replied thoughtfully. "But this isn't just about her; it's about the town, too. We have to consider the implications of what we're digging up."

"True. Maybe we should visit the historical society," he suggested, tapping his fingers on the journal. "They might have more records or even descendants of the people involved. A little chat with the locals never hurt anyone... except maybe the locals."

I chuckled, appreciating his wit. "Alright, let's make that our next stop. But first, let's grab a snack. I think I've earned at least one cookie after confronting my potential demise."

As we wandered toward the nearby café, the streets seemed alive with the chatter of the evening crowd, people filtering in and out of stores, their laughter mixing with the rustling leaves above us. But as we stepped into the café, a sudden chill swept over me, a stark contrast to the warmth of the atmosphere.

"Julia, you okay?" Liam asked, his brow furrowed with concern.

"Yeah, just... felt a shiver," I said, trying to brush it off, but the feeling lingered, an unsettling omen clinging to my skin. "Let's just hurry."

Once we had our cookies—decadent chocolate chip that melted in my mouth—I suggested we sit outside, needing the fresh air to clear my mind. We settled at a small table, and I pulled the journal out again, riffling through the pages, the musty scent of old paper filling my senses.

"So, what are we really looking for?" Liam asked, leaning back, a half-eaten cookie in hand. "A key to set her spirit free? A magic incantation? Or are we just hoping for a really convincing apology?"

I laughed, taking a moment to savor my treat. "Wouldn't it be great if it were that simple? Just say, 'Hey, sorry about the whole vengeful spirit thing; let's have a chat!' and boom, all is forgiven."

"Right? Ghosts should really take lessons from therapy," he quipped, his eyes sparkling with mischief.

But as I flipped to the last entry in the journal, I felt a prickle of unease creep back in. It read: "To seek the truth is to awaken the past. Beware the blood moon, for it draws out the shadows."

"Liam, look at this," I said, pointing to the ominous warning. "This is dated just days before the last disappearance. We have to figure out when the next blood moon is."

"Great. More ominous celestial events to worry about," he muttered, glancing up at the sky as if it might offer answers. "Do you have any idea when that is?"

"Let's check the almanac," I suggested, already typing furiously on my phone. As the data loaded, my heart sank when I saw the date. "It's tomorrow night."

"Tomorrow?" he echoed, his expression shifting from playful to serious in an instant. "We need to act fast. This isn't just about uncovering history anymore; it's about stopping something that might happen."

"Right. We need to get to the historical society before they close," I said, urgency filling my voice. We quickly finished our snacks and left a tip on the table, the laughter and warmth of the café fading as we stepped back into the chilling reality of our situation.

The historical society was a modest building at the end of the street, a quaint brick structure that appeared benign, but I couldn't shake the feeling that it held secrets darker than I could fathom. As we entered, the musty smell of aged books enveloped us, and I felt a wave of nostalgia mingled with dread.

"Can I help you?" a woman asked from behind the counter, her voice warm but her gaze sharp.

"Yes, we're looking for information about the woman in the portrait from the old library," I began, my voice steady despite the nerves dancing in my stomach. "And anything about the disappearances linked to the blood moon."

The woman's demeanor shifted; a flicker of recognition crossed her face, followed by an unreadable expression. "You might want to check the back archives. We have records of local legends and histories that might not be available elsewhere. But I should warn you..."

I felt a knot tighten in my gut, the way her eyes darted toward the darkened hallway hinting at something unsaid. "What?"

"There are some stories that are better left undisturbed."

"Isn't that what we're here for?" Liam chimed in, his voice light but with a firmness that suggested he wouldn't be easily dissuaded.

The woman sighed, casting a glance over her shoulder as if expecting something—or someone—to appear. "Just... be cautious. The past doesn't always let go."

Her warning hung heavy in the air as we made our way down the dim hallway, lined with wooden shelves crammed with dusty tomes and scrolls. Shadows flickered at the edges of our flashlight beams, stretching ominously against the walls.

"This feels like a scene from a horror movie," I whispered, glancing around uneasily.

"Great. I knew we should have brought snacks for the ghosts," Liam quipped, trying to lighten the mood.

But the further we ventured, the more I felt the weight of unseen eyes upon us, a sensation that crawled under my skin. We searched through the archives, flipping through brittle pages and fading photographs until finally, we uncovered a large, ornate book titled Legends of Ashwood.

"This has to be it," I breathed, my fingers tracing the gilded letters. We carefully opened it, and the pages seemed to flutter as if they had a life of their own.

"What's the first entry say?" Liam asked, peering over my shoulder.

I scanned the page, my breath hitching as the words leapt out at me: "The blood moon brings with it the vengeful spirit of Eleanor Blackwood, her rage entwined with the bloodline of those who wronged her."

"What does that even mean?" Liam asked, frowning.

Before I could respond, the lights flickered ominously, plunging us into semi-darkness. My heart raced as a cold wind rushed past us, the air growing heavy and electric.

"Uh, did you feel that?" I said, my voice trembling slightly.

"Yeah, it's like someone just walked through us," he replied, his gaze darting around the room.

In that moment, the shadows coalesced into a shape at the far end of the hallway, something dark and looming, flickering just at the edge of the light. I could barely breathe, my heart pounding in sync with the dread curling in my stomach.

"Liam..." I whispered, gripping his arm as the shape seemed to flicker closer, its features obscured, but the energy was palpable, a heavy shroud of rage and sorrow.

And just as I opened my mouth to scream, the figure lunged forward, the air thick with an overwhelming chill, and everything around us went dark.

Chapter 15: The Illusion of Safety

The storm arrived with a fury that turned the familiar streets of Ashwood into a treacherous maze of fallen branches and shattered power lines. The wind howled like a wounded animal, rattling the windows of Liam's studio, where we had sought refuge. It felt oddly intimate, the two of us huddled together amidst the chaos, candlelight flickering in the dim room, casting dancing shadows that mimicked our racing thoughts. I had never felt so close to him, yet the storm raged outside, threatening to upend everything we had built.

Liam sat across from me, his tousled hair backlit by the soft glow of the candles. I watched as he absently ran a hand through his hair, a habit I had grown to adore. There was something captivating about the way he moved, every gesture infused with a certain magnetic energy that drew me in. He glanced up, catching my gaze, and the intensity in his blue eyes sent a shiver through me that had nothing to do with the chill in the air.

"Do you think it'll ever stop?" he asked, his voice low and laced with an uncharacteristic vulnerability. The question hung between us like the heavy scent of rain-soaked earth.

"Eventually," I replied, trying to sound more certain than I felt. "But storms like this... they leave a mark." My words felt heavier than I intended, a reminder of the chaos swirling outside and the chaos simmering within.

He nodded, his expression turning contemplative, as if the storm had unleashed more than just wind and rain. The night wore on, filled with the occasional crack of thunder and the haunting sound of the wind's fury. In those moments, the world outside felt like an entirely different realm, one that could swallow us whole if we let it.

"Remember that time we went camping by the lake?" he asked, a half-smile breaking through the tension. "I thought the tent was going to fly away, and you were convinced we were going to drown in the middle of the night."

I laughed, the sound bright and defiant against the storm's growl. "You were the one who insisted we could pitch it in the wind! I had every right to be concerned."

"And yet, we survived," he said, his smile widening. "You and your overactive imagination. Maybe you should write a book about our adventures. Title it 'Surviving Liam's Bad Ideas.'"

"Only if you're the cover model," I teased, but beneath the playful banter lay a deep yearning. The air between us crackled with unspoken words, each passing moment urging us to tread into deeper waters.

As the laughter faded, a heavy silence settled in, punctuated only by the rhythmic drumming of rain against the roof. I could feel my heart racing, the storm outside mirroring the tempest within. What was I waiting for? In this candlelit cocoon, surrounded by flickering shadows, the distance between us felt insurmountable and yet tantalizingly close.

"Liam," I said, the words spilling out before I could stop them. "What if... what if we're just putting on a brave face? What if everything we're trying to build is just an illusion?"

He met my gaze, the warmth in his eyes shifting to something more profound, something that sent a rush of adrenaline coursing through me. "What do you mean?"

"I mean, this... us. It feels so perfect, but maybe we're just two people hiding from the storm," I confessed, my voice trembling slightly. "What happens when the sun comes out again? Will we still be standing?"

For a heartbeat, the only sound was the relentless rain. He leaned forward, resting his elbows on his knees, eyes searching mine as if they held the answers to questions we both feared to ask. "What if the storm is what brings us together? What if we need the chaos to realize how much we mean to each other?"

His words settled in the space between us like a warm embrace, but the weight of uncertainty still hung overhead. I wanted to believe him, to let the flickering candlelight drown out the shadows of doubt. But the truth was, the storm outside wasn't the only thing threatening to pull us apart.

"I just... I can't shake the feeling that I'm not enough," I admitted, my voice barely above a whisper. "What if one day you wake up and realize you deserve someone better?" The confession tasted bitter, like old regrets surfacing at the worst possible moment.

Liam's brow furrowed, and he moved closer, the candlelight illuminating the sincerity etched into his features. "You are more than enough. You're everything I never knew I needed." He reached for my hand, the warmth of his palm igniting a spark that chased away the lingering chill.

"But what if—"

He squeezed my hand, silencing my doubts. "No 'what ifs,' just us. The storm might rage outside, but in here, it's just you and me."

In that moment, the storm felt like a distant echo. I focused on the heat of his skin against mine, the way his thumb traced circles on my palm, grounding me in the chaos. The intimacy of the moment wrapped around us like a cocoon, shielding us from the outside world.

We fell into a silence that was comforting, laced with the weight of our shared vulnerabilities. It was a fragile truce, a pause in the tumult that threatened to engulf us. Outside, the wind howled, a reminder of the world we would return to, but for now, we existed in this sanctuary of flickering shadows and whispered dreams.

As the candles burned low, illuminating the tender expressions on our faces, I felt the tentative beginnings of hope. Maybe, just maybe, we could weather this storm together, navigating the unpredictable tides of our hearts. The night was far from over, and with it, a fragile promise hung in the air: to face whatever awaited us—together.

The rain continued to pelt against the studio windows, each drop like a tiny drumbeat, echoing the rapid tempo of my heart. Candlelight flickered, casting wavy silhouettes on the walls, and the shadows danced to a rhythm that felt almost celebratory, despite the tempest outside. I couldn't shake the feeling that we were the last two people left on earth, lost in a world stripped of its noise and distractions. The intimate atmosphere wrapped around us like a warm blanket, urging me to lean closer, to surrender to the moment.

Liam leaned back in his chair, a teasing grin playing on his lips. "So, if I were to make a list of things I love about you, where would you like me to start? Your impeccable taste in disaster-prone camping trips or your knack for making mountains out of molehills?"

I rolled my eyes, unable to stifle my laughter. "I'd say the fact that you always take the scenic route when we're late is high on the list. And don't forget your impressive talent for misplacing your phone every single time we leave the house."

"Hey, that's just me being an eternal optimist. Who needs a phone when you have the world's greatest company?" His eyes sparkled with mischief, but as he spoke, the glimmer faded, and a more serious expression replaced it. "But really, I think it's your determination that amazes me most. You don't just go through life—you wrestle it to the ground and make it your own."

His compliment caught me off guard, warmth flooding my cheeks. It was easy to banter, but beneath the jest, his words held a depth that both thrilled and terrified me. "You're not too bad yourself, considering you once thought a s'more was an advanced culinary technique."

"I stand by that. Who knew roasting marshmallows could be so complicated?" he replied, laughing softly. But then he sobered, his gaze steady and intense. "But seriously, what's really bothering you?"

His question hung heavy in the air, and for a moment, the laughter faded. I could feel the walls I had carefully constructed begin to crack, allowing a flood of fears to seep through. The storm outside might have raged, but the storm inside me was even more daunting. "I guess I just wonder if we're fooling ourselves. You make it easy to get lost in the moment, but I'm scared it's just a moment. What if this is all there is?"

"Then let's make this moment worth it," he said, his voice unwavering. "We can face whatever comes next together. I'm not going anywhere."

His words wrapped around me like a lifeline, and I wanted to believe him. The truth, however, was like the storm outside—chaotic, unpredictable, and sometimes downright terrifying.

In that suspended moment, time seemed to stretch, and I felt a pull toward him, an undeniable magnetism that urged me to close the distance. I leaned forward, catching the scent of cedar and something distinctly him—warmth, security, an unspoken promise. "Liam, if we're going to do this, I need you to understand something." My voice wavered slightly, the gravity of my thoughts weighing heavily on my chest. "I've never really let anyone in. Not like this."

He tilted his head, his expression both earnest and patient. "Then let me in, one layer at a time. We'll peel back the walls together."

As if that simple promise had unlocked something deep within me, I felt my heart begin to race with excitement and fear. "Okay," I said softly. "But you should know, I'm not exactly a walk in the park."

"Then we'll need to bring a picnic basket," he shot back, his eyes dancing with humor, but I could see the resolve behind his playfulness. "Just promise you'll save me some cake, because I have a feeling it's going to be a bumpy ride."

"Cake?" I laughed, the tension easing as I realized how easily he could shift the atmosphere with just a few words. "Are you really trying to bribe me with dessert?"

"Desperate times call for desperate measures," he quipped, feigning seriousness. "Plus, if we're going to face the world, we might as well do it with cake. It's practically a superfood."

We shared a warm laugh, and for a moment, it felt like the storm outside was nothing more than a distant background noise. But as the laughter faded, an uneasy silence filled the room, the kind that crept in like a shadow just as the sun dips below the horizon.

"Liam," I began hesitantly, the weight of unasked questions pressing down on me. "What if... what if we're not strong enough? What if the storm does get in?"

His expression shifted, the playful facade giving way to something raw and unguarded. "Then we'll find a way to fortify our walls. Together. I don't want to rush anything, but I can't pretend I don't want to be with you. I want to know all your storms, and I want you to know mine."

I felt my heart flutter, caught between exhilaration and the dread of exposing myself completely. "You don't understand—my storms can be pretty intense."

"I can handle intense," he replied, his voice steady. "Just promise me that you'll let me in, no matter how crazy things get. Because believe me, I've been through my fair share of tempests."

Before I could respond, a bolt of lightning illuminated the room, casting us in stark relief against the darkness. The power flickered and then died, leaving us in a sudden darkness punctuated only by the flickering candles. My pulse quickened, the absence of light amplifying every sound—the creak of the studio, the howl of the wind, the soft rustle of my own breath.

"Looks like we're officially cut off from civilization," Liam said, his voice low and playful, breaking through the enveloping darkness. "Guess we'll have to rely on our charm and good looks to survive."

"Right, because that worked so well last time," I quipped, but beneath the banter, I felt an unmistakable tension building again. "What are we going to do if this storm doesn't let up?"

"Simple," he said, the seriousness returning to his tone. "We ride it out. Together. Just like we always do."

But as the wind howled outside, echoing the turmoil within me, I couldn't help but wonder if this storm might be different. If it might reveal something I wasn't ready to face.

The darkness thickened around us, making the candlelight flicker as if trying to assert its dominance over the encroaching shadows. Liam's eyes sparkled with a mix of determination and mischief, illuminating the contours of his face and drawing me closer to the warmth of his presence. "So, are we going to let a little tempest ruin our evening, or do we dig in and face it head-on?" His tone was playful, but I could see the underlying challenge, a spark that ignited something fierce within me.

"Given the circumstances, I'd say we're already knee-deep in chaos," I replied, my voice teasing yet laced with an edge of truth. "But I've always been one for a good adventure. Let's see how far this rabbit hole goes."

Liam grinned, and the atmosphere shifted, charged with an electric energy that filled the air. "Adventure it is then! Let's turn this storm into something memorable." He grabbed a few candles and arranged them on a low table, transforming our temporary refuge into a makeshift candlelit haven.

As he busied himself, I took in the studio—his sanctuary, filled with eclectic art pieces and books piled haphazardly on every surface. Each painting told a story, reflecting the vividness of his imagination. The chaos outside was a stark contrast to the cozy charm of this space. The storm felt like an invasion, a reminder that while we could create our little bubble of warmth, the world outside was still turbulent and unpredictable.

Liam returned, holding a deck of cards. "Let's play a game. Loser tells a secret." His eyes danced with mischief, and I couldn't resist the thrill of the challenge. "Oh, I'm good at secrets," I replied, a grin spreading across my face. "But you should know, I'm also very good at winning."

The game began, laughter punctuating the tense air as we played, the tension easing as we lost ourselves in the moment. Each hand dealt was a new opportunity, each round punctuated with playful banter that made me forget, if only for a moment, the storm swirling outside.

"Alright, my dear opponent, what's your secret?" Liam asked after I managed to win the first round, a triumphant smile lighting up his face.

I leaned back, considering my options. "Well, I once accidentally set off the fire alarm during a cooking class. They told me I had a gift for creating smoke signals."

Liam chuckled, his laughter rich and contagious. "I knew you were destined for greatness! But fire alarms? Really? I can only imagine the chaos."

"Hey, it wasn't my fault the instructor got distracted. Besides, I'm pretty sure they didn't want to hear my rendition of 'Oops! I Did It Again' while I was flambéing." My eyes sparkled with mischief, and the laughter felt like a balm, soothing the frayed edges of my anxiety.

The game continued, each round revealing layers of our personalities, peeling back the protective shells we'd built over the years. But as the laughter echoed, the wind howled outside, reminding me that the storm was relentless, waiting for the perfect moment to intrude.

Finally, it was my turn to ask for a secret. "Alright, Mr. Charmer, your turn. What's your secret?" I leaned forward, curiosity piqued.

Liam hesitated, the playful spark dimming slightly. "Well, if we're being honest…" He paused, a flicker of vulnerability crossing his face. "I've been running from my past, trying to create a new me out here in Ashwood. I didn't want to be defined by who I was back then."

The admission hung heavy in the air, a revelation that shifted the atmosphere from light-hearted banter to something deeper, more profound. "You don't have to hide from me," I said gently, my heart aching for him. "I've felt the weight of that same burden."

He met my gaze, the intensity of his expression making my breath catch. "I know. It's just hard to let go. I want this—to be here with you—but every now and then, the ghosts of my past creep back in."

Before I could respond, the wind outside whipped into a frenzy, slamming against the windows with a violent crack. The candles flickered dangerously low, and for a moment, darkness threatened to engulf us. My pulse quickened as the shadows swirled, feeling less like a comforting embrace and more like an impending doom.

"Did you hear that?" I whispered, glancing toward the window where the world had been reduced to a swirling mass of wind and rain.

"Just the storm," Liam reassured, though his eyes betrayed a flicker of uncertainty. "But we're safe in here."

"Safe until a tree decides to pay us a visit," I replied, the teasing tone masking my rising unease. I tried to shake off the feeling, but a sense of foreboding settled in my gut.

Suddenly, the lights flickered back to life, casting the studio in a harsh glow that felt disorienting. For a moment, I felt exposed, the shadows retreating but leaving behind a stark reality. Just then, the unmistakable sound of shattering glass pierced the air, followed by a loud crash from the direction of the front door.

My heart raced as I exchanged a frantic look with Liam. "What was that?" I barely managed to whisper, the sudden fear tightening my chest.

"I don't know," he said, rising to his feet. The playful banter had evaporated, replaced by a palpable tension that electrified the air between us.

We moved cautiously toward the door, every creak of the floorboards amplifying the rising dread. "Stay behind me," he whispered, an unspoken promise of protection.

The world outside had transformed into a wild nightmare, the wind howling like a banshee as we approached the front door, now cracked ajar. The storm had breached our sanctuary, and I couldn't shake the feeling that something, or someone, had taken advantage of our vulnerability.

Just as Liam reached for the doorknob, a loud, booming crash erupted from within the studio, causing us both to jump back. "What was that?" I gasped, my heart racing in my chest.

"Stay here," Liam commanded, his voice low but firm. I wanted to argue, to insist on facing whatever storm had come for us together, but fear rooted me in place as he edged toward the door.

"Be careful," I urged, the anxiety clawing at my insides.

He nodded, his jaw set in determination. As he pushed the door open, the wind shrieked, and in that split second, the shadows outside seemed to stretch and twist, warping the very air around us.

Then, a figure emerged, silhouetted against the storm's fury, drenched and wild-eyed, the unmistakable outline of a familiar face cutting through the chaos.

"Help!" the figure shouted, their voice barely audible over the roar of the storm. "You have to help me!"

My heart plummeted as I recognized the voice.

Chapter 16: The Fracture

The morning light filtered through the cracked windowpanes, casting slanted shadows across the studio floor, each beam a reminder of the fleeting night. I rubbed the sleep from my eyes and reached instinctively for the space beside me, but it was cold and empty. Liam was gone, and the sudden absence echoed in the silence like a haunting refrain. I sat up, the weight of unease settling heavily in my stomach. Had I dreamt the warmth of his presence? The whispers of our conversations lingered in the air, and I could almost hear his laughter bouncing off the walls, but it was just an illusion, a cruel trick of memory.

The storm outside had transformed from a gentle patter into a full-blown tempest, the wind howling like a pack of wolves, thrashing against the old oaks that stood sentry outside. I pulled on my boots, the soft leather creaking in protest, and bolted out of the door. Each step felt heavy with dread, the wooden stairs creaking ominously beneath my weight. My heart raced as I rushed down the cobblestone path, my breath visible in the crisp morning air.

"Liam!" I called, the name echoing back to me like a mocking whisper. The park was shrouded in thick mist, each tree looming like a sentinel cloaked in gray. This was where we had first met, where our laughter had mingled with the rustling leaves, but now it felt like a ghost of that moment. I felt exposed, as if the shadows themselves were conspiring against me.

As I moved deeper into the park, the wind whipped through the trees, sending leaves swirling like confused spirits. My pulse thudded in my ears, and with each passing moment, the panic clawed at my insides. I could almost convince myself that he was hiding, playing a trick on me, but the knot in my gut told me otherwise. Something was wrong. I had seen the flicker of unease in his eyes before he left, the way he glanced over his shoulder as if expecting someone—or something—to follow.

"Liam!" My voice cracked, a desperate plea that felt swallowed by the ominous silence. The park seemed to close in around me, the branches reaching like gnarled fingers, grasping for something I couldn't see. I pressed on, a sense of urgency guiding my every step. I rounded a bend, and then, through the thick mist, I saw a figure standing beneath the old willow tree, its branches sweeping like a shroud.

"Liam?" I hesitated, dread pooling in my chest. The figure turned, and I felt my heart leap into my throat, though the face was not one I had expected. It was Nora, her dark hair whipping wildly in the wind, eyes wide with a mixture of fear and defiance.

"What are you doing here?" I demanded, my voice sharper than intended. She stepped forward, her expression unreadable, and the tension in the air thickened as I scrutinized her.

"I came to warn you," she said, her voice barely above a whisper, yet it carried an urgency that made my skin prickle. "They're looking for him. For both of you."

"Who's looking for us?" My mind raced, jumping to conclusions that twisted and turned like the branches overhead. The weight of her words sent a shiver down my spine, and I searched her face for answers.

"The people who want to keep this town's secrets buried. They know he's been asking questions." Nora glanced around, her eyes darting nervously, as if the trees themselves were listening. "It's not safe for either of you."

"Liam wouldn't just disappear," I shot back, my voice trembling with a mix of fear and anger. "He wouldn't leave without telling me."

Nora stepped closer, her voice low, urgent. "That's just it. He's in trouble, and if you don't find him soon, you might lose him for good." The gravity of her words sank in, a stone dropped into the depths of a well, sending ripples of dread across my heart.

"Where do I even start looking?" I felt a familiar surge of determination rise within me, mingled with the cold grip of fear. "What do you know?"

She hesitated, her eyes narrowing as if weighing the cost of her next words. "There's a place, an old cabin deep in the woods where people go to... disappear. If he's been taken, that's where they'd take him. But it's dangerous. You shouldn't go alone."

The thought of trekking into the woods alone sent another wave of dread washing over me, yet the alternative was unbearable. "I have to try. I can't just sit here waiting." My resolve hardened, and I turned back toward the path leading out of the park, the storm raging above me, matching the tempest in my heart.

Nora grabbed my arm, her grip surprisingly strong. "Wait! You need to promise me something." She searched my eyes, and for a moment, I saw a flicker of the girl I used to know, buried beneath layers of distrust and betrayal. "Promise you won't go in without backup. Call someone you trust."

I nodded, even though my thoughts were already racing ahead, fueled by the urgency of the situation. "I'll call Jenna. She knows these woods better than anyone." My heart sank at the thought of dragging my sister into this mess, but she was strong, resourceful.

As I broke away from Nora and sprinted toward my phone, a heavy feeling settled in my stomach, mingling with the storm brewing above. Each step echoed with the weight of uncertainty, and I couldn't shake the feeling that this was just the beginning of something far more sinister than I could have ever anticipated.

Jenna answered on the second ring, her voice muffled as though she had just rolled out of bed, and I felt a flicker of guilt for interrupting her slumber. "You sound like you've seen a ghost," she murmured, and I could almost picture her running a hand through her disheveled hair, her eyes narrowing at the day's unwelcome demands.

"Not a ghost, but definitely something worse. It's Liam. He's missing." The weight of those words hung heavily in the air, pregnant with an urgency that made my pulse race.

"What do you mean missing? Like, gone-gone, or just... he forgot to set his alarm?" Her tone shifted from groggy to alert in an instant. Jenna had a way of cutting through the fog of panic, a gift she honed through years of dealing with my overdramatic tendencies.

"No, I mean he's vanished. I woke up, and he was just—gone. I need you to meet me at the old cabin. Nora says that's where they might've taken him."

"Hold on. Slow down." The rustling on the other end told me she was getting out of bed, and I couldn't help but feel a surge of gratitude mixed with irritation. "What do you mean, 'they'? And why the cabin?"

"There's no time for explanations, Jenna! Just get dressed and meet me." My impatience bled through, and I could hear her inhaling sharply, possibly debating whether or not to push back.

"Fine," she finally replied, her voice a mixture of resignation and resolve. "But you owe me a very detailed explanation over coffee—preferably something strong enough to revive the dead. Give me twenty minutes."

I hung up and glanced back toward the misty park, now swallowed by swirling gray clouds. The storm seemed to thrum with anticipation, each gust of wind a reminder that time was slipping away. As I paced, the weight of fear settled in my chest, clashing with the flickering hope that I might still find Liam. The old cabin was a relic of the past, a place where secrets whispered among the trees and shadows danced in the corners.

I knew the woods well enough to navigate them, but the thought of what lurked in the darkness made my skin crawl. Every rustle of leaves seemed to mock my trepidation, and I swiped at my phone, trying to distract myself with the faint glow of notifications. Nothing important, just the usual chaos of the world outside—people arguing over breakfast recipes, pet videos, and the latest celebrity gossip. None of it mattered; all I could focus on was the gnawing sense of urgency that propelled me forward.

Minutes later, Jenna pulled up, her old Jeep rumbling like an overzealous beast. I could barely make out her silhouette as she climbed out, a vision of determined chaos in her flannel shirt and mismatched boots. She shot me a look that was equal parts annoyance and affection, as if she could read the panic etched into my features.

"Let's go before I change my mind," she said, already heading toward the path that led deeper into the woods. I followed, relief flooding through me at the sight of her steadfast presence, even as the storm clouds above roiled ominously.

The trail twisted and turned, the trees leaning in close as if sharing secrets in hushed whispers. The air was thick with moisture, the smell of damp earth mixing with the faint aroma of pine and something sweet and decaying. "Do you think we'll find him?" I asked, keeping my voice steady despite the fear gnawing at my insides.

Jenna shot me a sidelong glance. "If we don't, we'll at least have an interesting story for our book club," she quipped, trying to lighten the mood. "Although I'm pretty sure we'll have to switch genres from romance to horror if we find you covered in mud and running from ghost stories."

"Perfect. I can see the bestseller now: Chasing Shadows and Other Bad Ideas." I forced a laugh, but it felt hollow against the backdrop of uncertainty. We pressed on, the dense trees enveloping us in their cool embrace, but with each step, the unease clung tighter.

As we approached the cabin, the familiar outline loomed ahead, weathered and sagging under the weight of countless winters. It had been years since we'd last stepped inside, and memories flooded back—laughs shared over campfire stories and whispers in the dark, unspoken promises that felt both innocent and haunting.

"What if we're too late?" I murmured, the worry weaving through my thoughts like the vines that choked the cabin's edges.

"We won't know until we check." Jenna's voice was firm, cutting through my spiraling anxiety. "Stay close. If there's anyone in there, I'll handle it. You just keep your eyes peeled and remember: we're the heroes of this story, even if it feels like a horror flick."

The door creaked ominously as we pushed it open, revealing a dark interior thick with dust and the scent of stale air. Shadows danced in the corners, flickering with the occasional spark of sunlight filtering through cracked windows. I stepped inside, heart racing as I scanned the room. A small table stood in the center, littered with old maps and fading photographs that hinted at happier times—times that now felt almost foreign.

"Liam!" I called, my voice echoing back to me, swallowed by the silence. The cabin felt alive, as if it held its breath, waiting for the unfolding drama. I moved deeper into the space, every creak of the floorboards beneath my feet a reminder that I was not alone in this ghostly abode.

A faint sound made me pause. A rustle? My heart skipped, and I glanced at Jenna, who nodded, her expression grave. We shared a silent agreement, and I pushed open a door that led to a narrow hallway, shadows creeping along the walls as if alive.

Then, the unmistakable sound of muffled voices reached my ears, sending chills racing down my spine. Jenna and I exchanged a look, her eyes wide, a mix of fear and determination. We pressed ourselves against the wall, straining to hear the conversation filtering through the dim space.

"...shouldn't have come here," a deep voice warned, laced with an edge of menace that made my heart race.

"Neither should you," another voice responded, sharper, more familiar. It was Liam. The realization ignited a fierce hope within me, but it was quickly overshadowed by the urgency of the situation.

"We need to get him out," I whispered, adrenaline surging through me as I braced myself for whatever lay ahead. There was no turning back now; the shadows were closing in, and we were determined to chase them away.

With my heart pounding in my ears, I pressed my back against the cool wall, straining to hear every word exchanged between the shadows. Jenna stood beside me, her expression a mix of apprehension and fierce resolve, ready to spring into action at a moment's notice. I couldn't shake the feeling that we were teetering on the edge of something dangerous, a precipice where even the slightest misstep could lead us tumbling into darkness.

"Don't you understand what's at stake?" Liam's voice broke through the tension, raw and edged with urgency. "If you keep this up, you'll put everyone in danger, including her." My heart skipped a beat, the protective undertone sending shivers down my spine. He was talking about me, and I had to wonder just how deep the trouble ran.

A heavy silence followed his words, punctuated only by the distant rumble of thunder. I leaned closer, every fiber of my being eager to break through the threshold of uncertainty. "Liam!" I called, breaking the spell of silence, desperate to let him know he wasn't alone.

The rustling stopped abruptly, and for a heartbeat, I thought I might have gone too far. Then, to my utter relief, his voice came, barely above a whisper. "Is that you? Get out of here! It's not safe!"

"Not a chance," I shot back, emboldened by the fierceness that coursed through me. "We're not leaving without you." Jenna's eyes met mine, a flash of understanding passing between us. We were in this together, and together, we would face whatever lay ahead.

Suddenly, the door creaked open further, revealing a man I recognized, though I wished I didn't. Derek, the local businessman with an unsettling reputation, stepped into view, his face shadowed but the menace in his posture unmistakable. "Well, well, what do we have here?" he sneered, a predatory glint in his eyes that made my skin crawl. "The little damsel and her sidekick. How quaint."

"Let him go, Derek," I demanded, voice firm despite the tremor of fear creeping in. "This is between you and Liam. It has nothing to do with us."

He chuckled, low and mocking, his eyes darting back and forth between Jenna and me. "Oh, but you've wandered right into the middle of it, haven't you? This town has secrets, and trust me, you don't want to uncover them."

Before I could respond, Jenna stepped forward, her jaw set. "We're not afraid of you, Derek. What are you really after?" Her voice rang with conviction, and I felt a flicker of pride at her courage.

Derek's smile twisted, revealing a flash of white teeth that seemed more menacing than reassuring. "What I'm after is none of your concern, sweetheart. But your little boyfriend here? He's dug too deep, and now he's a liability." The words hung in the air, heavy with implications, and I felt a jolt of anger.

"Liam isn't a liability. He's brave enough to ask the questions you'd rather keep buried," I retorted, my voice growing steadier. "And I'll be damned if I let you intimidate us."

Derek's expression shifted, irritation flickering across his features. "Brave or foolish? You're playing a dangerous game, and the stakes are higher than you think." He took a step closer, and I felt a wave of dread wash over me. "You have no idea what you're up against."

In that moment, I caught a glimpse of something in Liam's eyes, a mixture of fear and resolve that ignited a fire within me. "You're not taking him anywhere, Derek," I declared, voice unwavering. "If you want to fight, then you'll have to go through me first."

"Very noble," he mocked, but I could see the tension coiling in his shoulders, a sign that I had struck a nerve.

"Enough of this," Liam interrupted, his voice rising, as if he were trying to break through the tension. "Just let them go. They don't belong in this."

The air crackled with electricity, and I could sense the pendulum swinging precariously. I took a deep breath, willing my heart to calm, while preparing for whatever may come. "Liam, I'm not leaving you," I said, my resolve as solid as the ground beneath us. "We're in this together."

Suddenly, the door behind Derek swung open wider, revealing a shadowy figure just outside. The new arrival's silhouette was obscured by the gloom, but the presence felt ominous, charged with an energy that set my nerves alight. "Derek, we need to move," the figure said, voice low and gravelly. "They're onto us."

"What do you mean?" Derek snapped, glancing back as the figure stepped forward into the feeble light. My breath caught in my throat when I recognized the unmistakable features of someone I hadn't seen in years. It was Marcus, an old friend turned adversary, someone who had slipped through the cracks of my life, leaving only memories tinged with bitterness.

"What are you doing here?" I blurted out, anger and confusion clashing in my chest.

"I'm here to help you, believe it or not," Marcus replied, his voice dripping with an insincere charm that I found hard to trust. "But it's time for us to leave, and now."

Derek's face twisted in irritation, but it was clear he was torn. "We don't have time for this, Marcus," he hissed, shifting his weight as if ready to pounce.

"Then let's go, before they call for reinforcements," Marcus urged, his eyes darting between us as if calculating the odds.

Before I could react, Derek lunged forward, his arm reaching for Liam, but I sprang into action, instinct taking over. "No!" I yelled, racing toward them as Jenna moved to flank me, her determination matching my own.

The cabin erupted into chaos, a whirlwind of shouts and movement, each moment stretching as if caught in a slow-motion reel. I heard Liam shout my name, the urgency in his voice fueling my adrenaline. Just as I reached for his hand, everything exploded into a flurry of shadows and sound.

In the chaos, I felt a surge of adrenaline and fear collide, my instincts screaming at me to act. But just as I grasped Liam's hand, a sharp pain shot through my side, and I gasped, stumbling back as darkness threatened to close in.

"Get out! Now!" I heard Liam shout, but the world around me dimmed, shadows swirling like a tempest as everything fell into chaos. The last thing I saw was Marcus's frantic expression, a mixture of urgency and dread etched on his face before everything faded to black, leaving behind nothing but the echo of my racing heart and the chilling question of what awaited us in the darkness.

Chapter 17: The Veil of Deceit

The air was thick with the scent of damp earth and the faint, sweet aroma of decaying leaves, a reminder that autumn had taken hold of Ashwood with its customary grip. I stood in the dim light of the old grove, the trees looming like silent sentinels around us. Clara's presence ignited a flicker of hope amid the shadows that had swirled around me since Liam and I began our perilous investigation. Yet, the moment I embraced her, the familiar warmth of her body was overshadowed by a cold dread creeping into my bones, as if the very roots of the trees beneath us were entwined with the dark secrets of our past.

"Clara," I breathed, pulling back to look into her face. Her auburn hair fell in messy waves around her shoulders, her once bright eyes clouded by the burden she carried. "What's happened? Why are you back now?"

Her fingers twisted together as she took a shaky breath, and for a fleeting second, I saw the little girl who had climbed trees with me, her laughter like the chime of delicate bells. "I had to come back, Ella. I stumbled onto something... something my family has kept hidden for generations." Her voice trembled, and my heart raced as I sensed the weight of her words.

We stepped further into the grove, the golden light of the setting sun filtering through the branches, casting elongated shadows across the ground. The world felt alive around us, yet I could only focus on Clara's words as she spoke of the dark history entwined with her family's legacy. I could hardly fathom what she was revealing—the town's oldest tales of betrayal and loss, steeped in blood and tears. As she unraveled the thread of her family's involvement, my stomach tightened, twisting painfully as the pieces fell into place.

"Do you remember the old Dawson estate?" she asked, her voice a barely audible whisper now. I nodded, remembering the crumbling mansion that had been the subject of many ghost stories whispered among children. The legend had it that a family member had gone mad, succumbing to the shadows of his own making.

Clara's eyes darkened. "It wasn't madness, Ella. It was the result of a pact made in desperation. The Dawsons thought they could control the dark forces that lingered in this town, but they only fed it. My family was entangled with theirs, and now—now I fear it's come back to haunt us."

A shiver raced down my spine as I considered the implications of her words. The very fabric of our lives seemed woven with deceit and hidden truths, as if Ashwood was a tapestry of pain and secrets yet to be fully revealed. "You've been investigating this? Alone?"

"I had to. I felt drawn to it. It was like the shadows called to me." Clara's voice grew softer, almost reverent. "I uncovered journals, letters... They spoke of rituals and sacrifices, of promises made to keep the darkness at bay. But the more I learned, the more I realized that my family had betrayed the very essence of what they sought to protect. The darkness hasn't just returned; it's been waiting."

Her admission was like a storm breaking, and I felt the first droplets of fear seep into my consciousness. The implications spun around my mind like autumn leaves in a tempest. I thought of Liam, of our late-night talks filled with hope and determination, and the way we'd brushed against danger without truly understanding its weight. "What do we do now?" I asked, my voice steady despite the chaos swirling within.

"I think we need to confront it," Clara replied, her resolve hardening into something unyielding. "There's a reason I came back now, Ella. The veil has lifted, and whatever is lurking is growing bolder. If we don't face it, it will consume us."

As I looked at her, the fear in her eyes mirrored my own. But there was something else too—an ember of bravery that I couldn't help but admire. I had always known Clara to be resilient, but this new intensity ignited a flicker of determination within me as well. "Together then," I said firmly, though my heart raced with uncertainty. "We'll uncover the truth, no matter what it takes."

The shadows around us deepened as we turned to leave the grove, a silent promise binding us to our fate. But before we could step into the fading light, a rustle in the underbrush caught our attention. My heart skipped a beat as I scanned the darkening woods, the eerie quiet amplifying my unease. "Did you hear that?" I whispered, my voice barely breaking the stillness.

Clara nodded, her posture tense. We both stepped back, instinctively seeking the safety of the trees. "It could be nothing," she murmured, though I could see the unease flickering in her eyes.

"Or it could be everything," I countered, adrenaline coursing through my veins. Just as I was about to suggest we head back, a figure emerged from the shadows—tall, broad-shouldered, and familiar. It was Liam, his brow furrowed, concern etched across his handsome features.

"Ella! Clara! Are you okay?" he called, rushing towards us. The sight of him sent a rush of warmth through me, mingled with confusion. He had been searching for me, his determination as palpable as the leaves crunching beneath his feet.

"Liam!" I exclaimed, relief flooding my senses even as tension rippled through the air. Clara shifted beside me, a silent acknowledgment passing between us, the gravity of our revelations resting heavily on our shoulders.

As Liam reached us, his eyes darted between Clara and me, concern giving way to an unspoken question. "What's going on? I felt something... something off in the grove."

"Clara knows about the Dawsons," I explained quickly, trying to bridge the gap between the two worlds that had collided in that moment. "She's been investigating. There's a darkness that's resurfacing, and we need to confront it together."

His expression hardened, a flicker of recognition crossing his face. "Then we're already in deeper than we thought."

Clara and I exchanged glances, the gravity of our intertwined fates settling in like a heavy fog. I felt a strange mixture of fear and exhilaration. The three of us were on the brink of uncovering something monumental, a revelation that could alter the very course of our lives in Ashwood. But as the shadows danced around us, I couldn't shake the feeling that we were being watched, that the darkness Clara spoke of was not just a myth whispered through generations. It lurked close, and we were about to plunge headfirst into its depths.

The tension hung in the air like a storm cloud, heavy and charged, as Liam's brows knit together in concern. "A darkness?" he echoed, his voice low, almost reverent, as if speaking the words aloud could summon it from the shadows. Clara nodded, her earlier bravado fading as she stood between us, caught in the web of her family's history and the town's secrets.

"More than just a story," she clarified, glancing around as if expecting specters to materialize from the underbrush. "It's alive, lurking just beneath the surface. I didn't come back just to reconnect with my roots. I came because I sensed it. I had to know."

Liam's gaze flicked to me, an unspoken question lingering there. He had always been the protector, ever ready to leap into danger, but the darkness Clara spoke of wasn't something to be trifled with. "And you think it's tied to the Dawson estate?" he asked, a flicker of recognition crossing his features.

Clara nodded, her eyes narrowing. "It's more than a haunted house, Liam. It's a portal of sorts—a channel for whatever malevolence has seeped into Ashwood's very essence. My family tried to harness it, but they didn't understand the cost. Now, it's our turn to pay that debt."

I felt a chill wash over me, a creeping realization that we had unwittingly stepped into a labyrinth woven with threads of deceit and desperation. "So what do we do?" I asked, my voice steady despite the whirlpool of dread threatening to pull me under.

"I believe we need to go to the estate," Clara said, her voice a mixture of trepidation and resolve. "If there's a way to confront this darkness, it's there. But we'll need to be careful. It's not just the stories that are dangerous—it's the truth."

Liam's expression hardened. "Then let's go before the sun sets completely. The longer we wait, the more power it gains." He reached for my hand, squeezing it tightly as if to tether me to him, to this moment, to the reality of what lay ahead.

As we began our descent from the grove, the world around us transformed. The vibrant colors of the leaves began to dim, turning into a muted tapestry of browns and grays. The chatter of the forest quieted, replaced by a profound stillness that felt unnatural, as though the trees were holding their breath, waiting for something to happen.

"You know, for a town that prides itself on its history," I mused aloud, trying to break the oppressive silence, "we're doing a bang-up job of ignoring the really juicy parts."

Clara let out a small, nervous laugh, the sound a brief flicker of light in the growing gloom. "If only the townsfolk knew what really went on behind closed doors. Maybe they'd stop complaining about my family's estate."

"Or maybe they'd just throw a festival about it," I quipped, my humor a poor shield against the heaviness creeping into my heart.

"'Ashwood's Haunted History: A Celebration of Fear and Folly,'" Liam chimed in, his smirk betraying the weight of our situation. "Sounds like a bestseller."

Our laughter echoed faintly through the woods, but it quickly faded into the quiet. The path grew narrow as we approached the outskirts of the estate, the trees parting like reluctant curtains to reveal the sprawling property before us. The mansion loomed ahead, its once-grand façade now marred by age and neglect, windows like dark eyes staring out into the encroaching night.

"What are we even looking for?" I asked, unease gnawing at my insides. "Do we expect the ghosts to welcome us with open arms?"

"Or maybe they'll just roll out the red carpet and serve us tea," Clara replied, her bravado flickering back to life.

With a deep breath, we stepped closer to the estate, the crunch of gravel underfoot the only sound breaking the heavy silence. As we neared the front door, I felt an invisible barrier pushing against me, a whisper of cold air that sent shivers down my spine. "This place feels... alive," I said, casting a wary glance at the surrounding shadows.

"It's more than alive," Clara replied softly. "It's watching."

Liam stepped forward, placing a hand on the door, which creaked open as if inviting us in. The interior was shrouded in darkness, thick dust cloaking every surface like a shroud. I hesitated, feeling the air grow colder, denser, as if the walls themselves were breathing.

"Ladies first?" Liam suggested, a playful grin tugging at his lips, but the underlying tension was unmistakable.

I rolled my eyes, unable to suppress a grin. "How chivalrous of you."

As I crossed the threshold, a chill swept through me, the hairs on my arms standing at attention. The foyer was expansive, the once-opulent chandelier hanging precariously from the ceiling, its crystals dim and dull. My heart raced as I stepped into the shadows, feeling as though I were trespassing not just into a house but into a history filled with anguish and betrayal.

Clara moved cautiously beside me, her eyes scanning the surroundings as if expecting a spectral figure to materialize. "We should look for any signs—anything that points to what they were doing here," she whispered, her voice barely above a breath.

"Like a room filled with ominous sigils and half-burned candles?" I quipped, trying to lighten the mood, but my voice wavered in the heavy air.

"More like a hidden journal or a letter," Clara replied, determination reigniting in her gaze. "Something that explains the connection between my family and the darkness. If we find it, we may have a chance to break the cycle."

We moved deeper into the house, the floorboards creaking underfoot, their sounds almost sounding like whispers of warnings. As we passed through rooms draped in shadows, Clara's intuition guided us toward a narrow staircase leading to the upper floor.

"Up there," she said, nodding toward the staircase. "That's where the family would have kept their most valuable secrets."

"Or where they stashed the bodies," I muttered under my breath, though my heart raced with a mix of fear and exhilaration.

Liam placed a reassuring hand on my back, urging me forward. "Let's find out what lies ahead. We'll confront it together."

With that, we climbed the staircase, each step a testament to our resolve. As we reached the landing, the air grew thick with anticipation, the shadows stretching toward us as if seeking to envelop us. A door stood ajar at the end of the hall, a sliver of light spilling from within like a beacon in the darkness.

Clara hesitated, glancing back at us. "Ready?"

"Ready as we'll ever be," I replied, bracing myself for whatever lay beyond.

As we approached the door, I felt the weight of our shared history pressing down on us, a reminder that we were not just confronting a darkness but unearthing the buried secrets of our lives, our town, and the tangled web that had drawn us all together.

The air was thick with a blend of anticipation and dread as we stood outside the ajar door, a faint light beckoning us from within. I felt a peculiar weight settle on my chest, a mix of fear and the faintest thrill of curiosity that had been my constant companion since this nightmare began. Clara's expression shifted from determination to something akin to terror as she stepped forward, her breath hitching in her throat.

"What if we find something we're not ready for?" she whispered, glancing back at us. Her vulnerability was a stark contrast to the brave facade she had donned just moments before.

Liam stepped closer, his hand brushing against mine, grounding me as I fought against the instinct to retreat. "We're already knee-deep in this. Running away now won't change anything. If there's a truth to uncover, we owe it to ourselves to face it." His voice was steady, filled with an assurance I desperately clung to, despite the tremors of doubt ricocheting through my mind.

"Besides," I added, attempting to inject a note of levity into our predicament, "what's the worst that could happen? Ghosts with unresolved issues? A family reunion gone horribly wrong?"

Clara rolled her eyes, but a slight smile broke through her anxiety. "Right. I'm sure they'll be thrilled to see us."

With a shared look of resolve, we approached the door, and as I pushed it open, a musty scent enveloped us, thick like the memories buried within these walls. The room beyond was dimly lit by flickering candles, their soft glow dancing across dusty shelves lined with books whose spines were worn and faded. Papers were strewn haphazardly across a large oak desk in the center, as if someone had left in a hurry—notes, sketches, and old photographs spilling over the edges like secrets begging to be uncovered.

"Looks like someone was doing some serious digging," Liam remarked, moving closer to the desk.

Clara stepped inside, her eyes wide as she absorbed the scene. "This must be where they kept everything—the journals, the records... anything related to the darkness."

"What exactly are we looking for?" I asked, my eyes scanning the cluttered surface. "A recipe for disaster? The family secret sauce?"

"Anything that connects my family to the Dawson estate," Clara replied, brushing her fingers across the top of the desk, gathering dust and memories alike. "If we can find something definitive, we can understand what we're up against."

As we sifted through the papers, a series of faded photographs caught my attention. I reached for one, revealing an image of a family gathered in front of the estate, their smiles frozen in time. "Clara, look at this."

She leaned over my shoulder, her breath hitching as she recognized the faces. "That's my grandmother... and her siblings. I didn't know they were involved here."

"They don't look like the kind of family that dabbles in dark rituals," I noted, studying the picture. They appeared ordinary, perhaps too ordinary for the twisted legacy Clara had uncovered.

"People wear masks," Clara murmured, her voice laced with sorrow. "Sometimes, the brightest smiles hide the darkest secrets."

Suddenly, Liam's voice cut through the heavy air. "What's this?" He pointed to a leather-bound journal peeking out from beneath a pile of old ledgers. My heart raced as he pulled it free, the leather creaking like the ancient wood around us. The cover was embossed with a symbol I didn't recognize, a twisting design that seemed to writhe under the candlelight.

"Let's see what it says," I urged, my curiosity ignited.

Liam carefully opened the journal, flipping through the brittle pages. The handwriting was elegant yet erratic, words spilling over one another in a frenzied script. "It looks like... a diary. Maybe from someone involved in the rituals."

Clara leaned in, her eyes scanning the lines feverishly. "This could be it. It could explain everything."

As we crowded closer, the room felt charged, each heartbeat echoing in the heavy silence. Words leaped out at us: "Sacrifice," "binding," and "the darkness grows." I exchanged a nervous glance with Liam, who shifted closer, his breath warm against my ear.

"What if this is exactly what Clara's family didn't want us to find?" he murmured, a hint of concern edging his tone.

"We have to read it," Clara insisted, determination rekindling in her eyes. "If we understand their motives, we might find a way to break the cycle."

My gaze flicked to the shadows gathering in the corners of the room, and a chill crept down my spine. "You mean, if we survive whatever darkness they stirred up."

Clara inhaled sharply, her eyes darting back to the pages as she read aloud, her voice trembling with the weight of her family's history. "It is with the blood of the kin that the seal will be broken, and the spirit will be bound. The balance must be maintained, or the darkness will rise again…"

The words hung in the air like an incantation, each syllable vibrating with a foreboding energy. Suddenly, the candles flickered violently, and the temperature in the room dropped, sending an icy blast that made us gasp. Shadows elongated and twisted, curling around us like tendrils seeking to ensnare.

"Clara, we need to—" I started, but my words were cut off as the door slammed shut behind us with a deafening bang.

Panic surged as we exchanged frantic looks, the flickering candlelight casting eerie shapes on the walls. "What just happened?" I exclaimed, heart pounding against my ribs.

"Something doesn't want us to leave," Liam said, his voice low and steady, even as his eyes betrayed a flicker of fear.

"Let's focus," Clara urged, her determination unwavering despite the chaos around us. "We need to finish reading this. Whatever is trying to keep us here can't be stronger than what we've already uncovered."

But just as she spoke, the temperature plummeted further, the shadows around us twisting into forms that flickered at the edges of my vision. I could almost hear whispers, faint and insistent, urging me to flee, to run. The very walls seemed to pulse with a dark energy, threatening to swallow us whole.

"Clara!" I shouted, fighting against the encroaching dread that wrapped around me like a vice. "What do we do?"

She was staring at the journal, her eyes wide, a realization dawning. "The answer... it's in the binding."

Before I could grasp the significance of her words, a violent gust swept through the room, extinguishing the candles in an instant, plunging us into darkness.

"Liam!" I cried out, reaching for him in the pitch black, but I felt only empty air.

"Stay close!" he shouted, his voice barely cutting through the silence.

The shadows closed in, the whispers growing louder, more insistent, until it felt as if the very walls were closing around us, and I was left gasping, adrift in a sea of terror, desperately trying to hold onto the last threads of light before the darkness consumed us entirely.

Chapter 18: The Confrontation

The town square buzzed with murmurs, a living tapestry of fear and suspicion woven tightly together. It was a swirl of faces, some familiar, others less so, all lit by the flickering glow of lanterns that cast an eerie light on the cobblestone paths. The scent of damp earth mingled with the sharp tang of pine from the towering trees surrounding us, grounding me amid the brewing storm of emotions. I could feel the weight of Clara's research pressing down on me like a heavy cloak, the evidence of the ancient spirit's malevolence fluttering in my mind like the pages of an old book, desperate to be read aloud.

Liam stood at my side, his presence both a comfort and a challenge. The warmth of his hand brushed against mine, a reminder of the bond we had forged through whispered secrets and shared fears. Together, we had uncovered threads of a dark tapestry that connected the town's past with its present, and now we were standing on the precipice of confrontation. I could see the crowd gathering, their expressions a volatile mix of curiosity and hostility. Old grudges simmered just below the surface, ready to boil over at the slightest provocation.

"Are you sure about this?" Liam whispered, his voice low and steady, cutting through the din.

"Not a doubt in my mind," I replied, though my heart raced like a wild stallion. There was something in the air, a charged energy that made every nerve in my body vibrate with anticipation. "They need to hear what we've found. This isn't just about us anymore; it's about everyone."

As I stepped forward, the crowd's murmurs shifted to a low hum, like the rustling of leaves before a storm. I took a deep breath, the cool evening air filling my lungs and hardening my resolve. The ancient oak that stood sentinel in the square felt like an anchor, its gnarled branches reaching out as if to shield us from the brewing tempest of distrust.

"People of Ashwood!" My voice rang out, cutting through the undercurrent of unease. I caught glimpses of familiar faces: Mrs. Hawthorne, her silver hair a halo of defiance; young Tommy from the bakery, eyes wide with a mixture of hope and fear. "We are here tonight not to incite panic but to share the truth—one that has been hidden for far too long!"

The crowd shifted, a ripple of uncertainty passing through them, but I pressed on, fueled by the urgency of our findings. "Clara's research reveals a chilling connection between the recent disappearances and the spirit that haunts our woods. For years, we've dismissed it as mere folklore, but it is far from a story; it is our reality."

The air crackled with tension as a figure emerged from the shadows—Mayor Thompson, his face pale and drawn, eyes gleaming with skepticism. "And what evidence do you have, Isabelle? You cannot expect us to take your word for it, not without proof!"

His words were like stones thrown into a pond, sending waves of doubt through the crowd. "We have the records," I said, my voice steadier than I felt. "The patterns in the disappearances match the folklore surrounding the spirit of Ashwood. Clara documented it all—dates, locations, descriptions. We are not alone in this fight."

A murmur spread through the crowd, some nodding in reluctant agreement, while others shook their heads in disbelief. It was then that I spotted Clara, her face flushed and determined, pushing through the throng to stand beside me. She clutched a folder to her chest, her fingers trembling slightly, but her eyes shone with resolve.

"I can show you," she said, her voice a clarion call that cut through the doubts. "I have proof that connects the spirit to the last three disappearances. We can't just ignore this anymore!"

As Clara spoke, I could see the seeds of fear taking root in the townspeople. They glanced at each other, whispers rising like smoke. The mayor scoffed, crossing his arms. "Folklore and tales won't save us from real danger. You're only stoking the fires of fear!"

"Fear is what has kept us silent," Liam interjected, stepping forward. "But silence only invites darkness. If we do not confront this, we risk losing everything we hold dear."

The tension escalated, a palpable charge in the air. I could feel the weight of their stares, each one a dagger aimed at the heart of our truth. A wave of determination washed over me. "We stand here not just for ourselves but for those who have been taken. We owe it to them to uncover the truth, no matter how uncomfortable it might be."

I felt Liam's hand squeeze mine, a silent affirmation that we were in this together, come what may. The air shifted, and for a moment, I thought I caught a glimpse of hope glimmering in the eyes of a few. Yet, before I could speak again, a voice cut through the gathering, sharp and accusing.

"What if this is just another story to scare us? You've always had a flair for the dramatic, Isabelle." It was Janet, a long-time resident with a reputation for stirring the pot. Her skepticism ignited the crowd, a fresh wave of murmurs and whispers washing over us like a storm.

"No, Janet, it's not drama!" Clara shot back, her voice rising above the chaos. "This is real! We have to face it head-on before it's too late!"

The tension was a living thing, palpable and electric. Faces twisted in uncertainty, shadows danced in the light of the lanterns, and the weight of history bore down on us all. I could feel the night wrapping around us, the ancient trees looming like watchful guardians. The past was at our doorstep, and the spirit of Ashwood hung in the balance, waiting for us to either rise together or fall apart.

The air was electric, the kind of charged atmosphere that made the hairs on the back of my neck stand at attention. As I glanced around the crowd, I saw faces painted with skepticism, uncertainty, and, buried beneath it all, a flicker of something akin to hope. Clara's folder felt heavy in my grip, a tangible embodiment of all the secrets we had unearthed, and I held it like a shield against the impending storm.

"Listen," I continued, desperation creeping into my voice, "we're not here to create panic. We're here because we care about our town, about our friends and families who are missing. Ignoring this won't make it go away."

The murmurs transformed into an uneasy silence, and in that moment, I could see a small opening. A few townsfolk exchanged glances, as if weighing the possibility that maybe, just maybe, the legends they had long dismissed could hold a grain of truth. But Janet, her arms still crossed defiantly, was having none of it.

"You expect us to believe that a spirit is responsible for all this? Where's your proof?" she shot back, her voice dripping with sarcasm.

A sharp retort danced on my tongue, but before I could unleash it, Clara stepped forward, her cheeks flushed but her gaze steady. "The records, Janet. We have eyewitness accounts and connections to every disappearance. I can show you the patterns, how the dates align with the old tales."

Her words hung in the air, a challenge, a dare for the crowd to reconsider their dismissals. I admired Clara's courage; it sparked a flicker of admiration that countered my own swirling fears. Yet, it was the mayor who rose to speak again, his voice booming over the crowd. "And if this is just a wild goose chase? If you're wrong, what then? You'd throw us into chaos for a handful of ghosts?"

In that moment, the crowd erupted into a symphony of dissent. Voices raised in angry protest, some demanding clarity, others simply dismissing us outright. My heart raced, but I refused to back down.

"If we don't confront this now, the chaos will find us anyway! The spirit won't just fade away because we ignore it. We have to fight for those who have been taken, for those who are still with us!"

I gestured towards the dark woods that loomed at the edge of the square, a reminder of the dangers that lay in wait just beyond the safety of the lantern light. There was a palpable shift in the crowd as some began to nod, their expressions softening with recognition. They knew the woods; they had whispered those tales to their children by the fire, and the fear of the unknown had always lingered, lurking just beneath the surface of their bravado.

"I say we listen to them," a voice called from the back. It was old Mr. Hargrove, his weathered face a roadmap of the town's history, filled with wrinkles that told stories of seasons long gone. "I've seen things in those woods, things I can't explain. If Clara and Isabelle have found something, we owe it to ourselves to hear them out."

The crowd quieted, the tension shifting like the wind. As more people began to voice their support, I caught Liam's eye, his expression a mix of relief and pride. But that brief moment of solidarity was swiftly undercut by Janet, who hadn't given up the fight just yet. "And what's to stop you from spinning this into a witch hunt? What if the spirit isn't our enemy? What if we're the ones who've brought this upon ourselves?"

Her words, while laced with fear, struck a chord in the crowd. The balance of support was precarious, teetering on the brink of chaos once more. The murmur grew louder, fueled by a mixture of anxiety and curiosity. I could almost hear the gears turning in their minds as they wrestled with the implications of Clara's findings.

"It's easy to blame a spirit when we're afraid," Clara interjected, her voice rising above the cacophony. "But the truth is, fear often brings out the worst in us. We have to face our fears, not let them dictate our actions. The spirit might have ties to our past, but we have to choose how we respond to it. We cannot become the monsters in our own story."

Her words resonated through the crowd, a reminder that fear could either imprison or empower. I sensed a subtle shift, a wave of resolve washing over the group. People began to stand taller, their shoulders squaring against the weight of the unknown.

"What do you propose we do?" a younger man asked, his voice cutting through the tension like a knife. "If we believe you, how do we fight something we can't even see?"

The question hung in the air, drawing my thoughts into the whirlpool of possibilities. What could we do? The town had relied on tradition for so long, ignoring the very spirit that could tear it apart. "We gather more information," I suggested, the words tumbling out. "We can track the places where people disappeared, look for signs, connections. Maybe we can find a way to appease the spirit or—"

"Or trap it," Janet sneered, crossing her arms tighter, her skepticism still radiating.

"Or communicate with it," I countered, a spark igniting in my chest. "If it's connected to our town's history, perhaps we can learn what it wants. Maybe it's not just about fear, but about reconciliation."

As the crowd shifted again, the energy had transformed, uncertainty mingling with an ember of hope. I could see a few nodding, murmurs of agreement stirring the air. Liam leaned closer, his breath warm against my ear. "You might just convince them."

"Maybe," I replied, casting a glance at the skeptical faces, but the fire of determination roared inside me. I wouldn't let fear silence our voice or drown our efforts in doubt. The night pressed on, heavy with expectation, and as I took a breath, I sensed the collective pulse of the crowd ready to follow where we dared to lead.

"Let's meet again," I proposed, my voice ringing out with conviction. "We'll organize a search party, gather more stories, and uncover the truth together. This is our town, our legacy, and we can't let fear dictate our future."

A wave of murmurs followed, some in support, others still hesitant. But amid the shifting tides of opinion, a sense of purpose began to take root. We could either let the darkness consume us or step into the light together, armed with the truth and the will to fight back. In that moment, standing alongside Liam and Clara, I knew we were on the brink of something extraordinary, something that could change the very fabric of Ashwood forever.

As I stood before the restless crowd, the night air was thick with anticipation, a palpable energy that buzzed like the static before a storm. The flickering lanterns cast shadows that danced on the cobblestones, mimicking the turmoil that churned within me. I could feel the weight of the townsfolk's scrutiny, their eyes like arrows aimed at my heart, each gaze heavy with the potential for either disbelief or belief. I straightened my shoulders, determined to anchor them in the storm of uncertainty that had gripped Ashwood for far too long.

"Tomorrow," I declared, my voice rising above the din. "We will gather at the edge of the woods, where the last disappearance took place. I invite anyone who believes in our town's history and its people to join us. We will look for signs, collect stories, and uncover the truth together."

The response was immediate; a murmur of agreement mixed with reluctant glances flickered through the crowd. I felt a swell of hope but knew it was fragile, a delicate bud threatened by the chill of doubt. Just then, a figure stepped forward from the shadows, his silhouette sharp against the light, eyes glinting with the kind of knowing that unsettled me.

"Are you prepared to face what lies in those woods?" It was Daniel, the town's long-time recluse, rumored to have wandered deeper into the forest than anyone dared. He had a reputation for eccentricity, a man with wild hair and an even wilder imagination, and the townsfolk often dismissed him as a mere storyteller. Yet there was something in his gaze that pierced through the disbelief.

"We've faced enough already," I said, attempting to sound more confident than I felt. "And if we don't confront it, we risk losing everything."

Daniel's laughter was rich, a sound that rolled through the crowd like thunder, causing some to jump. "Oh, I've faced things far worse than you can imagine, girl. Spirits, yes. But also the nightmares we create when we ignore the truth." His words sent a shiver down my spine, stirring echoes of the legends that had haunted my childhood. "You think this is just about the spirit? This is about the darkness inside us all."

As he spoke, I saw glances exchanged among the townsfolk, a flicker of unease mixed with intrigue. There was something raw and unsettling about Daniel's words, a challenge that rattled their carefully constructed walls of disbelief. "What do you know?" Liam's voice cut through the tension, steady and low, but I could hear the undercurrents of worry. "What do you know that we don't?"

"More than you could ever guess," Daniel replied, a cryptic smile playing on his lips. "I've watched Ashwood for years. I've seen what happens when fear runs rampant, when secrets fester in the dark. But I won't spoil the surprise." He stepped back, blending into the shadows, leaving behind a ripple of discomfort.

As the crowd murmured, a mix of curiosity and apprehension flooded the square, but I couldn't shake the sense of foreboding that hung like a cloud. "Tomorrow, we gather!" I called again, my voice stronger this time, seeking to banish the lingering unease. "Let's unravel this mystery together."

With that, the gathering began to disperse, the townsfolk drifting away, their expressions a kaleidoscope of emotions. As the last few lingered, exchanging hushed whispers, I felt a sense of camaraderie—one born from shared fear and uncertainty. Liam turned to me, his brow furrowed. "You really think they'll show up?"

"I have to believe they will," I replied, though I felt a flicker of doubt. "We can't do this alone."

As we walked back through the darkened streets, the moon casting silver beams across our path, I found myself lost in thought. The weight of the night settled around us, heavy with what lay ahead. We approached the edge of the woods, where the trees loomed tall and menacing, shadows swallowing the light. The wind rustled through the leaves, whispering secrets I longed to decipher.

"Tomorrow might change everything," Liam said softly, his voice barely above a whisper. "Or it could make things a whole lot worse."

"Or it could finally bring us peace," I replied, though I was aware of the tremor in my voice. I could feel the ancient spirit's presence lurking in the periphery of my mind, a chilling reminder of our shared history with this town.

We parted ways at the edge of the square, the night enveloping us like a shroud. I climbed into bed, tossing and turning as uncertainty gnawed at my insides. The shadows in my room danced as the wind howled outside, mirroring the chaos of my thoughts. I closed my eyes, desperate for rest, but sleep eluded me.

The hours passed, each tick of the clock echoing in the silence, and when the first light of dawn broke through the curtains, it felt like the calm before a storm. I dressed quickly, my resolve hardening with each passing moment. The woods waited for us, filled with the weight of ancient secrets and untold stories. As I made my way to the meeting point, I couldn't shake the feeling that we were stepping into a trap, one set by the very history we were trying to confront.

The gathering spot buzzed with a mix of excitement and anxiety, people murmuring as they exchanged stories and fears. Clara was already there, her energy a beacon amidst the tension. "I'm glad you're here," she said, her eyes bright with determination. "I think we can do this."

But as the minutes ticked by, I noticed a familiar face missing from the crowd—Daniel. I scanned the gathering, my heart pounding as dread seeped into my bones. "Where's Daniel?" I asked Clara, my voice tinged with urgency.

"I don't know," she replied, her brows knitting together. "He was here earlier."

The absence of his cryptic presence felt like an omen. The crowd was growing restless, and as I stepped forward to speak, my heart raced. "We're here to confront our fears and uncover the truth! We need to unite against whatever darkness lies within those woods!"

But just as the first rays of sunlight pierced the horizon, illuminating the gathering, a chilling howl erupted from the depths of the forest, echoing through the trees like a sinister laughter. Gasps swept through the crowd, a wave of fear crashing against our resolve.

"Did you hear that?" someone shouted, eyes wide with panic.

"What was that?" another voice trembled, anxiety rippling through the group.

I turned towards the woods, my breath hitching in my throat. The air thickened with an unseen presence, and the dark canopy of trees loomed like a curtain hiding the unknown. The shadows deepened, and I felt the pull of something ancient, something that beckoned me forward.

"Stay together!" I called, but as I looked back, I realized that Liam was gone, vanished into the thickening shadows. Panic surged through me, a wave of dread crashing against my chest. "Liam?"

Silence hung in the air, heavy and foreboding, and the woods answered with a whisper that felt like a warning. I stood frozen, the reality of our quest crashing down around me, the shadows swirling, and in that moment, I knew that we were not alone.

Chapter 19: The Dark Night

The cellar door creaked open, a hesitant invitation to a world draped in shadows and unspoken fears. My heart raced, a wild drumbeat echoing against the stillness of the night. I shone my flashlight into the dark, the beam slicing through the gloom like a knife, illuminating the cobwebs that hung like forgotten curtains. My friends shuffled in behind me, each footstep a cautious whisper on the damp stone floor, the chill in the air wrapping around us like a sinister embrace.

"Are we really doing this?" Claire whispered, her voice barely louder than a breath, quaking with a blend of fear and excitement. She gripped the flashlight like it was a lifeline, her knuckles white against the plastic casing.

"We have to," I replied, my own voice steadier than I felt. The decision to investigate the cellar had been born out of desperation, fueled by the mysterious happenings that had fractured our small town. Rumors of a vengeful spirit had spread like wildfire, igniting our imaginations and weaving a web of paranoia. What had once been a simple gathering of friends had transformed into a quest for answers, an attempt to confront the darkness that loomed just beyond our reach.

As we descended the rickety stairs, the air thickened with the scent of damp earth and decay, an aroma that clung to the back of my throat. The light flickered, casting elongated shadows that seemed to dance in mocking delight at our unease. I felt a shiver race down my spine, not from the cold, but from the weight of history pressing against us. This cellar held secrets, layers of time steeped in sorrow and desperation, begging to be uncovered.

We reached the bottom, and the beam from my flashlight caught on something glinting against the far wall. I stepped forward, the floorboards creaking beneath me like a warning. There, half-buried beneath a pile of dusty crates, lay a journal—its leather cover cracked and aged, as though it had borne witness to countless confessions. I reached for it, my fingers trembling with a mix of excitement and dread.

"Is it safe?" Marcus asked, his brows knitted together in concern. He was always the cautious one, the voice of reason that often tempered our more reckless impulses.

"Only one way to find out," I replied with a forced smile, trying to inject a note of levity into the heavy atmosphere. I opened the journal, the pages crackling under my touch like brittle leaves. The ink, though faded, was still legible, scrawled in a hurried, desperate hand that hinted at the chaos the writer had faced.

As I began to read aloud, the flickering flashlight revealed the chilling contents: accounts of rituals conducted in the very cellar we stood in, sacrifices made to appease a spirit whose rage knew no bounds. My heart pounded louder with each revelation, and I could feel the weight of my friends' gaze on me, their anticipation mingling with fear.

"'The blood must flow, the spirit must be fed,'" I read, my voice faltering. The words were heavy, laden with the despair of a people desperate for salvation from an unseen terror. "They thought they could bargain with it, but..."

"But it didn't work," Claire interjected, her eyes wide, a mix of horror and intrigue swirling in her gaze. "It never works, does it?"

"No," I murmured, a chill creeping into my bones. "It only ever leads to more suffering."

A sudden sound—a soft rustling, like the whisper of fabric or the flutter of wings—echoed through the cellar. We froze, eyes darting to the shadows. "Did you hear that?" Marcus whispered, his voice barely above a whisper, as if speaking too loudly would summon whatever lurked in the dark.

"Of course I heard it!" I snapped, though my heart raced not just from fear, but from the thrill of the unknown. "We need to keep going. There has to be more."

With each passing moment, the atmosphere grew thicker, the air electric with the tension of unsaid words. The shadows seemed to coil around us, drawing closer, eager to devour our courage. My flashlight flickered again, the beam dimming before it steadied, and I swallowed hard, feeling the heat of my friends' anxious breaths.

"I think we should head back," Claire said, her voice tinged with urgency. "This feels... wrong."

"No," I insisted, pushing against the doubt gnawing at my resolve. "We came here for answers. We can't turn back now." I could see the fear in her eyes, the flicker of panic beneath the surface, but I couldn't let that discourage me. The secrets of this place were waiting to be uncovered, and I felt an unshakeable connection to the history of it all—a need to understand what had happened, to confront the fear head-on.

With renewed determination, I continued reading, unraveling the twisted tale of anguish and betrayal inscribed in the journal. Each word seemed to weave itself into the air around us, creating a tapestry of terror that clung to our skin. As I read about the blood rituals and the haunting of the spirit, the temperature plummeted, and I could feel the hairs on the back of my neck stand on end.

Suddenly, a loud crash echoed from the far corner of the cellar, reverberating off the stone walls and sending us into a frenzy. Flashlights swung wildly, illuminating fleeting glimpses of fear etched on our faces. "What was that?" Marcus yelled, his voice cracking.

"I don't know!" I shouted back, adrenaline pumping through my veins as we turned towards the noise. The air was charged with fear, and I could almost taste the tension as we collectively held our breath. It felt as if the darkness itself had taken form, pressing in around us, suffocating our resolve.

In that moment, the unthinkable happened. The shadows seemed to shift and swirl, revealing a shape that lurked just beyond the reach of our lights. A figure—tall and ethereal, almost human but cloaked in a veil of darkness—stood watching us with eyes that glimmered like stars against the void. My breath caught in my throat as I realized we weren't alone.

The figure stood in the shadows, its presence palpable, like a heavy mist that pressed against our chests, constricting our breath. The air crackled with a tension that sent my heart racing and sent Claire stumbling backward, nearly colliding with Marcus, who had gone pale as a ghost. I could see the panic bloom in their eyes, mirroring my own burgeoning terror.

"Is that... real?" Claire's voice trembled, wavering like a candle flame in a storm. "Or are we just imagining things?"

"If it's imaginary, it's the best special effect I've ever seen," Marcus retorted, clutching his flashlight as if it were a sword, ready to battle whatever haunted us. His attempt at humor barely masked the tremor in his voice, and I admired his effort to lighten the moment, even as dread pooled in the pit of my stomach.

I took a step forward, driven by a mix of curiosity and fear. "Maybe it wants to communicate," I suggested, my voice steadier than I felt. "We've been reading about the spirit's past. Perhaps it's drawn to us—"

"Or maybe it wants to eat us," Claire interrupted, her eyes wide with alarm. "Let's not start a conversation with whatever that is."

"Great idea, let's all just stand here and stare at it like idiots," I said, biting back a smile despite the gravity of the situation. "What's the worst that could happen?"

The specter's gaze held us captive, its eyes twinkling like distant stars, both alluring and terrifying. As I stepped closer, the shadows flickered, revealing more details—an ethereal gown that flowed like mist, a face shrouded in an aura of sorrow that seemed to resonate with our own trepidation. My pulse quickened, the lines between fear and fascination blurring.

"Maybe it's a guardian spirit," I mused aloud, the words spilling from my lips like a reckless promise. "Maybe it needs our help to find peace."

"You think it needs our help?" Marcus scoffed, raising an eyebrow as he squinted into the darkness. "What kind of help does a ghost need? A therapist? Some sage burning?"

"Less sass, more focus!" Claire hissed, her eyes darting between us and the figure. "If it wanted our help, it could've just asked. It's not like we're fluent in ghost."

As we exchanged nervous banter, the figure shifted, the shadows writhing like smoke around it. I felt a pull, a strange connection, as if the air hummed with unspoken words, begging to be set free. "Please," I whispered, half to myself and half to the spirit. "Show us what you need."

And just like that, the atmosphere shifted. The temperature dropped even further, and a soft, haunting melody drifted through the cellar, wrapping around us like a lover's embrace. The sound was ethereal, filling the space with echoes of longing and pain. It was a lament, a melody steeped in sorrow that resonated within me, tugging at memories I didn't even know I had.

"Is anyone else getting chills?" Claire said, clutching her arms as if to ward off an unseen cold. "This feels... intimate. Creepy intimate."

"Creepy is definitely the vibe," I admitted, my pulse racing with the thrill of the unknown. "But what if this spirit is trying to tell us something important? What if it's leading us to answers?"

Just then, the ghostly figure lifted an arm, gesturing toward a small alcove at the far end of the cellar. It was as if the spirit were urging us to follow, drawing us toward the secrets hidden within the walls. My heart pounded in anticipation and dread. "We should go," I said, glancing back at Marcus and Claire, whose faces mirrored my apprehension.

"Lead the way, brave leader," Marcus quipped, attempting to mask his own fear with humor, though his eyes betrayed the tightness in his chest.

With one last, deep breath, I stepped forward, the beam of my flashlight flickering over the dusty ground as we approached the alcove. The spirit lingered, its presence enveloping us in a protective haze. As we drew closer, I noticed something glinting on the floor—an object half-buried in debris.

"What is that?" Claire asked, squinting to get a better view. The light caught the edges of a small box, ornate and intricate, adorned with symbols that seemed to pulse with a life of their own.

"It looks like a treasure chest," I murmured, kneeling down to examine it more closely. My fingers trembled as I brushed away the dirt, revealing its delicate carvings. "This could be it—the answers we've been searching for."

"Or it could be a one-way ticket to a ghostly curse," Marcus chimed in, peering over my shoulder. "I mean, if that thing is a treasure, I'd prefer to stay poor, thanks."

"Or maybe the treasure is just a box of terrible choices," Claire added, crossing her arms with a skeptical tilt of her head.

Ignoring their banter, I felt compelled to lift the box, the weight of it both reassuring and ominous. "Let's find out what's inside," I declared, feeling an electric thrill at the thought of uncovering a secret long buried. I struggled with the latch, and finally, with a satisfying click, the box sprang open.

Inside, nestled among layers of velvet, lay a collection of artifacts—old coins, tarnished trinkets, and a delicate pendant that sparkled like the ghostly figure before us. I reached for it, entranced, as the spirit drew closer, the sorrow in its gaze deepening.

"What do you want from us?" I breathed, holding the pendant in the palm of my hand. The air grew thick, wrapping around me like a warm cloak.

A rush of wind swept through the cellar, and the spirit's features sharpened, revealing a glimpse of desperation, a silent plea that echoed through the very fabric of the air. The pendant seemed to pulse with energy, a heartbeat of its own, urging me to understand its significance.

"It's a piece of the past," I said slowly, the realization dawning upon me. "This was important to you. It's a connection—a link between your suffering and ours."

Marcus and Claire fell silent, the weight of my words settling in the space between us, heavy and unyielding. The cellar felt charged, the shadows swirling in a dance of revelation and fear. I could sense the spirit's anguish, the history that had led to its unrest.

"We have to help it," I declared, my voice trembling with determination. "Whatever it takes."

The moment I spoke those words, the air shifted again, a palpable wave of energy vibrating through the cellar as if we had touched something deep and ancient. The pendant in my hand felt warm, almost alive, and I could sense the spirit's sorrow coiling around us like a thick fog. Claire's breath hitched as she stepped closer, her curiosity momentarily overpowering her fear.

"What if it's a curse?" she whispered, her brow furrowed with concern. "What if we're unleashing something terrible?"

"Or," Marcus countered, rolling his eyes with a hint of bravado, "we could be the first people in history to make a ghost happy. Think of the headlines! 'Teenagers Find Way to Lift Curse and Become Town Heroes!'"

"Right, because that's how the horror movies start," Claire shot back, crossing her arms tightly against her chest.

I tuned out their banter, focused instead on the pendant, which shimmered with an ethereal glow. "This has to mean something," I said softly, my heart racing with possibility. "It's a part of whatever was lost. Maybe it's a key to setting this spirit free."

The spirit seemed to respond to my words, its shape becoming clearer, more defined. It swayed gently, a ghostly dance that stirred the shadows around it, inviting us closer. As I gazed into those otherworldly eyes, I felt a rush of empathy that flooded through me, pushing back against the chill that had seeped into my bones.

"Okay, I'm convinced," Marcus said, his voice faltering as he took a small step back. "But how do we help it? What does it want from us, a group of teenagers with little more than enthusiasm and a flashlight?"

"Maybe it's more than that," I replied, brushing my thumb over the pendant. "What if this belonged to someone who was wronged? We need to figure out who it was."

Claire took a deep breath, her skepticism wavering as she glanced around the room. "All right. Let's start piecing together this ghost's life, and if it gets too scary, I'm sprinting back up those stairs."

With a small laugh, I nodded, grateful for her willingness to stay. The three of us gathered in a huddle, the pendant resting heavily in my palm like a puzzle piece waiting to click into place. I could sense the weight of history surrounding us, the stories yearning to be told, begging for recognition.

"Let's think," I began, my mind racing through the fragments of the journals I had read earlier. "There were names mentioned—people who performed the rituals, those who sacrificed to the spirit. Maybe if we find out who they were, we can uncover the truth behind all of this."

"Rituals? You mean those bloody ones?" Claire grimaced, her face scrunching as if she had tasted something sour. "You want us to dive into that again?"

"It's all connected," I insisted, fueled by a sudden surge of determination. "We owe it to this spirit to understand what it went through."

"I think you just want an excuse to keep playing detective," Marcus teased, a grin breaking through the anxiety that had settled on his face. "But fine, lead the way, Sherlock."

As we moved back toward the crates, I pulled out another journal, its leather cover cracked but intact. Flipping through the pages, I found sketches that detailed the rituals—symbols, names, and even accounts of the sacrifices that had taken place. The spirit lingered closer now, its energy crackling in the air like static, urging us on.

"There!" I exclaimed, pointing at a sketch of a woman adorned in the same intricate designs that embellished the pendant. "This has to be her—the one who wore this pendant."

"Do you think she's the spirit?" Claire asked, leaning closer to see the drawing. The sketch showed a woman with a serene expression, but her eyes were shadowed by a veil of despair.

"Possibly," I replied, tracing my finger over the lines. "Her name is Lyra. The journal mentions her sacrifices to protect the town, but it also talks about betrayal—she was wronged by those she sought to save."

Marcus's brow furrowed. "So, it's a classic tragedy—loyalty met with treachery. Sounds like a lot of drama. What do we do with that information?"

"Maybe it's not just about uncovering the past," I suggested, my mind racing. "If we can find out who betrayed her, we might be able to restore her honor. Perhaps that's what she needs to find peace."

"Great," Claire sighed, rolling her eyes. "Now we're ghost lawyers too."

"Better than being ghost snacks," Marcus replied, trying to inject some humor into the situation. "Though I still vote we don't stick around if things get hairy."

Just as I opened the journal again, the spirit flickered, and the air thickened, pulling us into a sudden hush. A new sound crept through the cellar—a low, rumbling noise that reverberated like a growl, echoing off the stone walls.

"What the heck is that?" Claire gasped, her bravado momentarily forgotten.

"I don't know," I replied, gripping the journal tightly. The hairs on the back of my neck stood on end, and I could feel the temperature plummeting, a cold breath wrapping around us like a warning. The spirit wailed softly, its form shimmering with agitation.

"Let's get out of here," Marcus urged, his earlier bravado faltering as panic seeped into his voice. "I don't like this. I really don't like this."

"No, wait," I said, my instincts screaming at me to stay. "What if it's trying to warn us? We can't run away now, not when we're so close."

Before I could finish, the growl escalated into a deafening roar, shaking the very foundations of the cellar. The shadows twisted and contorted, forming dark shapes that swirled around us like a storm.

"Get ready!" I shouted, adrenaline surging through my veins. "Stay together!"

As the noise crescendoed, the shadows burst forth, engulfing the spirit, and with one final cry, it dissipated into the darkness. My heart raced as the very ground beneath us trembled, dust and debris falling from the ceiling like rain.

"Run!" Claire screamed, but as we turned to escape, the entrance to the cellar vanished into an impenetrable wall of shadow, trapping us within. The air crackled with energy, the echoes of the past threatening to consume us as we stood on the precipice of an unknown terror, our breaths quickening in the suffocating dark.

In that moment, I realized we were not just uncovering a story; we had become part of it. And as the shadows closed in, I understood the true weight of what lay ahead—our very lives hanging in the balance, entwined with the fate of a spirit desperate for resolution.

Chapter 20: The Broken Seal

The air crackled with an electric tension as we stood there, each breath laden with the weight of the relic's presence. I glanced at my friends, their expressions mirroring my own cocktail of dread and exhilaration. Liam's jaw was set, determination carved into the lines of his face, while Clara's wide eyes glimmered with a mix of fear and curiosity that made my heart race. It was a strange sensation, this merging of anxiety and exhilaration, as if we were teetering on the precipice of something grand and terrible.

The hidden compartment yawned open before us, revealing a box ornately carved with swirling designs that seemed to move in the flickering candlelight. Dark wood, aged and warped, contrasted sharply against the dust motes swirling in the shafts of light, as if the very air whispered secrets of the past. I felt an odd tug at my consciousness, a compulsion to reach out and touch it, but a voice—a whisper, barely a murmur—cautioned me to hold back. "Careful, Zara," I heard Liam say, his voice low but urgent, breaking the spell that wrapped around me. "We don't know what this thing is."

"Or what it's been waiting for," Clara added, her voice trembling slightly. She took a step back, her gaze darting around the dimly lit room, as if expecting the shadows to spring to life.

There was a palpable pause, a heartbeat where time seemed to stretch, before I felt an irresistible pull to that relic, like a moth to a flame. "We have to see what's inside," I breathed, glancing back at my friends. "It's the only way to understand what's happening in Ashwood. If we don't confront this, we'll never escape it."

Liam hesitated, the muscle in his jaw twitching as he weighed my words. Finally, with a resolute nod, he stepped closer, and I followed, each step filled with a mixture of trepidation and anticipation. As we knelt before the box, the air thickened around us, pressing down like a weight. I could feel the energy pulsating from the wood, an eerie heartbeat that synchronized with my own.

With a trembling hand, I reached out, brushing my fingers against the intricate carvings. The moment I made contact, a shiver shot through my body, a current of raw energy that sparked something deep within me. The world around us blurred, the edges softening as my mind was flooded with visions, dark and vivid. I was no longer just a bystander in this ancient tale; I was plunged into the depths of its sorrow.

Visions unspooled before my eyes—a woman, her face etched with grief, standing alone in a dimly lit room. Her hands, delicate and shaking, clutched a faded photograph. I could feel her anguish, the isolation that wrapped around her like a shroud. The echoes of her despair reverberated through my soul, a haunting melody of loss and longing.

"Zara!" Liam's voice cut through the haze, his hand gripping my shoulder, grounding me. The vision shattered, and I gasped, blinking back tears that threatened to spill over. "What did you see?" he pressed, concern etching deeper lines on his forehead.

"I... I don't know. It was a woman, she was... she was suffering." My voice trembled, the weight of her pain still clinging to me. "There was so much sorrow."

Clara stepped forward, her eyes bright with a mix of fear and determination. "This relic—it's not just a thing. It's a vessel of emotions, a keeper of stories. We need to know why it was sealed away."

I nodded, the gravity of our task settling around us. With a deep breath, I lifted the lid of the box. It creaked ominously, echoing through the room like a warning. Inside lay an assortment of objects—each one more peculiar than the last. A rusted locket, its clasp broken; a yellowed letter, edges frayed; a small, cracked mirror that caught the candlelight and shimmered like a dark star.

But it was the dark crystal nestled at the bottom that drew my gaze. It pulsed with a dull, sickly light, as if it held the remnants of the anguish I had just witnessed. "What is that?" Clara whispered, leaning closer, her breath hitching in her throat.

"I think it's the source," I replied, unable to tear my eyes away from its dark beauty. "The spirit... it's trapped here, bound to this object."

Just as the words left my mouth, a chilling wind swept through the room, extinguishing the flickering candles and plunging us into darkness. My heart raced, and I felt the world tilt as an icy dread wrapped around me. "What the hell was that?" Liam shouted, his voice a mix of bravado and fear.

"Stay together!" I urged, but the room felt alive, thrumming with energy that pulsed like a heartbeat, echoing my own panic. I could feel the relic's power coursing through me, a blend of fear and rage that threatened to spill over.

Suddenly, the walls trembled, and a low, mournful wail filled the air, rising like a specter from the shadows. It resonated within me, a cry of desperation and longing that seemed to claw at the very fabric of my being. "This isn't just about us," I said, my voice steadying against the rising tide of chaos. "We have to listen to it. This spirit wants to be heard."

Liam squeezed my hand, and I felt his warmth against the chill. "What if it doesn't just want to be heard?" he asked, his brow furrowing. "What if it wants revenge?"

In that moment, the world shifted once more, the relic before us shimmering with a malevolent glow. I could feel the air thickening, a storm brewing on the horizon, and I knew we had only begun to scratch the surface of the horrors that awaited us in Ashwood.

The wail echoed in the shadows, wrapping around us like a cold fog. I felt the hairs on my arms stand at attention, each minute tremor pulsating in rhythm with the haunting cry. "Maybe it's just asking for a cup of tea," Clara quipped, her voice shaky but trying to break the tension that thickened the air. It was a brave attempt, but the fear in her eyes betrayed her.

"Right, because what every malevolent spirit needs is a proper British tea service," Liam shot back, though a hint of a grin tugged at the corner of his mouth. The moment felt fragile, the kind where laughter could either diffuse the dread or shatter our focus. I chose to latch onto the fleeting levity, drawing courage from it.

"Let's just... let's try to communicate," I suggested, my voice steadier than I felt. "Maybe it doesn't want to harm us. Maybe it's trapped." I leaned closer to the relic, the crystal pulsing with an ominous glow, inviting and threatening in equal measure. The air was thick, vibrating with unspoken words that yearned for release. "I can feel it, you know? This spirit—its pain is woven into the very fabric of this place."

"Great, just what I need," Liam muttered, crossing his arms. "An emotional ghost with abandonment issues. Sounds like a blast."

Clara snorted, the tension breaking just enough to let a sliver of light through. "Maybe it needs a hug," she said, stepping a little closer, her hand hovering over the relic as if it could provide comfort.

I laughed softly, though I couldn't shake the ominous feeling that loomed over us. "If only that were the solution."

As I spoke, the air shimmered around the crystal, and the ghostly wail transformed into a series of fragmented whispers, swirling in my ears like leaves caught in a tempest. "Zara... help..." The voice was barely above a whisper, filled with anguish and desperation.

My heart pounded, each beat a reminder of the urgency that surrounded us. "Did you hear that?" I looked up, meeting Liam's wide eyes. "It's asking for help!"

Liam took a deep breath, running a hand through his hair, a gesture that always betrayed his nerves. "So what do we do? Do we just start talking to it? Because I'm not exactly fluent in ghost."

"We start by asking it what it needs," I replied, the words tumbling out before I could think better of them. "We need to break whatever binds it here." I felt a surge of confidence, fueled by the urgency of the spirit's plea.

"Alright, let's give it a shot," Clara said, stepping forward. "We're here for you," she called, her voice steady, though the tremor lingered. "We want to help. Just... tell us what you need."

As the last word left her mouth, the crystal flickered violently, the shadows around us twisting and swirling like a dark whirlpool. The whispers morphed into a cacophony, a chorus of anguished voices pleading and shrieking in dissonance. I pressed my hands over my ears, trying to block out the overwhelming sound.

Suddenly, a sharp crack split the air, reverberating through the room. "That's not good," Liam said, his bravado faltering.

"Stay back!" I shouted as the relic surged with energy, the glow intensifying until it illuminated the room in a blinding light. The walls trembled, and I could feel the very foundation of the house vibrating beneath our feet.

Then, just as abruptly as it began, everything stopped. The silence was deafening, thick with the remnants of what had just occurred. Cautiously, I lowered my hands, glancing at my friends. "Are we still alive?"

"Last time I checked, yeah," Clara replied, her voice barely above a whisper. "But I think we just triggered something."

A pulse of energy emanated from the crystal, drawing my gaze back to it. The once-ominous glow softened, revealing a swirling image within—visions of the woman I had seen earlier, her face streaked with tears, reaching out as if grasping for something just beyond her reach. I felt an ache in my chest, the weight of her sorrow pressing against my heart.

"What is she trying to tell us?" I murmured, stepping closer. The image flickered, momentarily morphing into dark figures standing behind her, their faces obscured, but their intent was clear. They loomed like shadows, threatening to swallow her whole.

"Zara, don't," Liam warned, but I couldn't pull myself away. I was entranced, tethered to the moment.

"She needs our help," I insisted, my voice gaining strength. "If we can reach her, we might understand what's binding her spirit."

"But how?" Clara asked, fear threading through her words. "What if we're just making it worse?"

"Then we face it together," I replied, my determination rising. "We can't let her suffer alone."

With that resolve, I took a deep breath and closed my eyes, centering myself. "We're here for you," I said, my voice a soothing balm in the oppressive silence. "You're not alone. We will help you."

The image in the crystal flickered again, the woman's expression shifting from despair to cautious hope. A moment passed—one fragile, shimmering moment—before the shadows surged, enveloping her like a shroud. A low rumble echoed through the room, and I felt a sudden chill seep into my bones.

Liam stepped closer, his hand clasping mine, grounding me. "What now?" he murmured, his eyes darting around, still on edge.

"Now we listen," I replied, a mixture of fear and anticipation coursing through me. "Whatever this spirit needs, we have to be ready to confront it."

But even as I spoke, the energy in the room shifted, crackling with intensity. I could feel it rising, swelling like a storm about to break. My heart raced, caught between the thrill of discovery and the dread of what lay ahead. Whatever happened next, I knew we were standing on the brink of something monumental, a confrontation with the very essence of grief that had lingered too long in Ashwood.

The shadows flickered in response to our collective breath, each inhale laden with anticipation. I could feel the temperature plummet, an icy draft swirling around us as if the very walls were alive, breathing in sync with the pulsating energy of the relic. Clara shivered beside me, and I caught a glimpse of her biting her lip, a gesture of anxiety that felt all too familiar.

"Okay, so let's put our collective heads together here," Liam said, attempting to steer us back to some semblance of rationality. "What do we actually know about this woman? Other than the fact that she's apparently suffering from some serious abandonment issues."

I couldn't help but chuckle, even in the face of danger. "Right, because that's the first thing on the agenda. But honestly, we need to find out who she is, and why she's here. Maybe she's connected to Ashwood's history."

Clara's eyes widened as a flicker of inspiration struck her. "There were those stories we uncovered at the library—the ones about the Ashwood estate and the family that lived here. They had a tragic end, right?"

"Right," I replied, feeling a spark of excitement. "The widow who lost everything. Perhaps that's her."

Liam groaned dramatically, rolling his eyes. "So we're dealing with a vengeful ghost, a broken heart, and some serious emotional baggage. Fantastic."

"Look at it this way," I said, trying to inject a bit of optimism into the conversation. "If we can help her find peace, maybe she'll stop haunting the place. We could be saving the town from a ghostly tourism fiasco."

Clara laughed, though the tension in her shoulders didn't ease. "You may be onto something there. But first, we need to figure out how to reach her."

We turned our attention back to the relic, now humming with energy, its dark crystal almost vibrating with an inner light. I took a deep breath, feeling a sudden rush of bravery wash over me. "What if we try to recreate the moment she was trapped? Maybe it will help us connect with her."

"Are you suggesting we reenact some tragic play?" Liam raised an eyebrow, a teasing smirk dancing on his lips. "Because I'm not sure my dramatic skills are up to the challenge."

"Just go with it," I replied, nudging him playfully. "Let's bring her story to the surface."

Clara's brow furrowed as she considered my words. "You mean like a seance? That's... not exactly foolproof."

"Yeah, because we're not already in a horror movie," Liam chimed in, his sarcasm thick. But beneath the jest, I could sense his eagerness to help.

"Let's just try it," I said, feeling a fierce resolve solidify within me. "We can't let fear dictate our actions. The only way to break this cycle is to confront it head-on."

Liam sighed dramatically, but I could see the glint of determination in his eyes. "Fine. Let's have ourselves a ghostly therapy session. Just don't expect me to take notes."

With the stage set, I took a step closer to the relic, the pulsating energy drawing me in like a moth to a flame. "We're here for you," I began, my voice steady. "We want to help you find peace."

The air crackled, and I could feel the shadows closing in, thickening around us. "Tell us your name," I urged, willing the spirit to reveal herself. "We're listening."

For a moment, silence blanketed the room, a taut string waiting to snap. Then, the whispers returned, flowing like a river of sorrow, echoing through the walls. "Adelaide..."

The name hung in the air, a fragile thread weaving us into the fabric of her history. "Adelaide," I repeated softly, testing the name on my tongue. "We're here to help you. What do you need?"

The room trembled, and the crystal flared with a brilliant light, illuminating the contours of our faces. Suddenly, a vision unfurled before us—Adelaide, a young woman draped in a flowing gown, her features luminous yet marred by grief. She stood in a grand hall, surrounded by echoes of laughter that faded into chilling silence as shadows crept closer, clutching at her dress like phantom fingers.

"What happened to you?" Clara gasped, her voice breaking the trance. "Why are you trapped here?"

The vision flickered, and I could see her eyes—filled with desperation and fear, searching for something lost. My heart ached for her, this spirit bound by sorrow, and I reached out instinctively, as if I could touch her essence through the barrier of time.

"I loved..." Her voice echoed, low and haunting. "I was betrayed..."

The shadows thickened, and a sudden rush of wind swept through the room, extinguishing the remaining candles, plunging us into darkness. Panic surged, but then a voice cut through, steady and calm. "Adelaide, you are not alone. We can help you find peace. Just show us what you need."

But before I could finish, the shadows erupted, swirling violently as the darkness materialized into a shape—a dark figure stepping forth from the void. The air crackled with tension as it loomed before us, its presence suffocating and filled with an aura of menace.

Liam instinctively stepped in front of Clara, a protective instinct surging through him. "What the hell is that?" he shouted, his bravado dissipating in the face of this new threat.

"Adelaide!" I cried, my heart racing as the shadows coalesced, taking on a grotesque form. The spirit's pain echoed through the room, and I felt my pulse quicken as the darkness encroached upon us.

"Help me!" The plea rang out, not just from Adelaide but from the darkness itself.

Just as the figure reached out, tendrils of shadow stretching toward us, the crystal flared one last time, illuminating the room in a blinding light. In that moment, everything froze—the world hanging in a precarious balance.

And then it shattered.

The force of it knocked me back, sending me sprawling against the wall, the air crackling around me as I gasped for breath. I blinked against the brightness, my vision swimming as I struggled to regain my footing.

"Zara!" Clara's voice broke through the chaos, panic lacing her words.

I looked up, dread pooling in my stomach as I met her terrified gaze. The figure loomed closer, and in that split second, I realized the truth: whatever had been unleashed was far worse than we had ever imagined, and the stakes were higher than we could have ever prepared for.

Chapter 21: The Heart's Battle

The air in the attic was thick with dust and the scent of old wood, a musty reminder of days long past. Sunlight slanted through the single grimy window, illuminating the motes that danced lazily in the stillness. I knelt among the scattered remnants of my childhood, searching through boxes filled with forgotten toys and tattered books. Each artifact held a memory—a tiny soldier that had once led an epic battle across my carpet, a worn-out teddy bear with one eye that had listened to my secrets through countless sleepless nights. They whispered to me now, drawing me into the labyrinth of my past.

"Found anything interesting?" Liam's voice, warm and teasing, broke through my reverie. He leaned against the doorframe, arms crossed, the sunlight casting an almost ethereal glow around him. I turned to him, an involuntary smile tugging at my lips. How could I not feel lighter in his presence? He had a way of grounding me, a steadfast anchor in the storm of confusion swirling in my mind.

"Just some ghosts of my childhood," I replied, chuckling softly as I held up a battered book with a faded cover. "This one was my favorite—'The Adventures of Wonderwort.' It was about a brave little elf who saved his kingdom from darkness." My voice faltered slightly at the mention of darkness, memories creeping in like shadows. "Funny how I thought that was just a story back then."

"Sometimes, the scariest stories turn out to be the most real," he said, a hint of gravity in his tone. His eyes searched mine, as if probing the depths of my fears. I felt exposed, the way we used to feel when our parents would ask us to share our dreams in front of the family at dinner—vulnerable and uncertain.

I glanced down, tracing my fingers over the embossed letters on the cover, feeling the weight of my past pressing in on me. "There were monsters lurking in my closet," I confessed, the admission tumbling out before I could stop it. "I would sit up for hours, convinced they were waiting for the perfect moment to pounce."

Liam stepped closer, the warmth radiating from him wrapping around me like a comforting blanket. "Did they ever come out?" he asked, his voice low, as if afraid to disturb the fragile atmosphere that enveloped us.

"No," I replied, the honesty surprising even myself. "I guess I realized eventually that the real monsters were in my head." I laughed softly, but it felt hollow. The revelation was bittersweet, a reminder of the battles I had fought alone, shielded from the chaos of reality by my own imagination.

As we sifted through the remnants of my childhood, I felt a connection deepening between us—a tether binding our stories together. Each revelation felt like a step closer to unraveling the mystery of the relic, but it also felt like I was stripping away layers of myself, revealing the scars I had hidden for so long.

Just as I uncovered an old photo album, its pages yellowed and brittle, a sudden chill raced through the attic. I glanced at Liam, whose expression had shifted from playful to serious in an instant. "Did you feel that?" he asked, his voice barely above a whisper.

"Yeah," I admitted, the hairs on my arms standing on end. A shadow flickered at the edge of my vision, and I turned, heart pounding, to see a figure looming at the entrance of the attic.

The air grew heavy with tension as the figure stepped into the light. Cloaked in darkness, a hood obscured its features, but the malevolence radiating from it was palpable. My heart raced, panic clawing at my throat. "Who are you?" I demanded, my voice steadier than I felt.

Liam instinctively moved closer, positioning himself between me and the encroaching threat. "You shouldn't be here," he stated firmly, the protective instinct flaring in his voice.

"Ah, but here I am," the figure replied, voice smooth like silk, yet laced with malice. "And you two are meddling in matters that are far beyond your understanding."

"What do you want?" I shot back, anger flaring as I took a step forward, emboldened by Liam's presence. I could feel the weight of the relic's mystery pressing down on us, its energy crackling in the air.

"The relic belongs to the one who knows how to wield it," the figure said, each word dripping with condescension. "And you are woefully unprepared for the truth it holds."

In that moment, the room shifted—the walls seemed to pulse with energy, and I felt an overwhelming urge to reach for the relic, hidden deep within the confines of my heart. "We're not afraid of you," I declared, my voice rising with newfound resolve.

"Oh, you should be," the figure retorted, stepping closer, revealing a glint of something sharp in its hand. "Fear is a powerful weapon, and you're about to discover just how sharp it can be."

Liam's presence beside me was electric, and as we exchanged a glance, a silent understanding passed between us. Together, we were stronger. "Whatever you're planning, you won't succeed," he said, his voice a steady rumble of conviction.

With that, the shadows around the figure seemed to pulse, feeding off the tension in the room, and I could feel the weight of our destiny pressing down upon us. The heart's battle was just beginning, and we were standing on the precipice of something far greater than we could ever have imagined.

The figure before us loomed, a specter of menace wrapped in layers of shadow that clung to it like a shroud. The air thickened, charged with an electric tension, and I could feel my heart thudding in my chest, each beat a reminder of my vulnerability. "You think you can simply unearth what is buried?" it taunted, voice smooth but edged with a cruel laughter that echoed in the rafters.

"What's buried deserves to stay buried," I shot back, though I felt the tremor in my hands as I spoke. Liam stood firm beside me, an unwavering fortress against the encroaching darkness. I appreciated his resolve, but it also ignited a fire within me—this was my past we were dealing with, my fears unearthing themselves in the most literal of ways.

"I can sense your fear," the figure hissed, stepping into the light, revealing a face twisted with malice. A jagged scar ran down one cheek, and its eyes glowed with a predatory glint. "You're tethered to a legacy of nightmares. The relic—" it paused, savoring the word like a fine wine, "—will be my gateway to power, and I intend to reclaim it."

"Reclaim? You mean steal," I replied, my voice sharper than I felt, the words fueled by desperation and defiance. "You don't belong here. You're not welcome."

The figure laughed, a low, mocking sound that ricocheted off the attic walls. "Welcome? Child, I didn't come to be welcomed. I came to take what is mine."

Before I could formulate a response, a rush of wind swept through the attic, scattering dust motes like frightened butterflies. The figure's cloak flared, the shadows swirling around it as if they had a life of their own. "You're too naive to understand the power you're meddling with," it continued, and with each word, I felt the weight of its intent pressing against me, like a physical force trying to drive me back.

"Naive?" I echoed, astonishment flaring. "I've faced more than you can imagine. You think you can intimidate me with some dramatic flair?"

"Dramatic flair?" Liam's voice, a steadying current amidst the chaos, cut through my rising frustration. "This is not a stage, and you're not the main act. You're just a bad afterthought in her story."

The figure's eyes narrowed, surprise flickering across its face before it twisted into a scowl. "You should tread carefully, boy. Your fate is intricately linked to hers."

My pulse quickened as I glanced at Liam, realizing the weight of those words. What did it mean for him to be intertwined with my destiny? Would our bond strengthen us or expose us to greater danger?

I steeled my resolve, grounding myself in the moment. "Whatever fate awaits us, we face it together," I declared, my voice ringing with conviction.

"You think that unity can shield you from the inevitable?" The figure took a step forward, shadows stretching toward us like greedy fingers. "Love is a weakness, and you are both weak."

"Funny, I thought the only weakness here was your comprehension of love," I shot back, my voice laced with sass, surprising even myself. "And I've seen stronger monsters than you hide behind their shadows."

With a flick of its wrist, the figure unleashed a wave of darkness, a swirling vortex that threatened to engulf us. I braced myself, instinctively reaching for Liam's hand. Our fingers entwined, a spark igniting between us as the shadows crashed against an unseen barrier.

"Together!" he shouted, and the command echoed in my mind. I could feel the energy of the relic surging within me, awakening something I had buried deep. The connection between us pulsed like a heartbeat, a lifeline that resonated through the chaos.

As we stood united, I felt the shadows recoil, as if stung by our determination. "You think love can withstand the darkness?" the figure hissed, a tremor of fear threading through its voice.

"Not just love," I replied, my voice stronger now, clarity cutting through the haze of panic. "Hope and courage are far more powerful than you realize."

Liam's grip tightened around my hand, and together, we focused our energy, channeling our strength toward the swirling darkness. The room began to glow with an otherworldly light, illuminating the corners of the attic that had long been lost to shadow.

With a fierce yell, we pushed back against the encroaching darkness, the relic's energy surging between us like a river breaking free from its dam. The shadows shrieked, twisting and writhing as we forced them away, banishing the figure momentarily into the recesses of the attic.

"Run," Liam urged, eyes blazing with urgency. "We have to get to the relic!"

As we sprinted toward the corner where the old trunk lay, I could hear the figure recovering, its voice a low growl. "You can't escape me, little girl. You're tethered to me, and I will always find you."

I shuddered at the threat lacing its words, a chill creeping down my spine. "You're wrong," I yelled back, racing toward the trunk. "I'm not defined by my past! I'll forge my own destiny!"

With trembling hands, I fumbled with the latch of the trunk, feeling the weight of what lay inside. The relic pulsed against my fingertips, a heartbeat echoing in time with my own. The trunk creaked open, and I caught sight of the shimmering object nestled within—an ornate pendant, glinting in the dim light, as if calling to me.

Just then, the figure lunged forward, shadowy tendrils reaching out, desperate to reclaim its power. Liam moved in front of me, a barrier of strength, determination etched on his face. "Not today," he growled, and I felt a rush of gratitude swell within me, mixed with fear.

In that moment, the relic seemed to respond to our combined will, the light expanding outward, illuminating the entire attic in a brilliant glow. The shadows recoiled, and the figure let out a howl of fury, momentarily staggering back.

"Together," I whispered, knowing that whatever happened next would define us. Our hearts beat as one, and with a shared breath, we drew upon the strength of our bond.

As we unleashed the energy, the relic flared with light, casting the shadows away, illuminating the path to a future we could shape together.

The light from the relic burst forth, illuminating every corner of the attic and banishing the shadows that had been a physical manifestation of my fears. The figure shrieked, its voice a dissonant chord in the otherwise vibrant space. It staggered back, retreating into the dimness as if the brightness were a tangible force, a wall it could not penetrate. I felt the pulse of the relic in my hand, urging me to harness its power, to stand firm against the encroaching darkness.

"Now!" Liam shouted, and I didn't need to be told twice. Together, we stepped forward, the energy of the relic swirling around us, creating a protective barrier that pushed the shadows further back. My heart raced, not just from fear, but from a burgeoning sense of purpose that surged through me.

"What are you waiting for?" the figure hissed, its tone dripping with contempt. "You think a little light can protect you? You are nothing but a flicker in the abyss!"

"Flicker or not," I retorted, fire igniting in my belly, "we'll shine bright enough to burn you out." My voice was steadier than I felt, the courage swelling inside me like a tide.

With a determined flick of my wrist, I focused the energy of the relic, drawing upon the memories that had once haunted me. Each recollection—fear, loneliness, the childhood nights spent peering into the darkness—added weight to my resolve. I could hear Liam's voice beside me, steady and strong, murmuring words of encouragement, reminding me that I wasn't alone in this fight.

The shadows lunged forward, their twisted forms writhing like snakes. I could feel their cold touch brushing against my skin, trying to snuff out my light, but I pressed on, channeling the relic's energy, my own will intertwining with Liam's unwavering presence.

"Together!" I shouted, and we released the energy, a vibrant cascade of light that shot forward, illuminating the figure and forcing it back against the far wall.

"Your light may be strong, but it is not enough!" the figure roared, launching itself at us with a speed that left me momentarily breathless. It collided with our barrier, the force sending a shockwave through the attic that rattled the old beams overhead. Dust rained down like confetti, but I stood firm, feeling the heat of the relic humming beneath my palm, urging me to press forward.

"Stay close!" Liam yelled, and I could see the strain on his face as he braced himself against the dark tide. "We need to push it back! Focus on the relic, remember what it represents!"

The figure's eyes burned with a malevolent fury, and I could see it coiling itself, preparing for another attack. "You'll regret this! The past never truly dies; it merely sleeps, waiting for its chance to return."

With those words, the shadows surged forward once more, a wave of darkness that seemed almost alive, a creature desperate to reclaim its territory. I felt a flicker of doubt creep in, but Liam's hand tightened around mine, anchoring me to the moment.

"Remember the elf, the bravery, the light?" he reminded me, and I recalled my childhood hero, Wonderwort, who faced down darkness with nothing but courage and a glimmer of hope. I could almost hear the old tales echoing in my mind, the wisdom of those stories lending me strength.

The relic pulsed violently, responding to my thoughts, the air around us crackling with energy. "Let's give it a taste of what real light can do," I declared, resolve solidifying within me. We drew upon our combined strength, letting the relic's energy surge through us, and released it with a fierce cry.

A brilliant beam shot forward, slicing through the shadows and hitting the figure square in the chest. It screamed—a sound that chilled my blood, reverberating against the attic walls as the light exploded, a supernova of defiance that momentarily blinded us all.

When the light subsided, I squinted through the haze, and for a moment, the attic lay still. The figure lay sprawled against the far wall, shadows retreating, the glow of the relic illuminating its twisted form. I could hardly believe we'd done it; we had pushed back the darkness, at least for now.

"We did it!" I exclaimed, exhilaration rushing through me. "We actually—"

But the triumph was short-lived. With a sudden jolt, the figure rose, its form flickering like a flame on the brink of extinguishment. "You think you've won?" it sneered, a dark smile spreading across its lips. "The darkness is always waiting, biding its time. You may have struck me down today, but I am merely a shadow of the true darkness that lurks in your past."

Liam's grip tightened on my hand, his expression a mix of shock and determination. "What do you mean?"

"The relic was never yours to wield," it spat, and in that moment, I felt the air shift, a chill creeping back into the room. "It belongs to the one who knows how to control its power, and that's not you."

The shadows surged around us, a torrent that seemed to swallow the light, and I realized with a start that the figure was gathering strength. "We have to go!" I urged, panic surging through me.

As we turned to flee, the figure lunged forward, shadows twisting like a serpent, snaking toward us with unnerving speed. "You cannot escape your fate!" it shouted, voice echoing in a cacophony of rage.

"Run!" Liam yelled, pulling me toward the staircase that led down into the house. I stumbled, the urgency of the moment propelling me forward, but a sudden gust of wind blew through the attic, slamming the door shut behind us with a deafening bang.

We were trapped.

The figure's laughter filled the space, dark and mocking. "You may have light, but here, in my domain, shadows reign supreme."

As I turned, my heart pounding in my chest, I caught a glimpse of the figure's eyes—feral and alive, reflecting the flickering light of the relic, now dimming against the oppressive darkness. The atmosphere crackled with energy, and I could feel the weight of its presence bearing down on us, tightening like a noose.

"Liam, what do we do?" I gasped, feeling the dread coiling around me as the shadows began to swirl, forming a vortex that pulled at my very essence.

He looked at me, determination flaring in his eyes, but even he seemed to waver as the darkness surged. "We fight. We fight for each other, for the light, for everything we are."

But just as he spoke, the shadows surged forward, enveloping us in a suffocating grip. I could feel the weight of the darkness pressing down, suffocating, blinding, and in that moment, I knew—this battle was far from over.

As the shadows engulfed us, a single thought pierced through the chaos: We might be united against the darkness, but how long could our light hold out against the encroaching shadows?

Chapter 22: The Reckoning

The air hung thick with the scent of damp earth and fallen leaves, each breath drawing in the weight of history and the chill of impending dread. Ashwood had always thrummed with a heartbeat of its own, a gentle pulse that wove through the cobblestone streets and the crumbling facades of ancient buildings. But now, that pulse was erratic, haunted by a malevolence that clawed at the very essence of the town. I stood at the edge of the old town square, my heart hammering against my ribcage as Clara and Liam flanked me, their faces set in grim determination.

"Do you feel it?" Clara whispered, her eyes wide, flickering between the shadows that danced in the flickering light of the streetlamps. "It's alive, and it's angry."

I nodded, the words lodged in my throat, heavy with the reality of our situation. The relic we had uncovered, a seemingly innocuous trinket tucked away in the dusty attic of the old library, had become a beacon for something darker. Something that had slumbered for centuries, now awakened and vengeful, seeking to reclaim its dominion over Ashwood. The townsfolk had been blissfully unaware of the storm brewing beneath their feet, lulled into a false sense of security by the very beauty of their surroundings. But as the skies darkened and the wind howled like a wild animal, I understood that their ignorance was a dangerous luxury.

"Whatever it is, we can't let it take Ashwood," Liam growled, his jaw clenched, muscles taut under the weight of the impending confrontation. His strength had always been a comfort, a steadfast presence in the chaos that surrounded us. I glanced at him, his blue eyes shimmering with intensity, and felt a flicker of hope amid the dread. Together, we had faced countless trials, and this would be no different.

The spirit's anguished cries pierced the air, reverberating through the square like a siren's call. It was a sound of loss, betrayal, and an insatiable thirst for revenge. The townspeople, now aware of the disturbance, peeked cautiously from behind their curtains, their faces ghostly pale, their whispers mingling with the wind. Fear rippled through them like a wave, yet they remained rooted in their homes, unwilling to confront the darkness looming just beyond their doorsteps.

"Get ready," I murmured, my voice steady despite the tremor of my heart. I reached for the charm that hung from my neck, the only tangible remnant of our bond with the town. It felt warm against my skin, as if it too pulsed with a heartbeat, one that synchronized with the very essence of Ashwood. "We have to show it we're not afraid."

"Easier said than done," Clara replied, her usual sarcasm laced with an undercurrent of tension. She adjusted her glasses, the frame slipping slightly down her nose, giving her a slightly comical yet endearing appearance. "What's our battle plan? I don't have a PhD in exorcism or anything."

"Right, we need a plan," I replied, my mind racing. "But first, we need to draw it out." I glanced toward the old fountain at the center of the square, its waters long dried up, the stonework overrun with moss and vines. It seemed the perfect spot for a confrontation, a stage set for the chaos that was about to unfold. "If we can just lure it into the open..."

"Great idea," Liam interjected, his voice tinged with urgency. "But how?"

Before I could respond, a cold gust swept through the square, sending shivers down my spine and making the leaves dance in a frenzied whirl. The ground trembled, the cobblestones beneath our feet vibrating with the force of an unseen presence. "Now!" I shouted, instinct taking over. "Clara, do you have the relic?"

Clara fumbled in her bag, producing the relic, its surface glinting ominously under the dim light. It was a small, intricate piece, adorned with runes that seemed to writhe and pulse with energy. "I've got it! But how do we use it?"

"Just hold it up," I instructed, my heart racing as the spirit's howls crescendoed into a deafening roar. "We need to show it we're not afraid. We have the power to banish it."

Clara nodded, raising the relic high above her head. As she did, the winds began to swirl violently around us, howling like a banshee, and the ground shook more fiercely, threatening to swallow us whole. Shadows elongated, twisting into grotesque shapes that darted from the edges of our vision. I could almost hear the spirit's furious laughter, a cruel mockery of our bravery.

"Stay together!" Liam shouted, grounding us as we formed a tight circle, our collective strength pulsing in the air like an electric current. I could feel Clara's hand trembling beside mine, and I squeezed it, offering what little reassurance I could muster.

The spirit manifested before us, a swirling mass of darkness, eyes like glowing embers glinting with malice. "You think you can challenge me?" it hissed, a voice that dripped with ancient resentment. "This town belongs to me! I was the heart of Ashwood long before you dared to tread its soil."

"No," I shot back, my voice gaining strength as the fear began to ebb. "You were a shadow, a fragment of a memory, and we're not here to surrender."

With that declaration, a surge of courage unfurled within me, intertwining with the energy of the relic in Clara's hand. The air shimmered around us, and a brilliant light erupted from the trinket, illuminating the square in an ethereal glow. The spirit recoiled, its form shimmering and wavering as it struggled against the brilliance.

"Together!" I shouted, and as one, we focused our energy into the relic. The light expanded, engulfing the spirit, and for a moment,

I could see its true form—a tortured figure, wracked with pain and longing. A flicker of sympathy washed over me, but it was drowned out by the need to protect our home.

The spirit howled, a sound both anguished and furious, and I felt the ground beneath us tremble violently as it writhed against the light. "You cannot defeat me! I will reclaim what is mine!"

As the battle escalated, I knew this was only the beginning. The fight for Ashwood would demand everything from us, testing our limits and unraveling secrets that lay hidden in the town's history. But at that moment, standing with Clara and Liam, the weight of our fears lifted just a fraction, replaced by an unshakeable resolve. We would not let Ashwood fall into darkness—not today.

The brilliance of the relic pulsed with a fierce intensity, casting long shadows that flickered and danced across the cobblestones like playful spirits. I held my breath, heart racing as the light enveloped the spirit, its form shifting between solid and vaporous, like smoke curling in the breeze. The air crackled with energy, a static charge that prickled against my skin, urging me forward.

"Can you feel that?" Clara exclaimed, her voice a mixture of awe and terror. "It's like the town is holding its breath."

"Or it's about to scream," I retorted, adrenaline coursing through me as I clenched my fists, willing the light to strengthen. The spirit loomed larger, its malevolent eyes boring into us, a storm of rage and desperation swirling in its gaze.

"You foolish children," it hissed, its voice a low growl that rumbled through the square like distant thunder. "You think your light can vanquish me? I am the keeper of this town's secrets! I am the darkness that birthed Ashwood!"

"No, you're the reason we're standing here fighting," Liam shouted, his voice a steady anchor amidst the chaos. He took a step forward, his imposing figure blocking out the flickering streetlamp behind him. "You're a parasite, feeding off the fear and despair you create. This ends now!"

As his words hung in the air, the relic began to hum, the sound vibrating through the stones and into my very bones. It was a resonance that ignited a flame of hope within me, urging me to channel that energy into something powerful. "Liam's right!" I called, feeling the tension ripple around us. "We've had enough of your torment! Ashwood deserves to thrive, not be shackled by your ghostly chains!"

The spirit recoiled, its fury morphing into something more akin to panic. "You think you can erase me? I am woven into the fabric of this town. I will not fade!"

"Woven, maybe," Clara interjected, her voice steady despite the trembling in her hands. "But that doesn't mean you own it. It's time to untangle you from this place, to free Ashwood from your grasp."

With that, I felt a spark of something within the relic, as if it understood Clara's words, recognizing the truth in them. The light surged, illuminating the entire square, a beacon of defiance against the encroaching darkness. The spirit writhed and screamed, its form twisting in agony, eyes wild with rage and fear.

"Together!" I shouted, summoning every ounce of strength I had. "Focus your energy! We can do this!"

In unison, we poured our resolve into the relic, the light exploding outward in a brilliant flash. The air shimmered, crackling with energy as we stood resolute against the tide of darkness that threatened to consume us. The spirit shrieked, a cacophony of pain that clawed at our sanity, but we pressed on, fueled by an unwavering determination to save our town.

As the light enveloped the spirit, a sudden shift occurred, a moment of clarity that broke through the chaos. I saw it then—fragments of memories playing out in the air, scenes of the town's past unraveling like an old film. A young couple laughing beneath the very fountain we stood around, their joy infectious, their love pure. Children playing tag in the square, their shrieks of delight echoing in the crisp air. A town once vibrant, now shrouded in shadows.

"Look!" I cried, pointing toward the visions. "This is what you've stolen! You're not Ashwood; you're a relic of its pain!"

The spirit writhed violently, the memories colliding with its dark essence. "No! They are mine! They belong to me!"

A surge of compassion washed over me, mingled with the anger at what it had done. "You don't have to be this way!" I shouted, feeling the heat of the relic against my chest. "You can let go of your anger! You can remember what it felt like to love this town instead of loathing it!"

The spirit hesitated, its form flickering as if caught between two worlds—the past it clung to and the present we fought to reclaim. The wind howled through the square, the memories swirling around us like fallen leaves caught in a tempest.

"Enough of this!" It roared, summoning its power with a ferocity that rattled the very bones of Ashwood. The ground shook violently, and I stumbled, struggling to keep my footing as Clara and Liam steadied me. The shadows twisted, coiling around us like serpents, and I felt a chill seep into my bones.

"Stay strong!" Liam yelled, his voice slicing through the chaos. "Remember why we're fighting!"

With a sudden clarity, I grasped the relic tighter, feeling its warmth seep into my fingers. "Ashwood isn't just a town; it's a living memory. It's every laugh, every tear, every moment that brought us here!"

In that instant, I understood that this wasn't merely a fight against a spirit; it was a battle for the soul of our home. The relic pulsed with renewed vigor, its light a vivid counterpoint to the dark tendrils that threatened to engulf us. "Together, we can show it what love looks like!" I shouted, and as if in response, the memories around us brightened, igniting the square with a vibrant glow.

The spirit let out a final, anguished scream, the sound resonating through the very walls of Ashwood. I could feel the struggle within it, a fight against the chains it had forged over centuries. But the warmth of our bond, the strength of our unity, began to unravel the darkness it clung to.

"Let go!" Clara cried, her voice a fierce declaration. "You're free to choose another path!"

With one final surge of energy, we directed everything we had into the relic, our voices merging into a symphony of defiance. The light exploded outward, enveloping the spirit in a cascade of brilliant warmth, the shadows dissolving into nothingness. I held my breath, eyes wide, as the air shimmered with the remnants of the spirit's anguished wails, slowly fading into a haunting silence.

And then, just like that, it was over. The light receded, leaving behind a serene stillness in the square, the air warm and fragrant with the scent of blooming jasmine. I looked around, my heart racing with disbelief.

"Did we do it?" Clara whispered, her eyes wide as she surveyed the square, now bathed in the soft glow of moonlight.

"I think... I think we did," I breathed, unable to shake the feeling of awe that washed over me.

But even as the realization settled in, an undercurrent of unease twisted in my gut. The battle was over, but the war was just beginning. Ashwood had been saved, yet the echoes of its past lingered, a reminder of the darkness that had tried to reclaim its soul.

The soft glow of moonlight bathed the square in a tranquil luminescence, a stark contrast to the chaos that had just unfolded. I stood there, breathless and bewildered, the remnants of the battle hanging in the air like the aftermath of a summer storm. Clara's fingers trembled as she lowered the relic, its glow dimming until it resembled just a piece of ancient stone, nothing more than an artifact of our struggle.

"Did we really just do that?" Clara asked, glancing around as if expecting the spirit to reappear, its malevolence resurrected by our uncertainty. "I mean, I felt like we were going to be swallowed whole a moment ago."

"Just goes to show," Liam chimed in, a crooked smile breaking through the tension on his face. "Nothing like a good supernatural showdown to bring the neighborhood together."

"Right," I replied, trying to catch my breath, but my heart still raced like a runaway train. "And here I thought a nice cup of tea would do the trick."

But as the adrenaline began to ebb, I couldn't shake the feeling that something was off. The silence that blanketed the square felt too heavy, too profound. I stepped forward, scanning the shadows that clung to the edges of the street, half-expecting a specter to leap from the darkness. "What if it's not really over?" I murmured, my voice barely above a whisper.

Clara shivered, hugging her arms against the cool night air. "You know, I'm all for optimism, but you might be onto something. The spirit was pretty adamant about its claims. It could just be biding its time, waiting for us to let our guard down."

"Great, just what I need," I said, running a hand through my hair, feeling the sweat cool against my skin. "A ghost with a grudge. Just like my high school ex."

Liam chuckled, but his expression shifted as he stepped closer, his brows furrowing. "Let's not forget the history of this place. Ashwood's roots are tangled with dark stories and buried secrets. It might not just be that spirit we need to worry about."

The wind picked up, sending a chill that danced over my skin, and I couldn't shake the dread that lurked just beneath the surface.

"So, what do we do now?" I asked, looking from Clara to Liam, seeking some semblance of direction.

"We regroup," Liam suggested, his voice firm and steady. "We need to gather more information. If there's something else out there, we need to know what we're up against."

Clara nodded, a spark of determination igniting in her eyes. "We should visit the library. There must be more records, more about the town's history that can give us clues. We can't just sit here and hope for the best."

"Great idea, but let's go before I start to feel sentimental about that fountain," I quipped, trying to infuse some levity into the heavy air, but the truth was, I didn't want to linger in the square any longer. The shadows felt alive, as if they were watching us, waiting for us to turn our backs.

We made our way through the empty streets, the moonlight casting long shadows that seemed to stretch toward us, fingers of darkness clawing at our heels. My mind raced with the possibilities of what we might uncover. Clara's footsteps were steady, a rhythm that grounded me, while Liam walked with a sense of purpose that bolstered my resolve.

The library loomed ahead, its ancient façade both foreboding and comforting, like a wise old friend who had seen too much. The door creaked as we entered, the scent of old paper and dust enveloping us, a musty reminder of the countless stories waiting to be uncovered.

"Let's split up," Clara suggested, her voice echoing softly in the vast, quiet space. "I'll take the archives; they might have records about the town's past dealings with... well, whatever that was." She gestured toward the square, her expression serious. "Liam, you could check the local history section. I'll search for anything that mentions the relic."

"Got it," Liam replied, his tone brisk as he moved deeper into the library. "And you?"

"I'll see what I can find in the folklore section. Maybe there's something in the myths that can give us a clue about the spirit's origins," I said, though my stomach twisted at the thought of delving into the darkness of our town's past.

As I wandered through the aisles, the quiet felt almost reverent, each book a vessel of knowledge, secrets sealed within the brittle pages. I pulled a dusty volume from the shelf, flipping through the yellowed pages filled with stories of Ashwood's founding. Ghosts and legends danced across the text, each tale more chilling than the last, intertwining fact with fiction in a tapestry of fear and fascination.

I settled at a nearby table, my fingers brushing over the titles, when a peculiar sound echoed through the library—a low, mournful wail that sent shivers racing down my spine. It was a sound unlike anything I had ever heard, both sorrowful and haunting.

I froze, listening intently as the wail morphed into a low whisper, a voice calling from the depths of the library. "Help me..."

Heart pounding, I rose to my feet, glancing around to see if Clara or Liam had heard it too. The silence enveloped me once more, a thick blanket that smothered my courage. "Hello?" I called out, my voice wavering, echoing off the walls like a lonely ghost.

Then, without warning, the lights flickered, plunging the room into darkness before igniting again, casting shadows that twisted and swayed as if alive. My breath quickened, a sense of dread pooling in my stomach. "This isn't funny," I muttered, my voice barely above a whisper, but deep down, I felt the walls closing in, the air thick with the weight of something unseen.

"Annie?" Clara's voice broke through the silence, filled with urgency. "Did you hear that? What's going on?"

"I—" I started, but before I could respond, the room shook violently, books tumbling from their shelves like startled birds. The sound of glass shattering echoed through the aisles, and I instinctively took a step back, my heart racing as I braced for whatever chaos was about to unfold.

"Get out!" Clara screamed, her voice rising above the cacophony. "We need to go, now!"

But just as I turned to run, a figure materialized in the shadows, a flicker of movement that sent my heart plummeting. I squinted into the darkness, trying to discern its shape, and as the figure stepped into the flickering light, a gasp escaped my lips.

"Please," it whispered, its voice trembling. "You have to listen..."

And in that instant, I knew we were far from finished. The battle may have ended, but the true reckoning was just beginning.

Chapter 23: Ashes of the Past

The air shimmered with the remnants of battle, a delicate blend of charred earth and the sweet scent of blooming lilacs that filled my lungs. As I looked around, the once-terrifying landscape of Ashwood began to reveal its hidden beauty beneath the thin veil of morning mist. Each tendril of fog wrapped around the twisted branches of ancient oaks, as if nature herself was breathing a sigh of relief. I felt a surge of hope swell within me, fueled by the warmth of Liam's hand clasped firmly around mine.

"I never thought we'd see the day when we could breathe easy again," I said, casting a sidelong glance at him. His tousled hair glinted in the soft light, and the weariness etched in his features gave way to a burgeoning smile that could rival the sun itself.

"I always believed in us," he replied, his voice steady, laced with a hint of mischief that sent a thrill down my spine. "Besides, who could resist the charms of our fierce little band of misfits?"

I snorted, shaking my head as I gestured toward the remnants of our makeshift army strewn across the clearing—some were still catching their breath, while others exchanged stories of bravery and narrow escapes. The spirit we had confronted now lay at peace, a gentle whisper of wind reminding us of the battles fought not just against dark forces, but against our own shadows. "Fierce? More like fabulously chaotic. And don't think I didn't see you ducking behind a tree when the first wave of spirits appeared."

"Hey! Tactical retreat is a legitimate strategy." He grinned, and I couldn't help but return the smile, feeling the tension of the previous hours melt away.

As we stood together, the weight of our shared experiences began to settle comfortably upon us. Our laughter mingled with the early morning sounds of chirping birds and the rustle of leaves, creating a symphony of renewal that echoed throughout Ashwood.

The relic, a beautiful crystalline structure shaped like a teardrop, lay at the center of the clearing, glimmering in hues of violet and blue. Its presence felt both foreign and familiar, an echo of our triumph.

"Do you think it will always glow like that?" I asked, tilting my head as I observed the relic. It pulsed with an ethereal light, as if it held the very essence of our victory.

"Only if we keep it safe. It needs the energy of our hope and determination to thrive," Liam said, his voice softening. "We've got a responsibility now."

"Great. No pressure, right?" I chuckled, but beneath the humor lay an undercurrent of anxiety. The spirit's curse might have been lifted, but the whispers of what came next loomed over us like storm clouds gathering on the horizon.

As if sensing my shift in mood, Liam tightened his grip, grounding me in the moment. "We'll face it together. That's what we do." His eyes sparkled with an earnestness that made my heart race. I had always admired his ability to remain unfazed, even in the face of chaos.

Just then, our thoughts were interrupted by the loud clattering of hooves against the cobblestone path leading into the clearing. A rider approached, her silhouette framed by the soft glow of dawn. The unmistakable figure of Mara, our fearless leader and the first to charge into battle, emerged from the shadows. Her chestnut hair flew behind her like a banner, and her eyes, fierce and determined, held an intensity that could pierce the darkest night.

"Did we win, or did I just dream all this?" she called out, dismounting gracefully and surveying the scene. "I'm not sure if I'm more excited about the victory or the fact that my hair looks amazing right now."

"You're always the glamorous warrior, Mara," I teased, stepping forward to embrace her. "We did it. The curse is broken!"

"Of course, we did! Did you doubt us for a second?" She pulled away, her eyes glinting with mischief. "But I hope you saved some of the fun for me. I'm not too late for the after-party, am I?"

Liam snickered, "Just in time, as always."

Mara's laughter rang out like chimes, but beneath it, I sensed a seriousness that wasn't lost on me. "What's next for us?" I asked, casting my gaze toward the horizon, where the sun was now making a glorious ascent, splashing colors across the sky.

Mara's expression shifted as she regarded the relic. "Now, we rebuild. Ashwood needs us—needs its people to thrive again. But we must tread carefully; the shadows of the past can still linger if we're not vigilant."

"Vigilance? I'm all for that," I replied, a shiver of anticipation coursing through me. "But what about the relic? Shouldn't we find a place for it? Somewhere safe?"

Liam nodded in agreement. "We can't let it fall into the wrong hands. It's too powerful."

Mara's gaze turned steely, her voice dropping to a serious whisper. "There are those who would seek to exploit its power. We must ensure that doesn't happen."

The reality of our situation hung heavily in the air, suffused with an intensity that caused my heart to race anew. "So we're not just free; we're also protectors now?" I asked, incredulous.

"Yes," Mara affirmed, her tone unwavering. "It's a heavy mantle, but I believe we're up to the task."

I caught Liam's gaze, a spark of determination flickering between us. "Then let's get to work. We have a village to save and a future to build."

"Together," he added, his voice low and resolute.

With the first rays of sunlight bathing us in a golden glow, I knew in that moment that our journey was just beginning. The challenges ahead loomed like distant mountains, daunting yet alluring. Each step forward would be filled with new adventures, untold stories, and unexpected twists that would shape us into the protectors Ashwood needed. And as long as we stood united, I felt ready to face whatever came next.

With the morning sun now fully embracing the landscape, I felt a renewed sense of purpose. The remnants of our battle lay scattered around us like the debris of a thunderstorm, the ground still blackened in patches but sprouting tentative green shoots that promised rebirth. Nature, ever resilient, was already weaving its magic, and I couldn't help but wonder what stories these woods would tell in the coming days.

Liam, ever the optimist, nudged me playfully. "What's our first order of business, Captain? A victory dance or a strategy meeting?" His eyes danced with mischief, but the seriousness of our mission loomed just beneath the surface.

"Why not both? We can celebrate our triumph and then start plotting how to keep this place safe," I suggested, feeling a mischievous grin tug at my lips. "Maybe throw in a snack break. We definitely earned it."

"Snacks are essential for strategic planning," he agreed, feigning a scholar's gravity. "Let's see what culinary delights Ashwood can provide. I hear the local pastries are to die for."

"Or to cause a very dramatic sugar crash," I shot back, and he chuckled, shaking his head as we walked toward the village square, where the familiar bustle of our neighbors was beginning to stir.

The village had a unique charm, with cobblestone streets that wound like lazy rivers between cottages adorned with blooming flower boxes. The faint sound of laughter wafted through the air, and I could see figures moving about, their faces lit with the warmth of the morning sun. Ashwood was waking up, and with it, the energy of new beginnings thrummed beneath the surface.

As we approached the square, a small crowd began to gather, curious about the glow emanating from the relic we carried. I held it close, as if it were a newborn—fragile yet full of potential. The villagers eyed it with a mixture of awe and apprehension, reflecting the heavy history we had just unraveled.

"Is that the source of the light?" a familiar voice broke through the murmurs, drawing my attention. It was Clara, her wild curls bouncing as she rushed forward, her expression a blend of excitement and concern. "You did it! You really did it!"

"We did," I affirmed, feeling a swell of pride as I gestured to the relic. "But it's not just us. It's all of you, too. We need to protect this place together."

"Right! So what's next?" she asked, her eyes sparkling with enthusiasm. "Are we going to throw a party or a festival? Because I can make the best berry pies, and everyone knows it."

Liam smirked. "Sounds like an excellent plan, Clara. As long as you promise to save one for me."

"Only if you promise to actually help set up instead of just eating," she shot back, hands on her hips, but a playful grin broke her serious facade.

"We might need to combine the two, a 'victory festival' to celebrate our success and to honor what we've lost," I interjected, my mind racing with the possibilities. "A chance for everyone to reconnect and rebuild."

Clara's enthusiasm was infectious. "I'll get started on the invites! And I can organize games for the children—maybe a scavenger hunt themed around the relic!"

"Scavenger hunt? Just don't let them find the relic or the shadows it casts. We need to keep it safe," I cautioned, though I couldn't help but feel a bubbling excitement at the thought of bringing the village together.

As the ideas flew around like confetti, I caught Liam's eye. There was something almost electric between us, a shared understanding that this was more than just a celebration; it was a healing ritual for our community. Yet, in the back of my mind, a question lingered like a shadow. What truly awaited us beyond this moment of triumph?

"Let's not forget, while we're celebrating, we need to be vigilant," I said, bringing the conversation back down to earth. "We broke the curse, but we're still not out of the woods—figuratively speaking, of course."

"Always the realist," Liam murmured, though his tone was warm. "But I agree. We should set up watches, maybe even gather the villagers for a council. We're stronger united."

Murmurs of agreement spread through the gathering crowd. There was a palpable shift in energy, as if we had suddenly awakened a sleeping giant of collaboration and unity. As I watched faces transform from apprehension to determination, I felt a surge of hope. Perhaps Ashwood was on the cusp of a new era—a time to learn from the past while forging ahead into the future.

Suddenly, a loud thud echoed from the edge of the village, halting our jubilant chatter. All eyes turned toward the sound, a low murmur rippling through the crowd as unease crept into the atmosphere.

"What was that?" Clara asked, her brows knitting together as she exchanged worried glances with those around her.

"Probably nothing," Liam replied, but I could sense the tension in his voice, his shoulders taut. "But we should check it out, just in case."

"Count me in," I said, adrenaline igniting a spark of urgency within me. "Let's make sure it's not anything...unpleasant."

As we moved toward the source of the noise, the warmth of the village faded, replaced by a chill that slithered along my spine. The atmosphere thickened, charged with uncertainty, as the crowd parted like waves before us. We reached the clearing, and my heart plummeted at the sight before us.

A dark figure loomed near the edge of the forest, its silhouette jagged against the rising sun, like a broken shard of glass reflecting all that was wrong. It stood still, observing us with an unsettling calmness that sent a shiver racing through the air.

"What in the world...?" Clara's voice trailed off, her wide eyes locked onto the figure.

"Stay back," I commanded, instinctively positioning myself in front of her. The relic thrummed softly at my side, as if warning me of the danger ahead.

The figure stepped forward, revealing a face cloaked in shadows, the contours sharp and predatory. My breath hitched as recognition washed over me, a mix of dread and disbelief spiraling within. I had thought we were free from the grasp of darkness, but here it was, insistent and unwavering, threatening to unravel everything we had fought to protect.

"Did you really think it was over?" the figure drawled, its voice smooth and dripping with malice. "Ashwood belongs to the shadows now."

A sense of foreboding washed over me, mingling with the anger bubbling within. This was not just a threat—it was a call to arms, an invitation to a battle I hadn't anticipated. As the figure's laugh echoed around us, I felt a fierce determination rise within, igniting a fire in my belly that refused to be snuffed out. We had come this far; we were not about to back down now.

"Not if we have anything to say about it," I replied, my voice steadier than I felt. "Ashwood is ours."

As we stood together, ready to defend our home, the sunlight spilled over us like a shield, illuminating the path ahead. We would face this new challenge head-on, united as a community, determined to reclaim our future. The shadows might have returned, but we would rise to meet them, ready to embrace whatever came next.

The figure before us was an enigma wrapped in shadow, its form flickering at the edges like a candle flame struggling against a gust of wind. It seemed to absorb the light around it, pulling the sun's warmth into its depths, leaving a chilling void in its wake. I stood, heart racing, anchored by Liam's presence beside me, our hands clasped tightly together as if we could draw strength from one another in this moment of looming dread.

"What do you want?" I shouted, my voice ringing out, firm despite the anxiety pooling in my stomach. "You don't belong here."

It stepped closer, revealing a face that was both familiar and unsettling, the features warped by shadows that twisted around it like dark ribbons. "Ah, but isn't that where the fun begins? You think you've broken the curse, but you've merely stirred the pot." The voice was silky, wrapping around us, caressing yet threatening.

"Stirred what pot? We've lifted a curse that's haunted our village for generations!" Clara chimed in, her bravado echoing my own, yet her fingers trembled against my back.

"Generations? How quaint," the figure mocked, a smirk tugging at the corner of its lips. "But you see, curses are like bad habits; they don't disappear easily. They merely evolve, waiting for the perfect moment to rear their ugly heads again."

I exchanged a glance with Liam, who stepped forward, defiance written across his features. "We won't let you manipulate us. We've faced your darkness before, and we will do so again."

The figure laughed, a low, haunting sound that sent chills racing down my spine. "Oh, how brave you all are! But let's not forget who really controls the shadows here." It raised a hand, and the air thickened, shadows coiling around its fingers like serpents ready to strike.

I felt the energy shift, a wave of cold washing over us, making it hard to breathe. "Everyone, stay back!" I called, instinctively stepping closer to Liam, who stood resolute beside me.

"Ah, the gallant heroics," the figure said, its eyes glinting like shards of glass. "But remember, hope alone won't save you. You're swimming against a tide that seeks to drown you. And you've no idea what I have in store."

A flicker of movement caught my attention, and I turned to see Clara, determination etched on her face. "Whatever you're planning, you'll have to get through us first!" she shouted, fists clenched at her sides.

The figure turned its gaze toward her, momentarily distracted, and in that instant, I felt an opening—a sliver of opportunity. "We've defeated you before; we can do it again," I said, trying to harness the energy swirling within me. "We've changed. We've grown stronger."

It let out a low chuckle that sent a tremor through the crowd, a sound filled with mockery and menace. "Stronger? Perhaps. But strength means little when ignorance is your shield." It pointed at the relic, which still shimmered beside me, its light pulsing in time with my heartbeat. "You think that trinket can protect you? It's merely a reflection of your hope, a beacon drawing more darkness your way."

"No!" I yelled, anger flaring within me like a wildfire. "It's a symbol of everything we've overcome. You're wrong; we're not afraid of you."

"Fear is merely an emotion," the figure replied smoothly. "A tool I wield as effortlessly as I wield the shadows. You see, my dear, you are not the first to rise against me, nor will you be the last. I've seen countless heroes before you, each confident in their victories, only to be devoured by the shadows they tried to banish."

Suddenly, the ground trembled beneath us, the earth rumbling as if the very heart of Ashwood responded to the malevolence that stood before us. I staggered slightly, feeling Liam's grip tighten. "We need to push back," he murmured, urgency flickering in his eyes.

"Together," I replied, heart pounding in sync with his. I could feel the energy surging within the crowd as they rallied behind us, drawn together by the same fierce spirit that had ignited our fight against despair.

"Let's show this thing what we're made of," Clara shouted, and her words struck a chord, igniting a fire in the hearts of those gathered.

Liam and I raised the relic, its soft light illuminating our faces, casting away the shadows that tried to consume us. "We stand united!" I declared, channeling all the strength and love I felt for my home and the people around me. "This is our village, our future, and we will not be swayed by darkness!"

The figure snarled, its eyes flashing with something akin to rage, the shadows behind it swirling violently as if they were alive, hungry for the light we wielded. "Fools! You think you can dispel me with mere words and hopes? I am the reckoning you've invited into your lives, and you shall pay the price for your defiance!"

Before I could respond, a crack split the air, and the earth beneath us surged upward in a violent explosion. I was thrown backward, the relic slipping from my fingers as I collided with the ground. Everything around me turned chaotic, screams mingling with the growl of the earth as fissures tore through the village square, threatening to swallow us whole.

"Liam!" I gasped, scrambling to my feet, scanning the chaos for him. Panic clawed at my throat as I spotted him struggling to regain his footing, the shadows twisting around him like predatory vines. "No!"

In that moment of horror, time slowed, and I felt a rush of desperation. "Hold on!" I shouted, but the shadows were moving too quickly, enveloping him, pulling him into the abyss that had opened beneath our feet.

"Get the relic!" he yelled, his voice strained as he fought against the dark tendrils wrapping around him. "You have to—"

The figure laughed, a sound that echoed through the turmoil, a cruel reminder of our vulnerability. "You cannot save him. You cannot save yourselves."

With a final effort, I lunged forward, the relic now glowing with an intensity that was almost blinding. I reached out, my fingers brushing against its smooth surface, and the light surged through me like electricity. I could feel it resonating with the essence of Ashwood, the collective strength of our community channeling through the crystal, and I knew I had to harness it.

"Liam, hold on!" I screamed, my voice rising above the chaos. As the shadows closed in, I focused all my energy, my love, my determination into the relic, hoping to break the grip of darkness.

But the shadows surged forward, hungry and relentless, their laughter mingling with the howls of the wind. I couldn't fail; I wouldn't lose him like this.

Just as I felt the power building, the world around me erupted in blinding light, forcing me to shield my eyes. The shadows writhed and twisted, but then—silence fell. A breathless moment hung in the air, pregnant with uncertainty, and I dared to open my eyes, heart racing as I searched for Liam.

But he was gone.

The ground quaked, and from the depths of the fissure, a new figure emerged—a silhouette against the light, one that filled me with dread and disbelief. "Did you really think this was over?" it echoed, and I felt the world tilt beneath my feet.

In that instant, my breath caught in my throat, and the last shreds of hope slipped through my fingers like sand.

Chapter 24: A New Dawn

The morning air was crisp, tinged with the scent of damp earth and blooming wildflowers, as I stood on that familiar park bench, an unassuming slab of wood that had witnessed our transformation from strangers to lovers, from lost souls to warriors. The sun peeked over the horizon, spilling a cascade of golds and soft pinks into the sky, as if the universe was pouring out its blessings upon us. I felt the warmth of Liam's hand clasped around mine, a steady reminder that this moment was real, that we were here, and that the darkness we had battled was finally behind us.

Liam turned to me, his eyes reflecting the hues of dawn, a mix of warmth and mischief. "You know, if we keep this up, we might have to find a new bench. This one might get too sentimental." He flashed that dimpled grin that always set my heart racing.

"Sentimental isn't a bad thing," I replied, nudging him playfully. "Every scratch and groove on this bench is a memory—our memories. Besides, where else would we stand to plot world domination?"

"Ah, world domination via art therapy? Now that's a plan." He laughed, a sound that seemed to intertwine with the birdsong surrounding us, each note bright and joyful, heralding the beginning of our new chapter.

Clara's voice rang through my mind, buoyant with enthusiasm as she described our art program to revitalize the community. The vision she painted for us was vivid—a place where creativity could thrive, where the brushstrokes of our lives would intertwine with the souls of those who had long forgotten their own. Together, we envisioned murals splashed across crumbling walls, vibrant colors bleeding life into the dreariness that had settled over Ashwood.

I squeezed Liam's hand, a rush of exhilaration coursing through me. "We can really do this, can't we? Bring a little magic back into Ashwood?"

"Magic?" Liam raised an eyebrow, feigning seriousness. "Are you sure you're not talking about the community center's coffee? That stuff could wake the dead."

I rolled my eyes, the laughter bubbling up, contagious in its sincerity. "Hey, if we can awaken a few souls with a dose of caffeine and a splash of paint, then I'm all for it."

Our laughter mingled with the chirping of the birds, wrapping us in a cocoon of warmth. It felt good—so good to embrace the light after the shadows we'd faced. The memories of our struggles, the weight of the curse that had hung over Ashwood like a specter, were now mere whispers in the back of my mind. We had fought and clawed our way through, our resilience shining brighter than the sunrise before us.

Liam pulled me closer, his breath warm against my ear. "You know, I've been thinking…"

"Oh no," I teased, leaning back to scrutinize his face. "That's never a good sign."

He chuckled, a low rumble that sent butterflies dancing in my stomach. "I mean it. With your brilliance and my—well, my rugged charm, we could even host workshops. Get people involved in reclaiming their own stories."

"Rugged charm?" I repeated, a grin splitting my face. "What's next? You're going to tell me you're the next Picasso?"

"Why not?" he replied, mock bravado in his tone. "I've got the hair for it." He gestured dramatically at his tousled locks, which were still damp from the morning dew.

I laughed outright, shaking my head. "I think Picasso had a slightly different vibe."

"Touché," he conceded, amusement dancing in his eyes. "But that just means we need to channel our inner artists and make our mark."

His words sank deep into my heart, a flame igniting within me. We weren't just dreamers; we were doers, and together, we could create something beautiful. I could picture it—a sun-drenched space filled with laughter and creativity, a kaleidoscope of color flooding the walls, children giggling as they splashed paint across canvases, adults rediscovering the joys of their youth.

"Let's do it," I said, determination lacing my voice. "Let's start small. Maybe a community mural as our first project? We can invite everyone—show them that art belongs to everyone, not just a select few."

"Now you're speaking my language." Liam beamed, his enthusiasm infectious. "We'll need to gather supplies, spread the word, and then watch as the town transforms before our eyes."

Our conversation flowed effortlessly, weaving in and out of plans and possibilities, until I found myself lost in the idea of what Ashwood could become. The park, once a place of sadness and unease, could flourish with life and laughter. And the thought of Clara joining us—her fervent spirit melding with our vision—added an extra layer of excitement.

Just then, the vibrant colors of the sunrise deepened, spilling across the sky like molten gold, and I felt an overwhelming swell of gratitude for this moment. The curse that had once gripped our lives had loosened its hold, allowing us to dream anew.

"Are you ready for this?" Liam asked, his voice low, full of sincerity that sent shivers racing down my spine.

"More than ready," I replied, the weight of uncertainty falling away like autumn leaves in the wind. We stood there, hand in hand, ready to face whatever came next. It wasn't just about Ashwood; it was about us—our love, our commitment to each other, and the world we would create together.

The next few weeks unfolded with a whirlwind of colors and creativity, transforming Ashwood into a canvas of hope. As the sun dipped below the horizon each evening, casting a warm glow over the town, I found myself deep in planning sessions with Clara. Our vision for the community art program was taking shape, fueled by her infectious enthusiasm and my newfound determination.

"Picture this," Clara exclaimed one afternoon, her eyes sparkling with excitement as we spread out sheets of paper across the table in the quaint café where we often met. "We'll start with a mural on the community center. Something that embodies the spirit of Ashwood—a phoenix rising, colorful and radiant. A symbol of renewal!"

I nodded, caught up in her fervor. "A phoenix sounds perfect! It's a powerful image, and it speaks to everything we've experienced. But what about incorporating local artists? Everyone should have a say in what this represents."

"Brilliant!" Clara beamed, leaning forward as if the sheer force of her energy could bend the universe to her will. "We'll host a series of workshops, inviting everyone from kids to seasoned artists. Let them share their stories and contribute to the design. We want this mural to be a collective heartbeat, not just ours."

Our brainstorming sessions often flowed seamlessly into laughter, punctuated by the clinking of coffee cups and the occasional teasing from the barista, who had taken to watching our antics with amusement. The café, with its mismatched furniture and the aroma of freshly baked pastries, became our creative sanctuary.

"Just imagine," I said, savoring a rich bite of chocolate croissant, "a place where the walls breathe life, and every brushstroke tells a story."

"Let's not forget the snacks," Clara quipped, grinning as she stole the last bite of my pastry. "Art and pastries should always go hand in hand."

With our plan set, we dived into the logistics of gathering supplies and spreading the word, each new day filled with the thrill of potential. The more we spoke about the mural, the more the community began to buzz with anticipation. Flyers danced around town, colorful and vibrant, announcing our vision, and soon, we found ourselves inundated with eager volunteers.

Among them was Leah, a sprightly woman in her fifties, who had spent decades as a schoolteacher. She showed up one afternoon, her face a tapestry of laughter lines and wisdom, her spirit contagious. "I've been waiting for something like this," she said, her eyes glimmering with nostalgia as she reminisced about her childhood art classes. "Art saved me back then, and it can save this town now."

"I'm glad you're on board, Leah," I said, feeling the warmth of community beginning to envelop us. "We need voices like yours to help inspire the next generation."

As days turned into weeks, the mural began to take shape in our minds, its colors bursting forth like wildflowers after a spring rain. We decided to host a community meeting at the park, inviting anyone and everyone to share their thoughts and dreams for the mural.

When the day arrived, the park thrummed with energy. Families sprawled across picnic blankets, children dashed about with paint-splattered hands, and the sun bathed everything in a golden hue, just like that first morning. Clara and I stood at the front, both a bit nervous but bubbling with excitement.

"Welcome, everyone!" Clara began, her voice ringing out across the crowd. "Today is about you—your stories, your dreams, your colors! We want to create a mural that embodies Ashwood's heart. So, what does Ashwood mean to you?"

Hands shot up, voices chimed in, and soon we were engulfed in a beautiful cacophony of ideas. One elderly gentleman spoke of the oak tree that had stood sentinel in the park for generations, its roots deep in history. A little girl shyly shared her love for the butterflies that danced through the flowers each summer. With each story, my heart swelled, and I felt the richness of our community blossoming into something far greater than I had imagined.

As the sun began to set, casting long shadows and painting the sky in vibrant purples and oranges, I spotted Liam in the crowd. He was sketching fervently in his notepad, his brow furrowed in concentration. The sight of him, so absorbed in his art, sent a wave of affection crashing over me. I'd often marveled at how his creativity could flow effortlessly, bringing to life everything from abstract shapes to lifelike portraits.

After the meeting, I made my way over to him, the warmth of the day fading into a comfortable chill. "What are you working on?" I asked, peeking over his shoulder.

"Just some ideas for the mural," he said, glancing up at me with that familiar spark in his eyes. "I thought we could incorporate the oak tree, maybe even the butterflies. It could represent growth, resilience."

"That's perfect!" I exclaimed, my heart dancing at the thought. "You have a knack for capturing the essence of things, you know?"

"Only when I'm inspired." He smiled, his gaze intense and sincere. "And you inspire me."

I felt a blush creep up my cheeks, but before I could respond, Clara joined us, her arms overflowing with supplies. "Did you see the excitement out there? We're onto something incredible!"

"Yes! And Liam is going to help us channel that energy into something beautiful," I added, nudging him playfully. "Just don't let him take too much credit for the butterflies."

"Hey, I'll take whatever credit I can get," he teased back, that mischievous grin lighting up his face. "But let's not forget, I'm not the only artist here."

The warmth of camaraderie enveloped us as we discussed our next steps. Plans crystallized around us like morning dew, and for the first time, I felt a true sense of belonging—not just in Ashwood, but with Liam and Clara. Our paths had intertwined so intricately, each of us bringing our unique colors to the canvas of this community, ready to paint a new story together.

The days that followed our community meeting morphed into a vibrant tapestry of creativity and collaboration. Every morning, I awoke to the scent of fresh coffee and the faint sound of laughter drifting from the park, where Clara and Liam had already gathered eager volunteers. The rhythm of our lives began to sync with the pulse of Ashwood, its heartbeats echoing with hope and inspiration.

Each brushstroke on the mural became a celebration, a moment captured in color and spirit. Clara orchestrated the chaos, her laughter ringing like a bell as she guided children splattering paint with wild abandon. "More blue! We need the sky to match our dreams!" she would yell, arms wide open, encouraging everyone to embrace the joy of creation.

And amidst the joyful noise, there was Liam, a quiet force of nature. He often stepped back, sketching on his notepad, his brow furrowed in concentration. It fascinated me how he could blend into the background while simultaneously capturing the essence of the moment. One afternoon, while the sun painted golden highlights on the trees, I approached him, curious about his latest vision.

"What are you drawing this time?" I asked, leaning over to sneak a peek.

"Just a rough idea for the backdrop," he said, glancing up at me with a shy smile. "I thought a starry night might complement the phoenix. Something that represents the idea of rebirth—like we're all a part of something larger."

I marveled at how his mind worked, how he could take a simple idea and weave it into a narrative that transcended the canvas. "That's beautiful, Liam. It's like you're capturing our hopes and dreams."

He chuckled softly. "Or my desperation to make sure I don't accidentally paint a giant pigeon instead."

"Hey, if anyone can make a pigeon majestic, it's you," I shot back, feigning seriousness. "Just be sure to add a crown."

As laughter erupted between us, the mural transformed into a living tapestry of our stories. Strangers became friends, sharing secrets and laughter under the sprawling branches of the park's oak tree, which seemed to nod in approval at our burgeoning community. Every evening, as the sun dipped below the horizon, we'd gather to admire our progress. The once-blank wall now blossomed with swirls of color, vibrant shapes that echoed the heartbeat of Ashwood.

But as excitement filled the air, a sense of foreboding lurked at the edges of my mind. I couldn't shake the feeling that while we were building something beautiful, shadows still loomed. It wasn't just about the mural; it was about what had happened before. Whispers of the curse lingered in the corners of my thoughts, like a half-remembered nightmare. And then, as if the universe were tuning into my fears, the first storm of the season rolled in, dark clouds swirling ominously overhead.

"What a lovely day for a mural," Clara quipped, squinting up at the sky as raindrops began to patter softly on the ground. "Or a fantastic rendition of abstract art, depending on how the weather feels."

Liam chuckled, shaking his head as he secured our supplies. "Don't let the rain dampen your spirit. It'll add character. Plus, I'm sure that anything we paint now will eventually dry out."

"Unless it washes away," I added, unable to resist a teasing smile.

"Ah, but then it becomes a collaborative effort of nature and humanity," he replied, winking. "We're basically nature's artists now."

Just as the first drops fell, Clara clapped her hands together, summoning the group's attention. "All right, everyone! We'll take a quick break. Let's gather under the trees and brainstorm ideas for our next phase. Rain or shine, we're still committed!"

As we huddled beneath the oak's sprawling branches, the atmosphere crackled with energy, each person brimming with ideas. But then, as if summoned by our laughter, the sky darkened, and a rumble of thunder rolled through the park, cutting through our cheer.

"Okay, a little ominous," I murmured, glancing nervously at Liam.

"Nothing we can't handle," he assured me, though his voice carried a hint of uncertainty. Just then, a gust of wind blew through, rustling the leaves and sending a shiver down my spine. I could feel the tension in the air shift, like the quiet before a storm.

Suddenly, Clara's laughter faded as she glanced at something behind me, her expression shifting from playful to concerned. "What is that?"

I turned, following her gaze toward the mural wall, and my heart plummeted. Shadows flickered across the surface, twisting and writhing as if alive, dark tendrils reaching from the depths of the paint. Whispers echoed, faint yet chilling, wrapping around us like a cold breeze. The colors we'd poured our hearts into began to distort, swirling into a tempest of chaos.

"Everyone, step back!" I shouted, adrenaline surging through me as the once-joyful scene turned chaotic.

But it was too late. The shadows pooled together, forming an unmistakable shape—a figure draped in darkness, eyes glowing with an eerie light. It rose slowly, a menacing specter that loomed over the mural we had poured our souls into, as if drawn from the very curse we thought we had vanquished.

Panic erupted among the volunteers, gasps and shouts ricocheting through the park as they stumbled backward. "What is happening?" Clara yelled, clutching my arm, her face pale.

"I—I don't know," I stammered, fear gripping me like a vice. "We thought it was over. I thought we had lifted the curse!"

The figure solidified, a haunting smile twisting its features, and a low, rumbling voice echoed through the park, chilling my very bones. "You thought you could erase the past, but I am the shadow of what you've created. And I am here to reclaim what is mine."

As its words settled around us like a shroud, I felt a surge of defiance bubbling up within me. This wasn't just a battle against darkness; it was a fight for everything we had built, everything we believed in. "We won't let you," I shouted, forcing strength into my voice.

The specter's laughter rang out, a hollow sound that sent shivers down my spine. "You may try, but shadows always find a way back into the light."

And just like that, it lunged forward, the air thick with an ominous weight, as if the world had drawn a collective breath, waiting for what would happen next.

Milton Keynes UK
Ingram Content Group UK Ltd.
UKHW030104081124
450874UK00001B/56